FIRST LADY

OF

JAMESTOWN

A YA HISTORICAL FICTION NOVEL
BASED ON THE LIFE AND ADVENTURES OF ANNE BURRAS
THE FIRST ENGLISHWOMAN TO SURVIVE THE NEW WORLD

BY

TRACY SMITH

Copyright © 2024 by de Tello Publishing

All rights reserved.

No part of this publication may be reproduced, distributed, or transmitted in any form or by any means, including photocopying, recording, or other electronic or mechanical methods, without the prior written permission of the publisher, except as permitted by U.S. copyright law.

First Lady of Jamestown

YA Historical Fiction Novel

ISBN:

- 979-8-9899183-0-0 (Paperback)

- 979-8-9899183-1-7 (Hardcover)

Book Cover Design by 100Covers

Illustrations by Grant Smith

Interior Formatting by de Tello Publishing, LLC

DEDICATION

To my supportive husband Grant and children Abigail, Asher, and
Gwendolyn.
Thank you for letting me fly. I love you to the moon and back.

Contents

PART ONE

ENGLAND

NORFOLK
LONDON

Chapter One
LIFE AT HOME

"So wise, so young, they say, do never live long." –
William Shakespeare

Norfolk, England, Sep 20, 1606

I closed my eyes and took in the rich scents of fresh grass and flowers as I slowly made my way to the field behind our house. My petite fingers caressed the peeling gray bark of the tall oak tree before I stopped in the shade of the giant elm. I sat down and leaned against it for support as I removed my too-tight black shoes and well-worn stockings to wiggle my toes free. The soft blades of grass felt cool beneath my feet. A tear ran down my cheek, and I closed my eyes, relishing the last memory I had here with my brothers and sisters one year prior; when I was eleven and felt innocent and unscathed. I let my mind wander as I relived the old memory.

"Ready or not, here I come!" Nicholas had called out eagerly. His seven-year-old voice was high-pitched and carefree. His curly light brown hair flapped in the wind as he ran barefoot across our lawn and looked around the fat oak tree.

Little five-year-old Mary giggled as she poked her head out from behind the brush. Her red hair matched the deep tones of Mama's rose bushes. "We're not there," she teased.

"Mary, shh," I said with an irritated huff. "You'll give us away!"

Nicholas darted around to our hiding place. "Gotcha!" he said and laughed as he crossed his sun-kissed arms that peeked out from the sleeves of his white linen shirt. "Now, where could Jack and Anthony be?"

"They're *not* over there," Mary whispered, quickly pointing to the elm trees behind us.

"Mary!" I shook my head in disbelief.

Her blue eyes sparkled, and her red curls bounced innocently. She shrugged. "What? I thaid they *weren't* over there."

I couldn't help but shake my head at her and laugh. Mary was seven years younger than me and her cute lisp through her two missing front teeth was almost too much for me to bear. I had to cup my hand over my mouth to stop laughing. Mama used to say, "God made Mary sweet so we wouldn't get so mad when she was naughty." Mama was right!

"Ha!" Nicholas laughed after he followed Mary's directions to Jack and Anthony. "Found you!"

Nine-year-old Jack, tall and thin for his age, emerged from his hiding spot and smacked his hands on his thighs. "Oh, drats!"

"Supper's ready, children!" Mama called out from the house, bouncing baby Ellen in her arms. "Time to come inside."

"Yes, Mama," my oldest brother, Anthony, said, sighing. "We're coming."

I smiled with my eyes still shut tight reliving the moment. If I closed my fist tight enough, I could still feel Mary's hand imprinted on mine as we ran back to the house with growling stomachs. Our house wasn't grand or elaborate, but it was home. It boasted two tall windows and a roof-gable dormer that let light in. The exterior was brown and white, and the steep thatched roof kept us warm and dry in the winter. Papa was born in this house and said he never wanted to leave it.

Grandmother Burras and Mama's parents died before I was born. All I had ever known were Grandfather Burras, Papa, Mama, and my siblings. Grandfather was a quiet but hard working man. He created a shipyard business and taught Papa the trade. They both worked long hours but were always home to eat supper with the family.

After supper that night, we had all sat together in the main room as Mama lit two tallow wax candles. Papa usually told us stories, or he would play the lute and Mama would sing to us. I loved hearing her voice, especially when she sang us songs before bed. Tonight, Papa said he would tell us a story.

"Tell us about the people of Roanoke," I said with a big, toothy grin. "It's my favorite!"

Jack's blue eyes lit up excitedly, and he scooted his chair closer to Papa. Anthony and I followed suit and gave him our full attention. Mary and Nicholas climbed up and sat on Papa's lap.

Papa smiled at us and chuckled. "That one again?" Mama walked by, picked a few plates up off the table, and tsked; "Remember, dear, we want the children to sleep tonight without nightmares. Please try not to scare them this time." Papa coughed into his hand to cover a laugh. "Yes, my love, I will try my best."

"But don't leave off the good parts," Jack insisted.

Papa grinned. "Very well then, let me see." He readjusted Nicholas and Mary on his lap and sat farther back in his seat to balance them. "When I was a young boy, a group of Englishmen set out to colonize land recently discovered by Sir Walter Raleigh in the New World. They called it Virginia after our great Queen Elizabeth, the Virgin Queen of England; God rest her soul."

"Isn't that where the Spanish made colonies?" Anthony asked eagerly.

"Yes, the Spanish settled in the south, near Florida; that's why Sir Raleigh sent a group north so they wouldn't run into them," Papa said.

Jack stood up and pretended to slash a fake sword in the air. "They didn't want to run into Spanish pirates."

I giggled at Jack. Then, the thought of being raided by pirates turned my laugh into a gulp instead.

"Wasn't it dangerous?" Mary asked as she stared up at Papa. He nodded down at her, "They wanted to make a permanent colony there like the Spanish did."

"And to look for gold," Anthony added. He folded his large arms over his chest and raised his eyebrows. "That's what I would look for."

Papa shook his head and laughed. "Yes, some people were there for gold, but that wasn't the only reason. Many were there because they wanted a better life for themselves and their family."

He leaned in closer, and his blue eyes sparkled; "But others went to have an adventure of a lifetime."

"Wow," Jack said in a whisper.

Anthony combed his wavy auburn hair back with his fingers, "I know I'd volunteer to go," he said in a deep, strained voice.

I chuckled to myself at the way he tried to sit up taller in his seat and sound more manly.

Jack nearly fell out of his seat with excitement, "I'd volunteer too!"

"Me three," Nicholas cried.

Mary's smile turned into a frown, "I'm scared to go but I'm going if Nicholas goes," she said, as if the thought of being anywhere without Nicholas would be too much for her to bear.

I looked around the room, first at my siblings, then at Mama in her pretty green kirtle dress who had sat down next to Papa. I loved my family and couldn't imagine what it would be like living without them. "I'm going if everyone else is going," I finally said.

Mama shifted on her wooden stool and turned to Papa. "What do you say, dear? It seems like five of our six children will be headed to the New World. Should we go too?"

Nicholas furrowed his eyebrows at Mama looking as if he might cry.

"What's wrong Nicholas?" she asked.

Nicholas huffed and glanced up at her, "You forgot about Ellen," he cried.

Mama gently ruffled his brown hair and tapped him softly on the nose. "I could never forget about Ellen, my love."

He smiled, then the tender moment was broken when Jack jumped up and down asking if we could really go to the New World.

Anthony clapped him on the shoulder and pulled him back to his seat. "Settle down now explorer. I don't think any of us will be going anytime soon."

Mama laughed, "I'm afraid Anthony is right, Jack." "Oh, drats," he said again like he always did.

Papa looked at Jack, and his mouth turned into a smile, "Shall I continue the story?"

Jack sat back down, "Yes, please."

"After Sir Raleigh found a safe location, he returned to London and hired men to help him form a group of colonists. He asked Sir White to be one of the leaders and gathered one hundred and twenty volunteers, men and women, for the journey."

I raised my eyebrows, shocked that so many people would volunteer to go.

"Then what happened?" Jack asked as he rested his elbows on the table to support his head with his hands.

"They called the place Roanoke and started building homes and trading with the local native people. At first, they were on friendly terms, then things turned bad quickly and they started to fight each other."

Mary twirled a strand of hair around her little finger and frowned. "Why did they fight each other?"

Papa paused, then his shoulders slumped; his voice came out soft and soothing. He pushed back a red curl from her face, tucked it behind her ear, and sighed. "I wish I knew why, sweet girl. If I did, maybe others would, too, and all the wars and heartache of the world could be prevented. My only guess is that both groups were frightened of the other, or desperate. When people get desperate, they unfortunately tend to make bad decisions."

Mary went back to twirling her hair, either satisfied with his answer or more confused, I couldn't tell.

"The colony started to run out of provisions, so Sir White and some of the crew decided it best to return to England to get help," Papa continued.

My heart raced, "What about his daughter and her new baby?" I already knew the story by heart, but I wanted to hear Papa tell it.

The candlelight flickered, and Papa's eyes filled with tears. "He left them with her husband in Roanoke. It must have been a terribly hard decision for him."

I nodded, feeling sad for poor Sir White and his daughter. "Why didn't he just take all of them back?" Anthony asked with a scowl on his face.

"They thought they would be fine if they returned with more provisions and that the journey would be quicker with less people. They didn't realize how long they would be gone."

Anthony scowled, "I would have made them go back with me."

"Anthony, you're ruining the story," Jack pouted. "Then what happened, Papa?"

"Sir White and his men arrived a few months later in London, only to find England at war with Spain!"

"The Spanish Armuda," Nicholas added.

"Close, the Spanish Armada," Papa chuckled. "Queen Elizabeth forbade him to return to Roanoke because they needed his ship, and any ship they could find, to fight the Spanish. It wasn't until three years later that he could get the provisions and ships to return to Virginia."

Papa had never shared this part of the story before. He shook his head, "That is the mystery. When they arrived, everyone was gone. He had told the people to give him a sign to know where to look for them if they left."

"Did they leave any signs?" I asked.

"Yes, they left two big clues; the word 'Croatoan' was carved into one of the palisade posts, and the letters CRO were carved in a nearby tree."

"'Croatoan.' What does that mean?" Anthony asked.

"There was an island named Croatoan where the natives were kind and helpful."

Jack's thin shoulders shrugged. "Then why didn't Sir White just go there instead?"

"He tried, but there was a large hurricane, and they had to turn back. When they arrived a year later, even the natives were gone."

His words hit me hard. "Gone? Where did they go?" I asked. Papa sighed. "No one knows. Sir White went back several times after that but never found them; then he died a few years later."

Mary's eyes filled with tears, and she nestled her head into Papa's shoulder. "Poor Sir White," she said.

Papa gave her a knowing squeeze. I wiped away a tear of my own. If I were his daughter, I would do everything I could to protect my baby and find my father. A burst of hope swept through me, *what if they set out to find him?* I thought to myself. "Maybe his daughter and granddaughter are still alive," I said, nearly shouting.

Papa placed a finger to his chin, "They could be. What do you think happened to them?"

"I think they got eaten by a giant whale," Nicholas said. Mary giggled, "I think they walked into the ocean and joined the mermaids you told us about."

"Oh, that would be fun," Papa said. "Would they have grown long tails, too?"

Her blue eyes sparkled as she nodded, "And their tails would be made of gold."

Papa chuckled. "And what do you think happened, Anne?"

"I think they joined the Croatoan people; they wrote their name in the tree after all. Maybe they knew a storm was coming, so they hid or sailed to a different place."

"Very observant of you, Anne," Papa said. "What about you, Jack and Anthony?"

"I think they found a secret sword with magical powers that transported them back to King Arthur's court. Like the sword of excel."

Anthony scoffed and pushed his thick hair behind his ear again. "It's Excalibur, silly, and that wasn't real."

We all laughed so hard that our sides ached.

Mama broke the silence, "My turn," she said. "I think the people magically walked all the way from Virginia back to England, then into their beds so they could get a good night's sleep like the rest of you."

"Mama," we moaned but ended up doing as we were told. "Goodnight Mama, Goodnight Papa," I said as I kissed each of them on the cheek, then waited for the others and headed to our room to say our prayers and go to sleep.

"Anne, Anne!" Jack's voice startled me from the daydream I was in.

I slowly opened my eyes and forced them to focus. The real world I lived in came back into view. I sighed and leaned my back against the rough tree one more time before I responded. I would give anything to go back in time and change things, but I knew nothing I did would ever bring them back, no matter how much I wished I could.

Chapter Two
THE LETTER

"Nothing is sweeter than love, nothing higher, nothing stronger, nothing larger, nothing more joyful, nothing fuller, and nothing better in heaven or on earth." – Thomas A. Kempis

September 20, 1606

"Ellen's crying again," Jack whined as he walked by me holding a basket full of apples.

"What?" I stood up and leaned against the tree. "She's crying again." He shrugged, visibly annoyed.

I moaned when I thought about the time I would lose taking care of Ellen. "I'll get her," I said, as I wiped my dirty hands onto my apron. I tucked back a strand of my dark blonde hair that had sneaked its way out of my white linen coif cap then headed toward the house.

I blew another wayward strand of hair from my face and made a mental note to readjust my coif when I got inside. I wished my hair was like Mama's, soft and brown with curls at the ends. Even Sarah Dixon, down the road, had waves in her hair. Mine never did what I wanted it to.

I cupped my hands and called up toward the window, "I'm coming, Ellen."

When I finally reached Mama's room, ready to come to Ellen's rescue, all thoughts of my hair disappeared.

A reminder of what happened a few weeks after that playful day in the woods flashed into my mind. The Black Death struck our village with a vengeance. Papa said, "The plague doesn't care who it takes, old or young, woman or man. It takes them all just the same."

It all happened so quickly, but even if I covered my ears, I could still hear Mama's screams in my head.

"Don't take them!" she shouted to Papa when he forced the lifeless bodies of Nicholas and Mary from her arms. The men in pointed masks would deposit their remains in a mass grave; we weren't even allowed to see where they buried them.

"The disease can still spread from dead to living bodies," one of the masked men said.

The other nodded. "It's best to let us handle it." When they took Nicholas and Mary out the door, Mama followed, then collapsed onto the floor. Papa had to carry her to bed.

The house was different and quieter after they died. Baby Ellen was too young to know the difference. Anthony went to work helping Papa and Grandfather with the family business. I took on the duty of Mama to little Ellen, and Jack followed me around the house. Mama—well, Mama never truly recovered from the horror of that day.

One morning, I had seen Papa alone at the table and gathered the courage to talk to him about Mama.

I pushed at the cuticles on my nails, squeezed my fingers, and quickly got the words out before I could talk myself out of it. I hated to upset him.

"Papa, I'm worried about Mama; she barely pays attention to Ellen, and I always hear her crying."

Papa sighed and patted the oak stool beside him for me to sit down. He placed a kind hand on my shoulder and said, "I know, sweetheart. But it's not your job to worry about her. She will get better; give her time." He hugged me and stood to walk away but turned around and placed his hand under my chin.

"And Anne—"

"Yes, Papa?"

"Don't grow up too fast," he said with a big grin. His thinning blond hair glistened in the morning sunlight coming through the window and his light blue eyes sparkled as he gave me a loving wink.

My thoughts were heavy, and I sighed. I felt like that was exactly what I had to do: grow up quickly so I could help Mama, but I remembered what it was like before, and I ached to be a child again. Papa had said to give Mama time, and that's all I could do.

Mama's bedroom door was ajar, so I knocked and pushed it open at the same time. My eyes had to adjust to the darkness as I stepped into the room. The air felt damp, with a slight draft coming through the side window. A large four-poster bed made of solid oak, with vines intricately carved up the posts, stood in the middle of the room. My favorite piece of furniture, Mama's hope chest, sat at the foot of her bed. I ran my fingers across its surface and traced the initials E.B.—for Mama's name, Elizabeth Burras. It was a gift from Papa on their wedding day. I longed for the day I would have a hope chest of my own with my initials carved on top.

"Hello, Mama," I said as I walked to where she sat hunched over the hearth in her linen shift, stoking the fire with a long stick and forcing the disobedient embers to cooperate.

Sweet baby Ellen stopped crying when she saw me. She squealed, pushed herself into a sitting position, then reached up with her soft chubby arms and tear-stained cheeks.

"Nan," she said, calling for me to pick her up. My face puckered into a silly expression, and I stuck out my tongue. She giggled. I hefted her out of her cradle and twirled her around and around. I bent down, picked up her small woolen blanket that had dropped on the floor, and draped it over her head, making her laugh even more.

My mood changed when I looked back again toward Mama. Timidly, I approached her and gently placed a gray shawl over her shoulders to keep her warm.

She shifted slightly and looked up at me in surprise. "Anne? I'm sorry, I didn't hear you come in."

My nose scrunched up in confusion. "Ellen was crying; didn't you hear her?"

Mama's eyebrows rose, and she looked dumbfounded. "She was? I must not have heard her." She sat up straighter and gently pushed a soft blonde curl off Ellen's face. "I'm sorry, my angel," she said as she hugged her in close. Ellen nestled into her and sighed, seemingly unscathed by the neglect.

My head filled with anger and frustration. How could she not know Ellen was crying? She was sitting right there! Mama promised Nicholas she wouldn't forget Ellen, but she did.

My eyes glared at Mama, but she didn't seem to notice; she was too focused on comforting Ellen. Seeing the two of them together nearly broke my heart. I knew Mama loved her, but why couldn't she care for her like she used to?

It made me miss Mama, the old Mama I used to know.

I took a deep breath and tried to shrug off my disappointment and hurt. "Mama, are you unwell?" I asked.

She looked up at me, her soft hazel eyes danced with the flames' reflection. I missed those eyes; they used to sparkle when they looked at me, but now the sparkle was clouded and sad. I ached to be looked at by Mama like that again.

Mama motioned for me to kneel beside her then cupped my cheek with her left hand and studied my face like she hadn't seen me in a long time. "I'm sorry, Anne; I know I haven't been the mother I should have been to you lately." She paused and stared back into the fire. "I will try harder and do the right thing by you."

My forehead furrowed. *The right thing?*

Mama sighed, and I could hear her take a small breath before continuing. "I received a letter today from my cousin's wife, Lady Catherine Eden." She gave another attempted half-smile showing a slight dimple on her cheek. "When Grandfather and Papa get home from work, we will talk with all of you— Anthony and Jack too."

I took a step back; she sounded so serious it scared me. My hands shook, and I began to sweat. "Mama, is everything all right?"

She rocked several times and took a while to respond. Her pause made me even more curious. "It will be," she finally said.

The two hours it took for Papa and Grandfather to return felt like an eternity. Multiple scenarios flashed through my mind with what the news could be. A new baby? Did someone die? Whatever it was, by the look on Mama's face, it couldn't be good.

When Papa got home, he and Mama talked for over an hour before they called us inside for a family meeting.

Grandfather sat in a chair next to Mama. Ellen sat on Mama's lap and played with a toy horse. Papa stood behind Mama with his hands cupped over her shoulders for support.

Whatever happened, this way, they were united.

Papa's lips curved into a chagrined smile, and he couldn't meet my eyes.

"Children, please have a seat."

We quietly shuffled around the table; I sat to the left of Mama and Ellen. Anthony sat on my right, and Jack sat on the other side of Anthony. His chair squeaked as he dragged it across the floor, and it cut the silent air like a knife.

"Your mother and I have big news," Papa said as he held up an open letter. "Mama received this letter today from her cousin, Lady Catherine."

I nodded in agreement; excited to finally know what it was all about.

Papa's lips started to quake, and his eyes filled with tears. I had only ever seen Papa cry once, and that was when I snuck out of my room the night Nicholas and Mary died. I wasn't used to seeing him so upset; my chin began to quiver, and I started to cry.

Papa took a deep breath to calm his nerves before speaking to us again. "Children, as you know, Mama is unwell; she hasn't been the same since Nicholas and Mary died, but there is more. There are some things—grown-up things—we haven't wanted you to worry about yet."

My breath caught in my throat. *What didn't we know about?*

I raised my right eyebrow, "What things?"

"Things you didn't have to worry about until this arrived." He waved the letter again. "We were hoping things would change, and we wouldn't have to tell you, but it looks like we were wrong. Grandfather's shipyard is struggling. Customers are afraid of the Spanish and money is hard to come by these days."

Anthony stood up to his full height. At seventeen, he was already an inch or two taller than Papa, though much thinner and smaller through his shoulders. He pounded his clenched fist on the table, and I flinched. "Struggling? What do you mean, struggling?"

Papa raised his palms toward Anthony. "Son, I understand your concern, but let me explain. Things have been difficult for many families in the past few years. Grandfather has done all he can to recover, but supplies are low, and jobs are scarce, making the need for shipments and equipment obsolete. Grandfather has taken on a lot of debt to recover the business, but it has only made matters worse."

Anthony sat down, but I could still see his fisted hands. "What does this mean for us?" he asked.

Jack stared at Anthony then back to Papa, his dark eyebrows creased with worry.

Papa picked up the letter again. The linen fibers of the paper crinkled under the weight of his strong hands. "It would make more sense if I read the letter aloud." He held the letter a few inches closer to the candle for extra light and took a deep breath before reading.

My Dearest Elizabeth,

I was sorry to receive your letter and to hear of your much fallen circumstances. Things have not been the same since our dear Queen Elizabeth's reign, God rest her soul. There are many here without work, and more and more businesses such as yours have found themselves in ruin.

We have experienced hard times ourselves. I regret to inform you that my dear Richard passed away a few months ago. I do not need to recount to you the despair I feel at his loss. You all too well know of my pain and burden which I bear.

Although I would love to help you financially, I fear I cannot. Were Richard still alive, I might be in a better position to help. However, what I lack in finances I have an abundance of in connections, and I offer you my services with the latter.

Your eldest son, Anthony, is to inherit, yes? I am sure that over time your husband and father-in-law can re-establish their shipyard business. Until then, pray tell, what are you to do? What of your Anne and young Jack? I believe they are both old enough to go into service, are they not? Many prominent families have also had to send their children off to work or learn a trade.

I understand your predicament, so I took the liberty of seeking employment for them. Without a doubt, you would not have them separated, so I managed to have them placed in the same household in London. Both will need proper training, but Sir and Mistress Forrest have agreed to take them on as a favor to our family.

Sir Forrest is an old friend of my late husband, and you will see that they are well cared for. He is doing very well for himself and is said to have taken on a new investment with the London Company. They plan to send a group of men to Virginia in the New World. The crew leaves in the spring and are to name the place where they land Jamestown after our new King James.

Sir Forrest recently married, and his bride requires an additional maid. He said that Anne would do nicely for her, and that Jack would be placed as a seven-year apprentice under his finest carpenter.

Anne will have an opportunity to learn house-wifery skills such as sewing, cooking, and cleaning. All to prepare herself to be a good wife and mother. Jack will learn a valuable trade, then be free to be a journeyman and find work elsewhere or even open his own shop one day.

I know you are still healing from the loss of your youngest son and daughter, but this truly is the better course. Think of the alternative. It is far better to send the children to a place where they can secure work and a future than to have them face poverty. Additionally, Anne can send some of her earnings home.

Please consider the Forrest family's proposal for employment for Anne and Jack and send them to London. It would be a great comfort to know that at least two of your children are being taken care of.

Your ever-devoted cousin,
Lady Catherine Eden

I wasn't sure who stood up first, me or Anthony, but before I could say a word, Anthony was on his feet. "You can't send them away!"

Papa closed his eyes and sighed, "Anthony, it is our only choice. They will have a much better future if they go."

Anthony pounded the table with his fist again. "Send me off instead!"

Mama sighed and rearranged Ellen on her lap. "You know things do not work like that. The law states that you will inherit Grandfather's business and this house." She motioned to the room around us. "Everything will go to you when Papa is gone. Jack must learn a trade, and Anne needs to prepare for motherhood."

Anthony pointed to the front door. "She needs to prepare to be a wife three hundred miles away, Mother?"

I winced. Anthony had never spoken to Mama like that before, and her face reddened at his words.

Papa stood up and pointed a finger at Anthony. "You will not talk to your mother in that tone!"

Anthony looked down. "I'm sorry, Mama. I just don't see how this is fair to Anne and Jack. Haven't you already lost a son and daughter?"

Papa and Mama grimaced. It looked like a dagger went straight through Mama's heart, and she reeled back.

"That is enough!" Papa growled. His face grew red, and his hands were shaking. I had never seen Papa so mad. Anthony hunched his shoulders and his mouth hung open.

"We are trying to do what is right for our family. Do you think this is easy? You will understand someday."

Anthony bit his lower lip and shook his head. He stood up to say something else but ran to the room where we children slept and slammed the door instead.

Papa started to go after him, but Mama grabbed his arm and said, "Give him time to calm down."

I hung my head low and silent tears ran down my cheeks. I didn't know what to think or how to feel. *Me, a maid? In London?*

I wanted to shout and run away like Anthony, but I felt frozen in place; my legs felt like heavy buckets of water, and my arms were limp like dough before baking. I stared back at Mama and Papa, then looked over to Jack in pity as he sat with his face in his hands, letting tears drop over the sides of his skinny fingers. For the first time in my life, I was utterly speechless.

Chapter Three
LEAVING HOME

"Externals I cannot control, but the choices I make
with regard to them I do control." – Epictetus

October 28, 1606

The next few days and weeks felt like a blur as we made
arrangements and finished up tasks around the house.

My heart ached with the pain of leaving home and saying goodbye to Mama, Anthony, and Ellen; I dreaded having to leave. "I
feel too ill to send them off," Mama said when it was time to say
goodbye. I bit my lower lip to keep from crying and kissed her
tear-stained cheek as she lay in bed. "Be good," is all she said. My
heart nearly broke. I wanted her to hold me in her arms and tell me
not to leave and that she loved me and didn't want me to go.

"Yes, Mama," was all I could say instead.

Tears pooled in Papa's and Anthony's eyes too. They walked us
out the door to the Hackney carriage Papa had bought tickets for.

I hugged Anthony goodbye and kissed sweet little Ellen on her cherubic cheek.

"Will she even remember me?" I said through tears.

"Of course she will," Anthony said. "She will probably be taller than you, too, just like the rest of us." He laughed at his own joke, trying to cheer me up.

"Ha, ha," I said and shook Ellen's chubby hand. "We'll see about that, Ellen, won't we?"

Papa and Jack loaded our things onto the carriage's roof and waved goodbye to Anthony, who was then holding Ellen on his hip. He coaxed her to wave goodbye to us and even blew us a kiss.

Fortunately, Papa managed to travel half of the way with us. He said he would get off in Cambridgeshire for a meeting with potential investors. I felt relieved that we didn't have to make the first part of our journey alone.

Jack and I leaned out the side window and waved for as long as we could until Anthony and Ellen were out of sight.

"Goodbye," I said, trying to be brave. My voice sounded almost happy, like I was merely going to visit another town with Papa and Jack, but I knew I wasn't and that this could be the last time I'd see Anthony, Mama or Ellen for years. My heart felt like it was being twisted from the inside out, but I knew there was nothing I could do but try to make the most of the situation. I hoped the money I'd send home would help and that Ellen could remain home with Mama and Papa.

En Route to London, October 28, 1606

The lush green English countryside stretched for miles outside our coach window as we made our way to London. We passed forests of birch, aspen, ash, and oak trees with leaves of golden yellow, purple, orange, red, and every shade between. I sighed and ached to be out in the forest, feeling the ground beneath my feet and breathing in the fresh air.

It took over three days of traveling to arrive in London. We spent the first two nights at various inns along the route. On day

two of our journey, the fatigue was already visibly wearing on Jack and me.

Mama used to say, "It's important to travel looking your best; you never know what the situation may call for." Papa must have taken her advice to heart because he wore his best matching crimson red short-waisted doublet and breech shorts with stockings. He even wore a lace ruff collar and leather shoes with bronze metal buckles to match.

It made me proud to be his daughter, even if his clothes were older and well-worn.

We couldn't afford much in the way of new clothing, so Mama let me wear one of her old dresses: a brown gown made from a soft silk material that opened in the front. I wore a cream petticoat underneath it that showed off brown embroidered flowers to match the dress. It had a square neckline with removable matching sleeves that tied over my shift. My petticoat skirt rested on top of a stiff Spanish farthingale hoop that gave my hips a fuller look. The laced-up bodice still hung loose on my petite frame, even after several attempts to pull it tighter.

I didn't mind that the dress was too big or out of fashion; it felt good to wear something of Mama's and reminded me of happier times when Mama used to wear it to dances with Papa. Besides, it looked much nicer than the plain linen work outfit I had stowed in my luggage. It made me feel like a proper lady wearing it.

Cambridgeshire's area was more prominent compared to our small county in Norfolk. We were able to get a quick peek at Castle Hill and the Roman ruins along the way. I let out a sigh when I saw the view, knowing the time had come to say our goodbyes. Knots welled inside me at the reminder that we would have to travel the rest of the way without Papa.

Bam! Bam! Papa's cane tapped twice on the coach roof, letting our driver know he had reached his destination. We all dismounted from the coach to stretch our legs and bid farewell. As we did, Papa pulled me in for a hug, smelling of rosemary and citrus. I closed my eyes to lock in the memory and hold back my tears.

"I don't feel right about the two of you making the rest of the journey by yourselves," Papa said, "so I've asked the lovely couple who are boarding the coach to watch out for you."

I looked over Papa's shoulder to see a stout-looking man with mahogany-brown hair and spectacles standing next to a kind-looking, plump woman with curly red hair and freckles. The two of them waved frantically in our direction. The woman carried one toddler on her hip, and another pulled at her skirt. I gave her a small wave before I turned back to Papa and sighed.

"We don't need help, Papa. I'm nearly thirteen!" "Anne," Papa said, "everyone needs help from time to time. You don't always have to do everything by yourself."

"I know," I said and hung my head low. In all honesty, I didn't know; I knew I was perfectly capable of taking care of Jack, and I didn't want or need to be babysat by anyone, but it was terrifying to be left alone.

As we said goodbye, I noticed strain and worry lines pressing at the corners of Papa's eyes and forehead. His once-striking light blond hair, blended with white, made him look much older than his age. I didn't want to make him worry about me, so I gave him a faint smile.

"This isn't what Mama and I would have wanted for the two of you, but it's the only way." He placed his hand under my chin and lifted my head to meet his eyes. "Sometimes, the world can be cruel, but don't let it get the best of you, Anne. There is beauty and adventure in it, too. Take heart, my girl; you are braver and stronger than you think."

I didn't feel brave, and I didn't feel strong, but I didn't want Papa to know that.

"Yes, Papa," I said, bowing my head with a short curtsy. I couldn't meet his eyes again or I wouldn't be able to fight back the tears. Instead, I looked down at my leather shoes, scuffing at the dirt beside our carriage.

"That's my girl," Papa said with a smile, and he softly kissed my forehead.

Jack visibly straightened, his hands squeezed into fists, and he rocked back and forth on his feet when it was his turn to talk to Papa.

"Remember to mind Anne," Papa told him. "And make sure she doesn't get into too much trouble." He winked in my direction but addressed both of us.

"The Forrest family will take diligent care of you both. Whatever happens, watch out for each other, and I'm sure we will all be back together again in Norfolk before too long."

He tried to smile, but his usually jolly blue eyes looked sad, betraying his true feelings as he reached out his hand to help me climb back onto the coach. We watched him standing and waving to us until we turned the corner, and then he was no longer in sight.

Jack tried hard to hold back his tears and put on a brave face. I discreetly handed him my handkerchief, then quickly turned my head to look out the window before he saw me cry. I wiped a tear with my hand and did everything in my power not to make eye contact with anyone else on the coach. From the corner of my eye, I peered at Papa's now empty seat, and a rush of panic waved over me. We were indeed on our own.

After a few minutes, I looked up and found the red-haired woman giving me a pitying look. As daintily as possible, I sat straighter in my seat, readjusted my petticoat, and then tucked my relentless hair into place before giving her a curt smile. I didn't want her or anyone else thinking we weren't capable of taking care of ourselves.

Chapter Four
BRAVING THE JOURNEY

"Being brave does not mean you aren't scared. Being brave means, you do the right thing even if you are scared." – Mama

October 30, 1606

The sights of London bewildered me. I had never seen so many people and buildings in all my life. It was terrifying and exhilarating all at the same time. When I thought of the transformation from country to city, I felt ill with homesickness. From the look in his eyes, Jack may have felt the same. His skin paled and dark circles formed under his once-bright blue eyes. His stillness was unnerving. I ruffled his curly brown hair, reminding him that I was still there.

"I'm gut-foundered," he whined.

"Exactness in our words now, Jack," I said, glancing at the red-haired woman. I wanted her to change her mind about us now that she could see how well I cared for Jack. "You know Mama does not like us using slang." I pulled a piece of bread from my bag. "I know you are hungry. Here, I saved some bread for you."

Papa's words rang in my ears. "You must be brave now, Anne."

"Be brave," I whispered to myself. "Be brave."

Our coach driver lurched the coach forward and then abruptly stopped, causing my heart to skip a beat. This part of the ride had been the worst of all. We had traveled over large potholes, mud, and rough stone. We had been tossed forward, backward, and sideways, causing a wave of nausea to build up in my throat.

The six of us passengers peered through the window at the disturbance to assess the damage, only to see that our luggage had flown off the carriage roof onto the dirty ground below. Bags and trunks lay open in the street.

"Time to get out!" the driver said gruffly, following his words with a loud belch. His unsteady, baritone voice told us that he wasn't joking. After opening the coach door, we could all see why. He had conveniently stopped in front of a tavern.

"But sir," cried the red-haired woman in a thick Scottish accent, giving me a pitying look again, "we have not yet passed Westminster, and we are nowhere near the Strands."

I was impressed with her resolve to get where she needed to go.

"It's time for me to have a drink," the driver said. "If you want to wait for me to be done, be my guest."

"But we paid our fee," the woman pleaded. "We could be waiting here for hours!"

"It be your choice. You know where to find me." The driver walked off toward the tavern.

"Now what will we do?" the woman asked, looking at her husband for help.

Her husband was a quiet gentleman with a black, wide-brimmed hat and a green feather plume that bent in a perfect arch. His voice was soft and stammered, so we all strained to listen as he spoke. "We-ee'd better do as he says and g-eeet out.

I'd ra-aather find another hackney or w-waa-alk than wait for this fellow."

Jack and I nodded in agreement; I motioned to Jack to exit first, and we all descended the steps, attempting to avoid the manure on the ground when we stepped off.

"The fresh air will do us all good," the man added as he helped his wife and children down the steps.

I tried to smile—if not for my sake, then for Jack's. Getting out of the carriage and stretching my tired legs felt good. Every part of my body ached. My knees wobbled, and I felt like a baby fawn on its first day of life.

My heart skipped a beat, and my hands and feet suddenly felt tingly from sitting so long.

We quickly picked our tossed luggage up off the street. One side of my leather bag was covered in mud, and my under-shift had fallen out and lay on display for all to see. My cheeks felt hot with embarrassment. I quickly grabbed the dress and shoved it back into my bag.

Jack grabbed one of his shirts off the ground, then quietly slipped it back in his case. He looked at me with a scrunched up nose and fear in his eyes. "What are we going to do now?" he asked.

I wasn't sure what to do, but I wasn't about to tell Jack that. If we were already in London, we had to be close.

I forced the corners of my mouth to turn up into a smile. "It can't be too far from here; come along now, Jack," I said, trying to sound more confident than I felt.

The couple from the coach gave us a vague direction of where to go.

"Not that far from here now, loves," the woman said. "Go a wee bit past this section of town, then head eastward; that is where all the large manors and estates be. You can't miss it." She gave us a big toothy smile that showed off her dimples and endless freckles.

Within minutes of walking, the nausea returned, but this time it wasn't from being jostled in the carriage ride. Waves of pungent smells and smoke congested the air. The aroma was so intense I had to cover my nose and mouth to avoid vomiting.

People huddled around fire pits, wearing tattered clothing, trying to stay warm. Smoke billowed up, stinging my eyes and burning my nose and throat. Row Houses with thatched hay roofs lined the streets, and people from all levels of society hustled down the busy roads and alleyways. Some of them ran while others wearily stumbled around looking for food, water, or money. Jack had to hurry out of the way as a woman tossed out her chamber pots full of human waste before him. Mothers cried alongside their babies as they attempted to stay warm and plead for money; each pink in the cheeks and nose from the cold, hands cupped out for donations.

"Yuck!" Jack moaned as he lifted his shoe off a manure pile. He covered his nose and tried not to gag.

Even the puddles smelled sour. I could hear shouts and moans from the beggars crying for food. People would walk past them and yell at them to "bugger off."

The noise was almost palpable! People pushed carts around, selling goods. Each made a loud noise as their wooden wheels bumped over the cobblestone streets, selling everything from flowers to fresh chickens. The latter often bounded out of their carts and cages.

"Ouch!" Jack yelled when I squeezed his hand too tight after a man with a toothless grin smiled at me.

This was a horrible idea, I thought.

I sighed and ached for home; I could still picture it if I closed my eyes tightly enough. Home before Nicholas and Mary were taken from us, before Mama became so sad. When we were free to run and play outside, the soft blades of grass damp under our bare feet. I could almost hear Mama's voice as she called us in for supper and my siblings' laughter as we played tag. Their voices played tricks on my mind, and I longed for our days together.

I forced the tears and aching in my heart away as we trudged through the rest of the streets. Papa's words echoed again in my ears. "No use in looking back; all you can do is move forward."

"Time to be brave, time to be brave," I said again, taking a deep breath.

Jack's words woke me out of my thoughts. "Anne, watch out!"

Two large boys, filthy from head to toe, stood right in front of us, intentionally blocking our way. The older one with chestnut brown hair and brown eyes gave me a crooked smile and grabbed me by my left arm. "What you got in the bag there, miss? Why don't you give it to me, and I will show you where you can get a warm meal."

"No, thank you," I said firmly, quickly pulling my arm away. "Oh, come on now. Just take it from her, Charlie!" the younger one, with freckles and red hair, presumably his brother, moaned.

"Miss, don't put up a fight. Just hand it over." The taller one said as he stepped closer to us.

Jack loosened his grip on my hand and walked straight up to the red-haired boy to make him move.

"She said, 'No, thank you,'" he said. "Now move out of our way!"

"Oh, really?" the younger red-haired boy replied. "Make us!"

Jack's nose scrunched up, and his hands went into fists. "No, Jack," I said, pulling him back. "It's not worth it."

"Ya, listen to your sister, Jack," the red-haired boy teased, sticking out his tongue and stomping his feet firmer into the mud. This time, he reached out for my leather bag and pulled hard.

Before I knew it, I had pulled my bag away from him and swung it around as hard as I could right into his jaw. He twirled around so fast that he landed face-first in the mud.

I gasped and Jack seized my arm. "Run!" he shouted.

The older boy quickly bent over to help his little brother up. It took me a few seconds to realize what had happened before I picked up my petticoat skirt and ran with Jack.

Behind us, I heard the younger brother shout, "Get 'em!"

We ran as if our lives depended on it. Luckily, we had a head start. We swerved between the crowds of people, causing a ruckus in our wake.

"Ill-mannered children. Watch your step. Now, see here!" people shouted at us as we plowed our way through.

We finally found a crowded alleyway and hid behind some crates. After a few minutes of panting and catching our breath, we laughed at each other.

"I can't believe you did that," Jack huffed and playfully punched me on the shoulder.

"Me neither." I said as I ruffled his hair again with my hand. "Now, don't forget it next time you don't want to listen to me." Then I gave him a wink like Papa and Anthony used to do.

Chapter Five
FINDING THE WAY

"All clouds bring not rain." – John Withals, 1584

October 30, 1606

We walked silently for several minutes, holding hands to ensure we'd stay together, both too terrified to let go. The sky looked a dark shade of gray, ominous and sad, as if the clouds themselves were ready to weep with us. When the clouds finally broke, we were both soaked to the bone.

My body ached as each step felt like an extra ten pounds of weight tugging on my feet. The rain finally subsided, but I couldn't wait to get to the great house and sit by a warm fire.

The sun finally returned, and after what seemed like hours, we reached the end of the lane where the estates started, but I didn't know which home was the Forrests'.

An older woman and gentleman passed us on a post rain stroll. The London rain had stopped just as quickly as it had come. The woman looked beautiful in a yellow bodice and petticoat.

Her gloved hands gripped a Chinese parasol decorated in tiny red pansies, quite the fashion for the wealthy. The man with her looked as refined as she did in a tight-fitting gray doublet coat, wide lace-trimmed collar, and a large black hat.

"Excuse me, madam, can you help us find the Forrest Family home?" I asked. We must have looked quite a sight, covered in mud well past my hem and wet through and through. I swiped at my hair and pushed it away as it clung to my face and neck and tried to look presentable.

The gentleman gawked at us, then lowered his thick eyebrows and pursed his lips. I couldn't tell if he was giving us a look of pity or disdain.

"'Tis not far," he said, and with a flick of his wrist, he pointed to a clearing near the far east side of the road. "Follow that road, and it will lead you there."

"We thank you, sir," I said, curtsying deeply. I elbowed Jack to give a polite bow, then turned in the direction he had pointed. Jack visibly relaxed after our conversation with the gentleman. It reminded me he was just a boy of ten and probably felt just as exhausted as I was. We both were still shocked at having to leave home and travel this far. What we needed were warm clothes and food in our bellies.

Jack squeezed one arm tightly across his chest to stay warm, his other clutching the handle of his leather bag.

"What are you thinking about?" I gently prodded, to take his mind off the cold.

He sighed. "I was thinking about Mama, Papa, and home. Anne, do you think we will ever see them again?" His light blue eyes sprang full of water, hopeful and fearful at the same time.

"Of course we will. Papa and Anthony will figure out the problems with the shipyard, and then they will send for us to come home. You'll see." I bumped his shoulder with my arm.

Memories of Papa's sad blue eyes told me otherwise, but I didn't want Jack to lose hope. I shook my head to force my thoughts elsewhere. It wouldn't do to dwell on that now; too much was at stake. We had to focus on what was ahead, not what was behind. We walked the rest of the way as if in a haze.

"I'm so hungry," Jack cried.

The smells from nearby kitchens we passed almost made me stop in my tracks and cry. One whiff of fresh bread and salty roasted meat filled my nostrils, and my stomach growled in anticipation.

"Me too," I said. "We're nearly there; I'm sure of it." *At least, I hope we are.*

It was well past supper when we arrived at the mansion. Besides eating, all I wanted to do was change out of my wet clothes and sleep.

Our arrival was a welcome reprieve. I ached for home but was so happy to have a place to stay that I wanted to skip to the large door and shout that we had finally arrived. I took a deep breath to get a hold of myself and grabbed Jack's hand to go around the back to find the servant's entrance.

Sure enough, a smaller door stood behind the great house. I knocked several times before an elderly woman with multiple missing teeth answered the door.

"And who you be?" she asked suspiciously.

"The name is Anne, ma'am; Anne Burras, and here is my brother, Jack," I said, trying to keep my teeth from chattering from the cold.

December 2, 1606

Dear Mama,

We had quite the adventure getting here, but you would be happy to know that we found our way to the Forrests' home unharmed and are now safe in their care. Some parts of London are truly terrifying, but now that I have met some of Mistress Forrest's friends and guests, I can see why people talk of it so fondly.

Mistress Forrest is not overly kind, nor is she cruel. It feels like I tower over her. I must be at least four inches taller, even though you and I know I am not very tall. My blonde hair is quite the contrast to her copper red, which is striking compared to her bright green eyes. She is nothing but class and grace—even though she is missing several teeth that show up when she smiles, which is a rare sight indeed.

She is much older than I expected, already in her mid-thirties; older than most new brides which surprised me. I kept trying to get a peek at her when I arrived. I'm usually cleaning the house with the other maids and don't see her often.

Her husband, Sir Thomas Forrest, seems like a funny man. He is much the opposite of her, tall and thin, over six feet tall. I tried not to laugh the first time I saw him with wild shaggy brown hair that likes to swoop over his right eye and a giant bald spot in the back. He is a jolly sort of fellow. We all know he is home because he whistles when he walks in.

He has a five-year-old son named Peter from his late wife. Every time Peter enters a room, he always causes an uproar for Mistress and the staff. He runs so fast that no one can seem to catch him. Not even his tutor can keep up. He tries relentlessly to make him sit down and stick to his lessons. He runs circles around Mistress, and her cheeks get red with anger. I try hard not to giggle, Mama, I do. She usually yells something at him and demands he pay more attention to his studies, but it never helps.

Do you remember when Anthony would act that way? I can still picture it now: his tutor's face contorting as he tried to hold back his anger and you pulling out your fan in front of your face to hide your laughter. Mistress threw a party a fortnight after we arrived.

Sir Forrest hired a small orchestra of violin, lute, and mandolin players, which sounded magnificent. There were twenty or so couples who attended. They had a grand feast and rolled up the rugs for people to dance. I got to watch from the stairs with some of the maids. I imagined myself in a delicate dress, escorted by a handsome young man onto the dance floor.

Mama, I wish you could have seen the dresses. Some ladies' dresses were made of silver taffeta embroidered with gold! Can you believe it? Gold, Mama!

What would it be like to be a grand lady? Wouldn't it be so fun to attend a ball? Can't you close your eyes and picture it? Papa would dance the first dance with you, then with me, and force Anthony and Jack to dance, even though they'd hate it.

Speaking of Jack, he is doing well in his apprenticeship. He usually has a few hours on Thursday afternoons off, which he spends running around with the neighborhood boys. He checks on me often, and I on him when I can. It's a comfort to have him nearby.

Being a maid is much more complicated than it looks; I rise before the sun and work on household chores: cleaning, sewing, tending to fires, and sometimes helping the cook or whatever is needed. I am doing my best, and the head maid and Mistress seem pleased with my work so far. Please do not worry about us. All is well. I am grateful for the work and have enclosed part of my earnings with this letter. It isn't much, but I hope it helps.

How is Ellen doing? Does she miss us? Please give her my love.

I also think of you, Papa, Grandfather, and Anthony often. I miss Papa's stories and playing the lute while you sang us songs. I love you, Mama.

Yours always,
Anne

Chapter Six
MISTRESS FORREST

"Do you not know I am a woman? When I think I
must speak." – William Shakespeare

April 16, 1608

Time seemed to pass by quickly at the Forrest estate, and weeks
turned into months and months turned into over a year.
Jack turned twelve and I was nearing my fifteenth birthday. The
work felt mundane, but I fell into a comfortable routine. I woke
up before the sun, started a fire in the large room, collected water
from the well, boiled the water, cleared and dusted rooms, swept
floors, helped cook and whatever else was asked of me. My daily
tasks seemed to never end, but working with the other maids made
it feel less daunting. I met Sir Forrest and his wife when we arrived
but other than that brief introduction, they didn't pay us much
attention. Then, one morning, I was tasked with bringing Mistress
breakfast when her lady's maid became ill.

My knees wobbled. *What if I drop the tray or trip?*

I shrugged my shoulders and furrowed my brow. "Me? Why me?" I asked.

The kitchen maid placed the tray in my arms and pushed me out the door toward the stairs. "Because you're the only one available. Now, get on with you."

I didn't stay around long enough to get pushed twice; I knew my place. I willed my hands and knees to remain still and went up the stairs without dropping anything, then knocked on Mistress Forrest's chamber room door.

"Come in," came a regal voice.

When I entered, my eyes opened wide because of the grandness of the room. The walls were lined in wainscoting with beautiful tapestries of lakeside scenes. Her bed was large and extravagantly covered with green satin cloth finished with fringe-trimmed edges. The fabric draped elegantly across the top and down the sides, tied by a ribbon at each corner. A portrait of Sir Forrest hung above her matching vanity set with hairbrushes and powders. Four heavy curtains covered two tall windows, and a carved oak wardrobe rested against the opposite wall.

"Good morning, Mistress," I said with a bob of my head. I strained to keep my face calm and proper. With shaking hands, I placed a tray with a bowl of porridge on her lap. She waved at her beet-red face rapidly with a Chinese silk-laced fan.

"Are you ill?" I asked her timidly.

"I fear this insufferable heat might do me in. However shall I endure it?" She moaned and threw several pillows off her bed onto the floor.

I hid my confusion. It was a mild spring morning. "Why don't we open your windows, Mistress? The fresh air will do you good." I walked to her windows, pulled back the shades, and let some air in. "What beautiful grounds you have." Her grounds were impeccable, vast, and built on a flat terrace. A small rotunda stood in the far corner of the garden; the daffodils of spring were out in full force, along with bluebells, purple and pink primroses, and wallflowers of every color. The view from her window took my breath away, and I felt as if I was transported somewhere else for a time. The white and yellow daisies felt like they were beckoning me to play. I stood there, entranced in the moment until I heard a cry come from behind me and realized I was still in Mistress's bedroom.

Mistress covered her face with her hand to block out the bright sun. "What are you doing?" she cried.

I took a step back, bowed my head, and looked at the ground when I turned to her. I prayed she wouldn't fire me.

"I'm sorry, Mistress; I didn't mean to offend," I said sheepishly. "Your grounds are impeccable, and I thought seeing them would lift your spirits."

She sat there in silence, fanning herself for what felt like hours. In a calmer tone, she said, "Yes, I suppose you are right."

My heart raced at what she would say next. When she didn't say a word, I asked, "Will there be anything else?"

She gave me a prodding, curious look and said, "That will be all." She continued to fan herself softly.

I dipped my head in a curtsy, felt my cheeks flush, and walked out of the room as quickly as possible.

After shutting the door, I pushed my back against the stone wall and breathed a deep sigh of relief. "I can't believe I did that," I whispered to myself.

When I returned to the kitchen to tell the cook and head maid that Mistress's food had been delivered properly, I didn't dare mention what had happened. I hoped the whole incident would be forgotten but my hope was in vain.

The following day, I heard a knock at my bedroom door in the attic.

"Sir Forrest wishes to speak to you, miss," a maid yelled.

Sir Forrest? That's it; he must be sending me back home for how I'd acted the day before.

With my heart pounding in my chest, I quickly slid my woolen red kirtle dress over my shift, laced the stays and pulled on my white stockings, tying them with ribbon garters above my knee. Then I slipped my feet into my black square-toed shoes, covered my hair with my linen coif, and ran downstairs to meet Sir Forrest.

"Miss Anne Burras, am I correct?"

"Yes, sir," I said, giving Sir Forrest a small curtsy.

"I was friends with your mother's late cousin, Sir Eden." "Yes, my mother told me such."

"Lady Catherine asked me to help your family." He had a bright look in his eyes and a gentle smile as he remembered who I was. "Have you been treated well here?"

"Oh, yes, sir, I have." I nodded. It was demanding work, but they treated me well, considering the circumstances.

"Good, that is good; and your wages, are they sufficient?" *Wages? Why would Sir Forrest ask me about my wages?* "Yes, sir; I send most of my pay home to my family in Norfolk."

"Excellent." He paced the floor for a moment and then asked, "Pray tell, what is your age?"

My eyebrows squeezed together in confusion. "My age, sir? I am nearly fifteen."

He nodded his head and held his hands behind his back as he continued to pace the floor. Then he paused and looked at me with a kind smile. "Miss Burras, I want to offer you the position of lady's maid for Mistress Forrest."

His offer shocked me, and I took a small step back. "Lady's maid, sir?"

Unknowingly, my right eyebrow rose higher than the left in a questioning look. Sir Forrest must have read my thoughts because he went on to say, "Yes, her current lady's maid is too ill to continue with us, and Mistress has taken a liking to you. She said you understood the importance of fresh air and maintaining a good lawn. Whatever you said or did for her had a calming effect, and it would be wise to give you the position. She, at times, can be—well, let's say that at times she needs to be reminded of what is most important."

My heart began to race with excitement, and I felt my face flush. "Yes, sir. Thank you. I consider it a great honor," I said with a deep curtsy.

Over time, I realized that it wasn't just the weather that upset Mistress. A lot of things did: smells, noises, food, and especially young Peter.

"Now, Thomas," Mistress would say, "if you do not get this child under control, I shall pull my hair out at once!"

Sir Forrest often replied, "Oh, come dear, do be sensible. He is but a child, and a little boy at that. Look here; he is just having a bit of fun."

Mistress generally turned red in the face, which was my cue to step in and help.

"Mistress," I'd say, looping my arm in hers, "pray, tell me more about the flowers we see outside this window."

Mistress loved her gardens and spoke fondly of them. I learned a lot from caring for Mama that it was better to prevent a sorrowful or anxious mood than try to put one out of it.

"Thank you," Sir Forrest usually mouthed after the fact. He never scolded Peter, which drove Mistress crazy. I thought it must have been because he reminded him too much of his late wife to get angry, and besides, he was too good-natured to stay mad at anyone.

Oh, how he doted on Mistress! I never understood the perplexities of marriage; yet I found myself thinking of it often.

Mama and Papa didn't write to me often, but when they did, I considered it a great treasure and kept it under my mattress. Occasionally, I pulled their letters out to read them when I felt homesick. Mama wrote one that had me feeling more homesick than ever:

My dearest Anne,

It pains me to have you and Jack so far away. I am starting to recover and don't want you to worry about me. I hope you and Jack are faring well and attending to your duties without complaint.

Anthony and Papa are working hard to restore the business. They have clients here and there, but we need more to sustain us long-term. Anthony has made it known that he is fond of Sarah Dixon down the road and may pursue marriage once he has earned enough money for her hand. It would be a love match that may be joyous for Anthony, but after losing the shipyard's primary customers, I doubt her prudent father would agree.

The bans of Rebecca Leigh and William Jones were read in church last week, as well as those of Mary Brown and Ezra Robison. Everyone waited till after Lent to marry and rushed before it was spring.

I do wish we had a dowry for you to marry well. Keep working hard; you will have skills to offer your future husband, as well as the little we are trying to save from your earnings. Please know that you are in our thoughts and prayers.

Love always,
Mama

Sarah Dixon! I huffed to myself as I sat down on my bed. *Of course, Anthony had to like Sarah Dixon. She and her beautiful curly hair.*

A tear rolled down my cheek and my hands started to shake. I didn't realize how much I missed home and how unfair it all felt that the world was moving on without me.

I couldn't help but feel sorry for myself. I wiped away a tear that slid down my cheek. Marriage was the natural course of things, but I still couldn't help being jealous of Rebecca and Mary both being married before me. Marriage gave them protection, a home, a name, and society's approval. What if I never married and became a spinster like old Lady Thurton at the market? What would society think of me then? I would be a lady's maid until my dying day. My worries only increased when I thought about the dowry that the other girls brought to their marriages. *What did I have to offer?*

Chapter Seven
My Lady

"We know what we are but not what we may be." –
William Shakespeare

May 1, 1608

My duties changed after becoming a lady's maid. Mistress Forrest was now "My Lady," and I only tended to her. Besides getting her dressed, mending her clothing, bringing her food, and tending to her bath, I was charged with taking care of her when she was in one of her moods. It was a lot of work, but the pay was much higher, so it was worth the extra responsibility.

My workload never seemed to end, but I relished Sundays when I went to church with the Forrest family and then had the remainder of the afternoon to myself.

My favorite time was when I could walk around the estate grounds. I loved to trace the path that led near the woods. It was peaceful there and reminded me of home. Spring was in full bloom, and little pink and white buds dotted the trees. I liked to take off my shoes and stockings and walk barefoot on the grass. It was the best feeling in the world—I could escape and feel free.

It rained often, not much more than in Norfolk, yet there was something different about the rain in London. The smell, the feel of it seemed different.

One day, the rain fell so hard I thought the roof would cave in on us. I was sick that day, and Mistress was a stickler against illness in her home. The plague had hit London hard three years prior, and anything as much as a sneeze would get you sent upstairs away from everyone else.

"Oh, Anne, do mind yourself," she would say, or "Get thee hence at once. One must not spread such a vulgar disease," then she'd point to the door for me to leave.

I didn't mind it so much; it allowed me to catch up on my other chores and escape the chaos. Occasionally, I was even able to see Jack on those days.

The day I was ill, all I wanted to do was lie down on my bed. I slept all day, and it was late at night when I awoke. The rain still fell, so much so that tiny droplets had made their way through the plaster beside my bed. When this happened, I put a copper pot underneath the drops. Unfortunately, I didn't have one in my room to use.

I lit a beeswax candle and had just opened my door to go downstairs to get a pot when I heard Mistress crying and yelling in the other room. She must have been having one of her fits. I cupped my hand around the flame to prevent the fire from blowing out and made my way in her direction.

I had almost reached her chamber when I heard Sir Forrest's voice. If he was with her, she wouldn't need me, and I certainly did not want him to see me in my night shift, so I slowly inched my way back down the hall to grab a pot. My heart thumped in my chest as I ran the rest of the way to my room, set the pot under the drip and blew out the candle I was holding.

As I turned to shut my door, I heard a loud thud from something Mistress had thrown across the room and her raised voice. It made me jump. I knew it wasn't my business, but I decided to listen anyway. I bit my lip to force myself to be quiet and left the heavy wooden door cracked open to hear.

"Do you intend to abandon me, Thomas, and go to the other side of the world? After all that we have been through?"

"Been through? What do you mean, been through? My dear, you have had nothing but the best, and I intend to give you such. You have a splendid roof over your head, food on your table, and clothing on your back. That is much more than the rest of the people in this country have. I must check on our investment if you intend to keep having such luxuries. It was an order from the Company."

"The Company, the Company; why must everything be about the *Company?* What about *me?*"

"It is about you, my dear; can't you see that? It is about our future."

"Then take me with you."

"Take you with me?" Sir Forrest paused. "To Jamestown? But you are a woman; it isn't safe!"

"What isn't safe is leaving me here while you go about the other side of the world. What about my nerves? Who will tend to them?"

"Why, Anne, of course, my dear, and the other maids." "Anne will come with me, then!"

"Come with you?" Sir Forrest sounded alarmed.

"She's the only one who knows how to calm me, and besides, it will be but a few months. You said so yourself."

I clasped my hands over my mouth and stepped back into my room. *Me, leave England and go to Jamestown?*

"A maid?" I heard Sir Forrest cry out.

"Why not? They have all sorts of workers there. Why not a maid?"

His steps echoed as he paced the hard wooden floor, and I could imagine the wheels spinning in Sir Forrest's head.

"What are we to do with Peter, then?" he asked.

"Peter is far too young to make such a journey, and you know how fragile my nerves are around him. He is safer here with his tutor."

After a few moments of silence, I closed my eyes and strained my ears to hear the rest.

"You're right, my dear. This may be your best idea yet. We will show the Company how successful and safe the trip will be if two women can make it. But I promised I would keep the Burras children together—if we are bringing Anne, we must bring her younger brother Jack with us too. Other craftsmen will be coming, including his master, so it would be sensible to bring him either way. Captain Newport said we need more crew and supplies. What a pleasant surprise you will be, my dear."

"I agree wholeheartedly, my love," she said, pleased with herself.

I quietly closed my bedroom door, too stunned to know what to say or think. My heart raced, and my palms began to sweat. I tried to compose myself, but too many thoughts ran through my head. I couldn't believe this was happening to me! Cross the ocean to the New World and live among the people there? It all seemed so exciting and terrifying at the same time. Papa's stories of the people who settled in Roanoke and the Spanish flashed through my mind.

Would we be abandoned there too? Were the stories I heard true? How would Jack feel? I was anxious to talk to Papa, and it made me grateful he had taught me to read and write, unlike most girls, who never got the chance. I immediately took out the quill and ink Mistress had given me and wrote a letter to Papa. Three weeks later, I received the following reply.

Dear Anne,

Thank you for your letter. I also received one from Sir Forrest on your behalf. He has promised to do his best to keep you and Jack safely together when you travel to Jamestown. The prospect does worry me; unfortunately, I have little say in the matter as you both are under his care and employment, seeing as how I do not have sufficient means to support you at this time.

I wish the circumstances were different. We are trying new ways of investing; I sold a portion of our estate to invest back into the shipyard. It should be enough to keep it going for the time being. If it does turn a profit, there may be a chance of you and Jack returning home.

Please remember that you are in their care, to listen and respect your duties, and remind Jack to do the same. It is fortunate that Cousin Catherine set up your job when she did. Otherwise, you would be going on something other than this grand adventure. I wish I were going with you. Please write and tell me all about it when you can; and Anne, please watch over Jack.

Until we meet again, my dear,

Papa

Chapter Eight
SETTING SAIL

"In a calm sea, everyman is a pilot." – John Ray

Docks of London, August 3, 1608

We set sail on a sweltering day in early August. The air was sticky and full of the stench of fish and human waste as we made our way from the city to the shore.

I could feel the moisture on my face and lips as we approached. The water sloshed against the deck while the men shouted at each other.

The names *Margaret and Mary* were painted in small black letters on the side of our ship. It was magnificent, made of white and yellow pine and painted with dark red designs.

Captain Christopher Newport was our guide. Seventy passengers waited to board; one was even a Virginia native named Namontack. It was my first time seeing someone from the New World. I bit my lip and tried to look away; I didn't want him to find me rude for staring.

"Good day," he said in a deep, raspy voice as I passed with Mistress and Sir Forrest.

"Good day," I replied with a smile, caught off guard by his welcome to me in English. I couldn't help looking back a few times after we passed to get another glimpse of him. Stories I overheard from Sir Forrest about the Virginia natives played tricks on my mind; before, I'd wanted to be as far away from him and them as possible, but something about Namontack's kind brown eyes and smile made me feel safe.

All sorts of people were at the docks waiting to say goodbye to their loved ones. I watched the organized chaos unfold in front of me as men loaded cargo and supplies onto the ship. Some raced back and forth on the deck, pulling at the masts and riggings. It was so loud I could barely hear what Sir Forrest said next to me.

"What an amazing sight!" he called over the noise. "Indeed, my love, it is," replied Mistress, squeezing his arm.

The excitement in the air was contagious! I looked around in awe; I had never seen this large a port before, let alone one of the biggest ones in Europe. It felt as if I was part of the royal family, admired and waved at as we boarded the ship. My cheeks blushed to bright pink, and I tucked my hair under my coif as I trailed behind Mistress and the massive amounts of luggage she had insisted we bring. She would have brought more luggage if the London Company did not limit the quantity of supplies we could bring.

Jack and a few of the craftsmen made their way toward us. "Jack!" I waved. When he reached us, I squeezed his hand.

"Isn't this exciting?"

His eyes widened. "Papa would have loved this!"

I nodded and leaned over the rail. "Remember the tales Papa used to tell us about Roanoke?"

Jack laughed. "How could I forget a lost colony of English set-tlers roaming around Virginia?" His blue eyes danced with excitement. "Do you think we'll see any of them when we are there? Maybe we can find them!" he said with a hopeful grin.

I smiled. "I hope we can. Could you imagine the look on Papa and Anthony's face if we did!?"

"They would have loved this." Jack added.

I looked around and nodded, "I think so too."

We looked out at the vast ocean in awe together. I couldn't believe we were about to visit the New World! Part of me was terrified, but it was comforting to know that Captain Christopher Newport had made the voyage several times and knew what he was doing. We'd received word several months ago that the first three ships, the *Godspeed*, the *Discovery*, and the *Susan Constant*, had made it to Jamestown. Captain Newport informed us that a fire had broken out after the first supply ship arrived a few months ago, burning much of their new supplies. I imagined they eagerly awaited our arrival with the replenishment of goods and supplies.

Sir Forrest may have been relaxed and passive with his wife and Peter at home, but here among the men he was treated with utmost respect. When they heard that a Company investor was onboard, they fawned over him and Mistress because they did not want to cause any trouble for themselves or the crew.

Sir Forrest looked polished in his green doublet jacket with matching breeches. He also wore a large black hat with two green feather plumes and a broad white lace collar around his neck. Mistress Forrest wore a beautifully embroidered cream bodice with swirls of intricately sewn flowers and a petticoat skirt with the same pattern to match.

The ship was full of men from all levels of society. There were gentlemen, artisans, and farmers. Most were English, but some were Polish, German, and Slovaks. There were glassmakers, soap makers, pitch-turpentine makers, carpenters who crafted clapboards, and artisans of every kind. The Virginia Company of London recruited them all.

We also carried over one hundred and fifty tons of supplies with us! It was a miracle we were able to float at all.

My heart raced with anticipation of what we'd see next and how we would get along during the next few months onboard the ship.

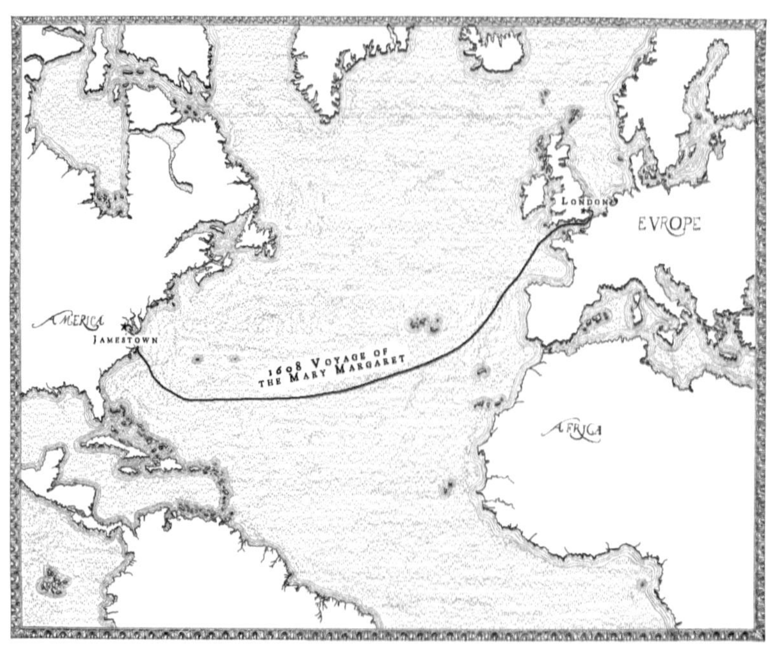

LONDON
EVROPE
AMERICA
JAMESTOWN
1608 VOYAGE OF
THE MARY MARGARET
AFRICA

Chapter Nine
Only a Fortnight Away

"Heaven and earth never agreed better to frame a place for man's habitation." – Captain John Smith

August 16, 1608

I never imagined something so grand as the open sea. It could be friendly one minute then fierce the next. The sunsets were amazing to watch; soft pinks touching over the glow of orange reflecting off blue water. Other times I felt tossed around like I was on a toy boat in a giant pond. Fortunately for us, the weather stayed primarily favorable, with occasional storms. I tolerated it well enough, but others were not so lucky. "Disgusting!" a man complained.

"These biscuits are hard as rocks," said another. "How do they expect us to live off of these?" He threw a biscuit against the wooden hull, shattering the food into tiny pieces. An argument broke out, and one of the men pushed another.

I retreated below to our corner of the cabin to get some space from the men. Sir Forrest closed the blue linen curtain set up for us to have some privacy from the others.

"Everything will be all right, ladies," Sir Forrest said.

"Oh, my poor nerves," Mistress complained, fanning herself again in distress. "To have to live among such people!"

"Now, now, dear," Sir Forrest said comfortingly. "We shall be there soon. You shall see."

I shook my head and tried not to laugh; for such an opinionated woman, Mistress sure didn't handle discomfort very well.

The water barrels smelled foul. We were only permitted to use plain water for cooking and cleaning; even then, I didn't want to touch it. When I investigated the wooden barrel, I saw a thick slime resting on the top, not to mention the bugs swimming and floating above the grime. It made me want to gag. We drank the watered-down beer water instead, and even that made me sick at times. Oh, how I yearned for fresh food and clean air!

Mistress gave her strong opinion of the water, and I tried to change the subject.

"Did you see the dolphin that jumped by our porthole yesterday, My Lady?" I asked. Mistress was happiest when she spoke about plants and animals; I hoped the conversation would distract her from the men's argument and the grumbling in our stomachs.

"Yes, I did." She smiled for a moment, then her lips formed a scowl. "'Tis a pity it didn't stay longer."

I forced a fake smile. "Yes, my lady. That is a shame." Then I turned and rolled my eyes. How did she always find a way to turn something positive into something negative?

My other favorite thing to look for was birds. Initially, wild birds had landed on the deck and distracted us. Jack told me how he and some other young boys would try to chase them away, but it had been weeks since we had spotted any.

"Captain Newport said when we start to see birds again, we are close to land," I told Mistress with a smile. The sea was beautiful, but I couldn't wait to see land again.

Jack was made for the sea; if he wasn't running around the deck with the other boys, he would swing from the ropes, getting pointers from the crew. As he put it, his confidence in being a "sailor" grew daily.

There was a constant watch assigned to look out for Spanish ships or pirates who wished to do us harm just as much as there was a watch for dangerous weather. Being as agile and energetic as he was, Jack was selected more than once for the lookout position. Luckily, his stomach did not disappoint, and he stayed alert when a small rainstorm came in. The storm passed quickly, but I thought that poor Mistress would die of fright.

"Alright, back to the hull with you," the sailors shouted whenever they caught the boys about. "Either that, or we'll put you to work!" And they often did, forcing them to clean the deck or climb to a high point on the sails that the men didn't want to reach. The rest of us, besides the crew, mostly stayed under the ship's deck to avoid the sailors; Mistress did not want the men gawking at us. When the weather was excellent and the water was calm, a few of us could get fresh air on deck if we weren't in the sailors' way.

Under the deck was a world of its own. I had never met nor heard so many different languages and cultures in my life! People spoke German, Dutch, Slovakian, and the like. There were men everywhere. They sat and lay around on pallets, chairs, and even the floor; most played card and dice games such as Shut the Box and Backgammon.

Mistress and I stayed to ourselves in the corner given to us. We'd brought our bedding, two mattresses full of goose feathers sewn into a linen sheet, which was placed on pallets made from the cargo the ship carried. Besides light from the portholes, it was dark, and the odor from the men and us permeated the air.

My skin itched from being unable to bathe or change my shift, and the ship's hull smelled awful. We had no privacy, and our clothes were stored in cedar chests underneath the other supplies. At times, claustrophobia set in, and I felt like I might explode if I didn't get off the ship soon.

September 22, 1608

We had spent roughly two months at sea when Captain Newport declared that we should reach land within a few weeks.

"Huzzah!" the crew shouted. I felt like shouting with them to celebrate but knew Mistress would think it improper.

I glanced down at her, her face had looked gray earlier but now her skin looked red and blotchy, and it worried me.

"Oh, Anne," she moaned, as she leaned over and vomited again into the copper pot I held for her.

I dabbed at her forehead with a wet rag to calm her fever. She was sweating something fierce and felt fiery hot to the touch. By the smells and sounds around me, I'd say that a few other people around us were in the same condition.

"Please drink, My Lady," I begged, offering her more watered-down beer. "All will be well; you shall see. Captain Newport said we should arrive within a fortnight."

She stayed in her condition intermittently for days until we finally heard shouts.

"Land ho!" called one of the men.

Oh, blessed land! My heart pounded in my chest. The excitement I thought I'd feel surprised me instead with a strong sense of urgency and panic. I yearned to break free from the confinements of the ship. Instead of feeling relieved, I felt trapped. It felt hard to breathe. I tried to peel off my linen shift from my sticky arms, and the walls within the ship felt like they were closing in on me. A sudden urge to climb the ladder to the deck and jump off the ship swept over me, even if it meant swimming to shore alone. I desperately wanted to plant my feet on solid ground.

I looked down again at Mistress's pale hand, holding tight to my own; her head moved side-to-side while beads of sweat dripped down her clammy face. Guilt swept over me. *How could I leave her like that? Even if I could, where would I go?*

We gradually made our way around the bend to Chesapeake Bay. I looked through the porthole and spotted more wild birds again: herons, wild geese, and ducks, some of the most beautiful creatures I had ever seen. I'd never been so excited to see birds flying overhead. I wanted to burst with joy and collapse from exhaustion from all the worry and care for Mistress. She was still very ill, but I prayed that getting off the boat would revive her body and spirit.

It took several more days until we were close enough for the ship to reach the shore. The men hustled in every direction to prepare for our landing. The rest of the passengers stayed in the hull to be out of the sailors' way as they worked.

"Get ready to strike the sails!" Captain Newport shouted.

There was a commotion of feet running above the deck as the crew prepared to follow orders and take the sails down.

PART TWO

THE NEW WORLD

Chapter Ten
AROUND THE PENINSULA

"Faire meadows and goodly tall Trees, with such Freshwaters running through the woods, as I was almost ravished at the first sight thereof." – Sir George Percy

September 28, 1608

The sky was a clear, bright shade of blue as we entered the bay toward Jamestown. The air shifted from crisp to heavy and wet. I could feel the thick moisture on my face and the taste of salt on my lips as it penetrated my skin. My heavy linen garments clung even more to my small frame; its weight reminded me of the burden I had felt these past few months taking care of Mistress Forrest. The excitement I felt at arriving in the New World boiled up in my chest. By the cheers and whistles of the men, I could tell the crew felt it too.

"Hurry, men; to your stations!" shouted Captain Newport as he put on his brown leather hat, guarding his wild blond hair against the sun and wind. His clean-shaven face stood out amongst the sea of beards from the men surrounding him.

Men busily ran around the deck, nearly colliding with each other. Shouts were heard in all directions as they lowered some of the sails and beckoned the wind to carry us gracefully the rest of the way.

My eyes grew wide, and I swallowed hard as I looked out at the vastness and depth of the trees sprawled across the coastline. The natives could have been hiding anywhere. What if they attacked?

The forest floor lay littered with leaves of every shade: sunset orange, soft pinks, deep reds, and burgundies. A few remaining ones clung to branches for dear life, defying autumn and turning their back on the prospect of winter.

The water from the James River gingerly trickled against the coarse sandy shore that hedged up against lush green grass. It was breathtaking yet terrifying at the same time! The pull of this New World was intoxicating.

"Is that Jamestown?" I asked as we looked out the porthole. Next to me, a man with greasy gray hair and pointy ears stood so close that I could smell his bad breath and feel the warmth of his words in my ear, and I took a step back. "I heard Captain Newport say it is Point Comfort, a lookout spot to warn against the Spanish before they'd reach Jamestown."

Point Comfort, hm? It looks beautiful, I thought. The name was fitting. Knowing there was some type of lookout to protect us against the Spanish did bring me comfort.

I nodded my head in the man's direction but kept my eyes locked on the world around me.

When we sailed past its small wooden posts and raised watch-tower, an odd feeling came over me, like I had been there before. Maybe it was the scenery or knowing we would be off the ship soon, but in a way, it felt like I was coming home.

We turned the corner one afternoon, and there she was: Jamestown. A fortress made of the same wood-bound material we saw at Point Comfort. The fort formed a triangle, with towers erected in each corner. The tops of the timber were carved into rugged pointed edges, and a large gate was situated in the front. As we docked, a tall man with a red padded vest, pointed waist, and short breeches with white stockings approached us. His unruly curly brown hair swept to the side and tucked behind his ears. He stood there for several minutes while we waited to disembark the ship.

"They said we may leave now, Mistress!" I said with excitement.

"Just leave me here, Anne," Mistress cried in distress. "I don't think I will ever be able to step foot on solid earth again."

I sighed and rolled my eyes. "Oh, come now. From what I can see, there are beautiful forests and many varieties of flowers and plants here. Would you like to see them?" I gently pulled her up to a standing position.

It took several attempts to persuade her, but in the end, I convinced her to get on her feet and off the ship.

I lifted her up with my right arm while Sir Forrest held her up with his left. Six men were there to greet us. Each dressed in heavy armor chest plates and metal helmets that formed a point in the front.

"Welcome to Jamestown," the man with the unruly hair said as he helped Mistress and me off the boat. "The men will show you the way while we unload the supplies and provisions." We followed suit with Sir Forrest and the rest of the men from the ship as we made our way toward the gate. A scream escaped my lips as we walked around the south side of the fort. I gasped at what stood before us.

A decaying body hung from the gallows, with a hangman's knot tied around his neck. The man's long black hair covered his face, and vultures had eaten away parts of his face and arms.

A shiver went down my spine, and I averted my eyes to look at the ground as we walked.

"What do you think the man did?" a sailor in torn blue breeches beside me asked his friend.

"It doesn't matter what he did. That there be a symbol to the rest of us that no one is to defy the Company."

The men caught me staring at them and stopped talking. The short one tipped his cap at me and said, "Do be careful, miss. They don't take kindly to those who do not follow orders or question them."

Something was unnerving about his comment, and I clutched my bag tighter to my chest. From time to time, men and women were hung similarly in London, but I made it a point never to watch the hangings. I felt it was too inhumane.

When we made our way through the gate of the fort, bile boiled up in my throat once more. Crosses, indicating graves, littered the ground, marking poor souls who did not survive to tell their tales.

A shiver ran up my spine again. *What kind of a place is this?* The impulse to vomit took over, and I could no longer hold down the pressure building up in my stomach. I relieved myself right then and there. Three other men did the same. Sir Forrest looked as pale as a ghost and just as appalled as I was. He held me up with his left hand and supported Mistress Forrest with his right.

"Why are they buried inside the fort?" I asked, looking up at Sir Forrest.

He shook his head, bewildered.

"'Tis orders from the London company to bury them inside the fort," a sailor nearby said as he slung a heavy bag over his right shoulder. "I imagine they don't want the natives knowing how many men we have lost."

We looked at each other in horror; there must have been fifty crosses. The haunting realization of the severity of the situation here took my breath away. I could make out a dozen makeshift homes made of mud and stud—wood with mud plaster used to keep it together. I'd seen poorer homes in London made of similar materials. They would build the houses right on top of the ground without digging to create a foundation.

In the middle of the fort was a small chapel, if you could call it that. It resembled more of a barn than a church, with mud and clay as its foundation, straw and hay for a roof; but it pleased me to see it. My heart rose to know that there was some influence and respect for God here—at least, I hoped there was.

Frantically, I looked around for Jack, ensuring he got off the ship and into the fort safely. From the corner of my eye, I saw him running off inside the fort with the other boys, and my worries subsided.

"He will be fine," Sir Forrest said, as if reading my thoughts. "What a marvelous adventure for a boy to have!"

A flood of relief rushed over me, and I nodded my head in agreement.

A few men arrived as we gathered in. I visibly stepped backward and nearly toppled into the mud at the sight of them. They looked more like men possessed than the gentlemen we thought would greet us. Most had long, thick, shaggy beards, with pale and sad-looking eyes, others filled with a fierce anger or craze. Each was as thin and frail as the next, many wearing heavy armor over torn shirts and doublets.

One of the men, a short fellow with thick brown hair and a full beard sprinkled with brown and red whiskers approached us. He wore an orange jerkin over his blue long-sleeved doublet with glass buttons. He stepped forward with a hearty smile and greeted Captain Newport and our group.

"Welcome, Captain Newport and Sir Forrest; I dare say, welcome!" he said as he firmly shook both of their hands. "You truly are a sight for sore eyes."

"Captain Smith!" Captain Newport smiled, with a vigorous handshake in return. "I dare say the same, my good man." The mood quickly shifted to more pressing matters, and Captain Newport jumped to business. "What happened here? I left you with over a hundred men and enough provisions till my return. Where is everyone?"

"'Tis not what it appears, sir," Captain Smith said. "We are immensely grateful for your arrival. As for the men and supplies, we have suffered many difficulties. The men became sick in droves, and we had to bury more than one daily. They should have taken the time to plant and grow their food correctly instead of obsessing over their search for gold. Our supplies quickly ran out after you left."

"How many men are still alive?" cried Captain Newport.

Captain Smith shook his head, and his brown eyes filled with sorrow. "I tried to send off men in different directions for food, but most never returned. The rest were starved or shot by the natives. There are but sixty of us left."

"Sixty!" Captain Newport echoed. "Sixty! I left you with over a hundred men."

"It's a great relief that you have brought us provisions and men, sir." As he said this, Captain Smith's eyes looked upon me and Mistress Forrest, and his face turned paler than my dear Mistress's had been. He realized his slip of the tongue. "My lord and ladies, I wholly apologize for not giving a proper welcome to Jamestown. Many of us are gentlemen, after all."

"I am here to change all that, Smith," boomed Captain Newport. "The London Company wants a return on their investment. They also want a more thorough search and effort put into finding the Roanoke settlers."

My curiosity piqued at the sound of Roanoke. Were they still alive? Could the rumors be true? Were they living among the natives? I ached to know more. Before I could listen in too long, a gentleman in an orange- and red-striped doublet jacket touched my elbow and guided the Forrests and me away from the conversation. I tried to turn my head back to hear the last words of Captain Newport, but their voices muffled as we walked away.

Men gawked back at us with sunken eyes and wan faces. Dark circles and loose skin hung from their faces. It was as if I was looking at ghosts more than men. A surge of fear rushed through me, and I clung to the handbag I was carrying.

We stopped in front of the church for a minute for Sir Forrest to speak with another leader he knew from the London Company. One of the guards carrying our supplies leaned in close to me. His breath smelled terrible, and he was missing several teeth. The ones he had left were yellow or black and covered in grime. I recoiled and tried to step away from him, which only made him snicker. "Do take care, miss. The natives are ever watching, and I don't think they would take too kindly to ladies. The men—well, let's say they've been away from home for a long time. Some are gentlemen, but many are not and might not treat you as they should."

The color drained from my face, and I took a step closer to Mistress Forrest, who sneered at the man.

"These men ought to be taught some manners before being allowed to travel here," she said.

For once, I agreed with her.

We continued our walk to the cabin, meeting the eyes of men under similar conditions: starving, lonely, and angry.

Chapter Eleven
A New Home

"He who does not work, will not eat." – John Smith

October 1, 1608

"Your cabin, sir." One of the guards gestured as if we were the most fortunate souls on the planet. "It's located in the far eastern corner of the fort for privacy. There are two adjoining rooms, so your maid can serve you." By the looks of the other cabins, we were living in luxury.

"This will do nicely," Sir Forrest said. "Thank you, my good man. Please bring our luggage and the rest of our supplies." He gestured to the two other men walking behind us with what we had brought from the ship.

The makeshift cabin did indeed appear more prominent than the others. It was also a mud-and-stud design and encased with plaster and hay for warmth. There was a rope tie in each corner of the bed to pull it tight for support. We'd brought our bedding from the ship and a wooden stand to place our water bucket on in the Forrests' bedroom; a walled-off area behind their room was for me, with a medium-sized pallet on the floor and straw bedding inside a linen cover. Men brought in Mistress's cedar chest and put it at the foot of her bed.

"Comfortable?" Sir Forrest asked as Mistress sat on a dark wooden chair with green upholstery. She feigned annoyance at his gestures, but she inwardly smiled at his concern.

For a couple so different, they seemed to be in love. I wondered if I could find love like that one day. It reminded me of Mama's letter with the wedding announcements, a reminder that I was not financially ready to marry and might not be for a long time.

October 2, 1608

A strange pecking sound woke me up. I was used to a rooster's crow doing the same, but this was no rooster. The sound was more like a hammer banging continuously on wood. Everything felt strange; the air felt different and heavy on my chest.

Yesterday on the ship, I felt nothing but excitement, but after our arrival and seeing the condition of the men, I felt terrified.

With a sigh, I fell back onto my pillow. I wished I could just sleep in. We were thousands of miles away from any English civilization, and there I was, still waking up early to do my chores. I intended to make the best of it; Papa always used to say, "No use dwelling on things you can't control."

As quietly as I could, to not wake Mistress, I slipped out of bed and changed out of my dirty shift into a new one. I'd never been so happy in all my life to change into a new shift. We couldn't change on the ship because our luggage was stowed in a different compartment, and even if we could reach it, we needed more privacy and room to change. The feel of clean linen against my skin felt amazing! I slipped a red kirtle dress over my head, fixed the attached skirt, and laced the bodice top. After it was secure, I tied the white linen apron over the front. Next, I pulled up my brown stockings and tied them each with a ribbon garter, slipped my coif linen cap over my hair, and grabbed my pouch as I left the room.

After a quick search, I found the source of the sound. "Why, hello, there," I said to a beautiful, white-bellied bird. Its pitch-black outer wings were painted with snow-white patches. Its head and neck were covered entirely in a majestic crimson red. It emitted a loud, high-pitched cry as it flew in flashing circles above the oak tree behind the fort. I could spend days studying that bird and wondered if it had any friends.

"Get back to work, Anne," I mumbled to myself and sighed.

With as much dignity as I could muster, I slowly grabbed the chamber pot from the corner of my room and the one placed under the Forrests' bed, trying hard not to wake them. I gagged as I saw a few drops slosh to the floor. This would have been the chamber maid's job in London, but because I was the only maid here, the duty fell to me.

After looking outside our door in both directions, I carefully stepped out and threw the human waste to the side of our cabin. The wind returned the foul smell to my nostrils, and I shuddered. I could never get used to emptying someone else's chamber pot.

Once they were empty, I placed both chamber pots back in their rightful places, grabbed the water bucket on the floor next to the table, and set out for my second chore of the day: collecting water.

Usually, I would go down to the well with another maid to fill my bucket, but seeing how I was the only one here, I had to make the journey alone. Holding on to both wooden buckets by their rope handles, I frantically walked around the fort looking for the well, not venturing too far from our cabin in case some native was out there to raid me, or one of the dirty, hungry men I saw yesterday wanted to hurt me.

"There be no well," a shaggy-bearded blacksmith said with a chuckle and a sneer when he saw me peek around the corner.

"What did you say, sir?" I asked timidly, holding tight to the buckets to keep my hands from shaking.

"There is none—well, that is—if that's what you're looking for. The men haven't finished digging it yet. You need to go collect it at the river like the rest of 'em." He gestured toward the fort's gate, which I saw was open wide.

I must have looked frightened because he let out another chuckle.

"I'll show him!" I mumbled.

Two men stood at watch near the entrance, one per each bulwark. They wore heavy metal armor that covered their chests and split into two longer pieces at the waist, reaching to their thighs. Their pointed helmets and large muskets certainly looked intimidating.

What if they closed the gate while I was out there? What if I got shot with an arrow in the process? They wouldn't do that, would they?

There was no way around it. I had to make it through that gate to get the water. I crept toward the gate, quickly looked around, and saw a few men collecting water. I hurried down with as much dignity as possible, filled the buckets as fast as I could, and nearly sprinted back toward the gate. I could hear the men laughing behind me but did not care. I wasn't about to get shot or stolen for their sake.

My heart pounded. Once inside the gate and out of sight, I placed my hands on my knees and leaned over to catch my breath. The guard on the right laughed and pointed to the other guard. I glared at him; I didn't care if he laughed, he's not the one who had to go out there to get water.

I sighed in relief and wiped dirt from my hands onto my apron, then made my way toward our cabin, trying not to spill the bucket as I went. I tried my best to remember how to get back to the cabin. I turned left past the blacksmith and then made a quick right. As I did, I saw two men, filthy from head to toe, sitting on a bench against the wall of a cabin. The man with the long, shaggy beard leaned over and whispered something into the other's ear; he, in turn, looked up at me and laughed. My cheeks immediately felt hot, and I turned and walked the other way as quickly as possible. The men laughed even louder, but I didn't stop walking until I found our cabin. I took a deep breath before I stepped inside; this would take some getting used to, I thought.

Chapter Twelve
A New Friend

"Bite a stone, not the hand that throws it." – Old
English Proverb

October 28, 1608

It had been nearly a month since our arrival at the fort, but Mistress Forrest had still not recovered her strength and was not fit to travel back. Even if she was physically able to go back to England, there were no ships leaving anytime soon.

She and several men in the fort complained of stomach cramps, fevers, and vomiting.

Some nights, Mistress' forehead felt like it would burn my hand. She couldn't keep food or water down no matter how much I fed her. I tried to cool her burning skin with a cold cloth and stayed with her to accommodate her needs, but it was exhausting. As much as I fought and aimed to improve her, there was no change.

There had been a few nights when I started feeling hot and sweaty; chills and body aches took over, and like Mistress, I couldn't keep anything down. All I could do was keep pushing on and tending to my work. I still collected water from the river every morning, made scant bread from the flour we brought, and tried my best to rinse out our soiled bedding. Luckily, I recovered after a few days.

So many of the men struggled with illness. A commotion occurred after our Sunday sermon concerning why so many were getting sick.

"It's our food," shouted one.

"No, it's the muggy weather," came another.

"It's our water," a man with long blond hair said. "It's full of salt and dirt. It looks more like mud than water to me." He smiled at his own comment; a few men joined him in a brief bout of laughter.

"Ya, when will the well be finished so we don't have to drink this filth?" another man shouted.

"It even oozes," a man behind me cried. "When are they going to be done with the well?"

"Brethren, brethren," Reverend Hunt said. "I'm sure the well will be finished in no time. Am I right, Captain Smith?" He gestured from the podium set up in front of the congregation.

Captain Smith walked to the podium and stood before our group. "Gentlemen, gentlemen, please listen. We are doing our best to dig a suitable well. In the meantime, the river is all we have. Fresh streams are too far east from the fort for us to reach for our daily drink. It's also too dangerous to venture out in the woods by yourselves. Go in pairs or small groups if you have to. We will continue to dig until the well is clear. In the meantime, please be patient."

The men grumbled to themselves when Captain Smith sat down. I didn't know what to think or what to blame the sicknesses on. All I knew was that clean water sounded heavenly.

I tried to collect water with Jack, but another young boy went to the river instead while Jack worked in the carpenter station.

In the weeks that followed, I occasionally saw him in the fort and talked to him after services on Sunday. He seemed to be doing well. We were both so busy with our daily tasks, we didn't have much time for each other.

Tending to Mistress Forrest all day was exhausting. I found myself not only missing home but aching for my life in London where I at least had the other maids to talk with and Peter to make me giggle. I still had chores to do on Sunday but was able to spend a few minutes in the afternoon walking around the fort with Jack.

One morning when I did my daily task of straining the water, I felt something slimy slip by my hand and bucket.

What was that?

I screamed and jumped back when I saw it was a snake with blotchy brown-and-black skin and a triangular head. My heart skipped a beat, and I slowly backed away from the water. I had just sat my bucket down and taken a few deep breaths to build up the courage to return to the water again when I heard a loud rustling sound and laughter in the distance.

Footsteps from boots loudly clopped over the dried-out red and yellow leaves left on the forest floor. I squatted down behind a bush to get a glimpse of what was happening. I heard a few boys' voices, including Jack's. Just as I was about to scold him, I heard a girl's voice.

"No, like this," the girl said. My ears strained to understand what was being said and by whom.

A girl? Another English girl? What was another English girl doing here? I shook my head in surprise; it couldn't be. Was I hallucinating?

It wasn't an English girl, but it *was* a girl—a girl speaking English!

"Hello," she said, waving toward my bush. "Hello." I hesitantly waved back.

Her short, cropped hair rested just below her ears. She wore a deerskin dress that covered one of her shoulders and had beautiful white shells sewn into the hem. Her deerskin leggings and shoes and the fox skin she wore over her shoulders protected her from the autumn chill. A feather was tied to a portion of her hair and dangled past her shoulder, adding to her beautiful appearance.

She looked to be about Jack's age, eleven or twelve. "Hello," she repeated, and she waved again before running off to chase one of the boys.

I stood up, in shock, to get a better glimpse of her playing tag.

"No fair," one of the boys said. "She cheated!"

"Being faster than you isn't cheating," Jack said as he ran by. My mouth hung open as I soaked in the scene.

"Jack," I yelled. "What are you doing?"

"Playing tag." He shrugged as he ran after the girl and boys. The girl dodged the other boys through the forest as they tried to catch her. I giggled when I saw her taunting them. She was significantly faster and nimbler than they were, and they had difficulty keeping up.

After a while, the group stopped racing and switched to playing wheelbarrows with their hands. One person would hold up the other's legs, and the one with their legs in the air would walk with their hands. They laughed so hard that they all fell to the ground holding their stomachs.

"Jack, this isn't safe," I said as I approached the group. Two other English boys were also playing. "You boys shouldn't be out here."

The girl and two native boys stood there watching me. They looked around the same age. The native boys were shirtless and wore deerskin covers around their bottoms. It made me uncomfortable.

"No one should be outside the fort except to get water," I said, trying to sound more grown up.

The young girl started to walk around me as I talked. She lightly touched my shirt sleeve and yelled, "Tag!"

I looked at Jack, who shrugged and said, "You're it."

I knew I'd get in trouble if Mistress found me, but I couldn't resist. I started chasing after the group.

"I almost forgot where we are," I said afterward, holding my stomach from laughing too hard.

"Me too," Jack said with a smile. He pointed to the girl resting by a tree.

The young girl stopped to catch her breath. I took a deep breath of air myself then walked over to her and smiled.

"Who taught you English?" I bravely asked. She looked at me and smiled. "Captain Smith." "You know Captain Smith?"

She nodded. "He taught me English. I teach him Algonquian."

"Algonquian," I tried, saying the word slowly.

"I, Pocahontas," the girl said, pointing to herself.

"I'm Anne," I said, pointing to my chest. "Nice to meet you, Pocahontas."

"Nice meet you, Anne." She smiled at me and gently touched a hair that had slipped from my coif.

Jack giggled and said, "I guess she has never met an English girl, and you probably look very different."

"Well, I have never met a native girl before, and she looks very different to me, so there we are." I smiled and gently reached out and touched a piece of her cropped hair in return. Her smile widened, and then we both started giggling.

I got a good scolding from Mistress for taking so long, but it was worth it! I felt so free and alive to run again, and for the first time in months, I didn't feel so alone. I met a new friend.

Chapter Thirteen
A Storm's a Brewing

"For in Virginia, a plain soldier that can use a pickaxe and spade, is better than five Knights." – John Smith

October 31, 1608

"A storm is coming!" Sir Forrest quickly reported to Mistress and me after opening our cabin door. He had been to a meeting with Captain Smith and the other leaders.

Mistress sat up in bed and coughed, "What else did he say?" she asked.

Sir Forrest pulled at the collar of his blue jerkin vest. "He said we need to fortify our dwellings and stick together. With storms such as these, the real danger is in the water it brings up from the river. Be mindful and keep watch."

I looked around the cabin. All we had in our cabin was Mistress Forrest's massive chest, which we could sit on to stay dry, and our two makeshift beds stuffed with bird feathers that Mistress had insisted must come with us.

Tiny drops of rain started to trickle down on us, and the wind blew in from the south, pushing open our cabin door.

I quickly closed it and asked, "What do we need to do?"

"Captain Smith suggested we all dig a trench around our cabins to keep the water out."

I nodded but had never dug a trench before.

"Anne, I'd hate to ask this of a Lady's maid, but I need your help. Here, take this," he said as he handed me a large copper pot. "I will dig, and you scoop up the dirt and throw it away from the cabin."

I nodded again numbly, not sure what to say.

The day was chaotic, with men frantically attempting to fortify their huts and supplies. Captain Smith ran around the fort, giving orders to prepare for the storm.

"You must dig a trench like this," he told Sir Forrest as he was running from cabin to cabin to show the men. "If you dig a trench around the outside of your walls, it will stop the water from flooding your cabin. The water needs a place to go."

Mistress still wasn't well, so Sir Forrest told her to stay inside while he and I dug the trench. The company provided one small shovel, a large metal pot, and a few wooden spoons to scoop out the dirt.

"Here, Anne," Sir Forrest said, "take the metal pot and scoop out the dirt as much as you can, like this." He demonstrated gathering dirt into the pot and then throwing it a few feet away from our cabin.

The rain poured down harder and harder, and the sky was an eerie shade of dark green. The wind blew in from all directions, like knives against my skin, leaving large puddles forming at the base of our cabin. We dug for hours, but the trench didn't seem deep enough.

Dirt turned to mud beneath our feet and made it difficult to walk without slipping. I had to catch myself several times from falling.

At one point, I got up to move a bucket of mud away from the walls of our cabin but slipped instead. My feet flew up in the air, and I landed hard on my back against the cold, solid ground below. For a minute, I couldn't breathe; it felt like the air had been kicked out of me. My body screamed at me to stop, and my arms and legs shook violently as the pain and cold seeped into my bones.

"Anne, I think this digging is futile," Sir Forrest shouted over the noise of the wind and rain. "You're hurt, and we aren't digging fast enough. We have done enough; we must go inside now and wait out the storm."

With tears streaming down my wet cheeks, I agreed. Then I jumped and screamed as the outline of a man came out of the darkness. He came in so suddenly and quietly that I hadn't noticed him.

"May I help?" he asked politely, his lace-trimmed collar smashed against his dark blue jerkin vest. His clothes were soaked and covered in mud and his right hand had a large trowel ready to dig.

"Yes, sir," Sir Forrest eagerly said. He took the man by the hand in a firm shake and added, "We would be much obliged."

I could not make out much more of what the man looked like. His silhouette showed that he was tall, shorter than Sir Forrest by only an inch, with broad shoulders and dark hair that clung to his head and ears.

I hesitated to go inside because I knew how dreadful things could get if we didn't have a proper trench around the cabin, but exhaustion took over and I conceded.

I wiped a wet strand of hair that stuck to my face and curtsied toward the men. "Thank you, sirs. I will retire inside, then."

The men nodded back, then went straight to work. I knew my formality was silly, but I felt it my duty to show Sir Forrest respect even though I was drenched head to toe.

I tried to wipe off the mud as best as I could before I entered the cabin, but clumps still fell to the floor when I walked in. I shivered from the cold and went straight to my room to change into dry clothes.

Rain and strong winds roared through the night. I pulled my blanket over my head to block out the sound and keep myself warm, then got up to tend to Mistress Forrest for the rest of the night.

The storm eventually subsided, but we didn't dare brave the outside until morning. When the sun broke out, I ventured out of our hut. My foot sank into at least two inches of water and mud, but it wasn't awful.

Water and sediment clung to the foot of our beds and Mistress's wardrobe chest. Most of her dresses were wet on the bottom and I promptly wrung them out and hung them on a line when it was safe to do so. I'd only brought two dresses with me, along with an extra change of sleeves to give off the appearance of another dress. The one I'd worn the night before sat utterly soaked with mud and rainwater. I hung that out to dry as well.

Debris and mud covered the ground. Most of the trees surrounding the fort had been cut previously to use for lumber. If not, they might have fallen on us during the night.

Fortunately, our mattresses, being a bit off the ground, were safe, and we were grateful for it! All would have been lost if it hadn't been for that trench.

Sir Forrest left a few minutes earlier to inspect the fort. He walked through the door just as Mistress was waking.

"Would you just look at this mess," Mistress Forrest said in a weak voice as she painstakingly sat up in bed.

"It could have been much worse my dear had we not had help with digging the trench. Some of the cabins are filled with feet of water," Sir Forrest said.

"Someone helped you dig the trench?" Mistress asked, confused.

"Yes, a gentleman came and helped, just in time if you ask me," he replied.

Mistress raised one eyebrow, "Who was the gentleman who helped us?"

"I... I didn't catch his name," Sir Forrest stammered, "but I believe he was one of the tradesmen."

"Didn't catch his name? My dear, how could you be so forgetful?"

"I will seek him out when we get our cabin under control, my dear," Sir Forrest said, obviously hurt by her rebuke.

I tried to conceal my grin. Mistress's scolding could frighten a grown man even in her weakest state.

But the next instant, she was coughing again.

"Oh, Anne," she moaned. "I don't know how much more I can endure."

"All will be well, My Lady," I said as I dabbed a cold cloth on her forehead. Her pale skin was warm to the touch, and as she handed me back her white handkerchief, I could see tiny drops of blood and yellow phlegm. Judging by the look on Sir Forrest's face, he saw it too.

Chapter Fourteen
WE MEET AGAIN

"Indians killed as fast [outside the fort] as Famine and Pestilence did within." – Sir George Percy

November 3, 1608

"Come on, Anne!" Jack said, waving at me to play with him and the others.

Pocahontas and her brother, Rusirur, ran after Jack and the other boys.

"Play," Pocahontas said, beaming as she turned sideways and stood on her hands.

"She can't," Jack said. "She's a lady's maid; she has to be proper."

"Proper?" Pocahontas asked. Jack just laughed and walked away.

My heart longed to play, to be able to run in the dirt and do a cartwheel like Pocahontas, but Jack was right. It would seem undignified for a person in my position to do so. I frowned and carried out my chores of collecting firewood and making dinner for the Forrests.

If I rose early enough, a group of men went together to collect water. When I first learned this, I decided to follow them out to the river. The men were crude and filthy head to toe, but it was either that or go by myself to the river and get attacked by a native.

"What are you doing here?" a long-bearded man asked one of the first days I ventured out with them.

"Getting water like the rest of you," I replied, then added, "sir" so he would overlook my annoyance. At first, the men stared at me, but after a while, they hardly noticed I was there.

One day, I woke up late and ran to the fort's gate. I peered out and saw some men scooping and sifting out water. A few of them wore heavy armor, making it hard to bend. I quickly made my way to the river and sifted out the rocks as I scooped the water into my pail. I grimaced at the bucket of murky brown water staring back at me. I shook my head.

"Yuck," I said. "There's no way I'm going to drink that."

I dumped the water back out and used my apron to filter the water one more time. My stomach growled, and I thought of the times when I'd bring Mama water while she cooked. Images and smells of fresh rolls, cabbage, potatoes, and carrots floated in my mind like a dream. My stomach growled again and brought me back to reality.

I shook my head, focused on sifting the water again, and sighed. It resembled a pot of tea more than water. I grabbed my pail and stood up. With horror, I realized I was alone. Panic gripped me. Before I could gather my things and go, two large hands wrapped around me, one on my waist and one pulling back hard on my right shoulder.

A scream escaped my lips. The rough hand on my shoulder quickly moved to cover my mouth. The man dragged me back away from the water toward the woods.

My eyes searched the tower and found the sentry on watch. He must have heard my scream because his wide eyes met mine. He was gone within seconds.

"No scream!" the man behind me said in broken English, pushing his hand harder against my lips.

Get away. I need to get away were the only thoughts going through my head. I had heard stories of natives taking men before. They either tortured then killed them or traded them as slaves. I wasn't about to discover what he intended to do to me, especially a woman.

I bit down as hard as I could on his hand. Blood filled my mouth, and he yelled out in pain. He tried to release his hand, but I bit harder. He jerked his hand back and let me go.

My heart pumped fast, and I seized the opportunity and ran as quickly as my legs would take me across the coarse sand toward the fort.

The man scrambled toward me and lunged, knocking me off my feet. He latched on to my right ankle and dragged me back into the sand. I flipped around and kicked him with my free foot as hard as I could.

I had a clear view of his face. His dark beady eyes stared back at me from under black war paint. The bottom half of his face was painted red. He was thin but strong. A sizeable wooden bow was strapped to his back, its string crossing over his left shoulder and chest. He wore leather leggings and moccasins, with no shirt, yet the cold didn't seem to bother him. With my hands clenched in fists, I punched and kicked him with all my might. I dug my hands, flailing for a grip, into the coarse sand, and kicked his hand hard with my left foot, trying to free myself from his grasp. He pulled me hard again, and I felt the left side of my head slam against a sharp rock. Something wet oozed down my hair, ear, and face. It was warm and sticky, but panic gripped my chest, and I flailed my arms and free leg again with all my might.

Chunks of sand clung to my face and mouth. I desperately screamed for help. I heard a loud *boom!* and saw my attacker's shoulder jolt backward. Blood splattered onto the sand and my leg. He tightened his grip on my ankle with his good hand and started to pull. He dragged me a few more inches when another *phtt-boom!* whizzed by. The man groaned loudly and then released his hold on me to cover his chest, falling backward with a loud thud.

I shrieked and scrambled away from his body.

With shaky hands, I wiped the sand from my eyes. When I looked down, I noticed my hands were covered in blood. I swatted frantically at the disheveled hair that covered my face to find the source of the blood—a deep cut on the left side of my head, a few inches above my ear. Not too deep, I imagined, but deep enough for blood to seep out.

I felt dizzy and nauseous. I tried to look up, but the sun burned my eyes, and my head spun. I panicked and started to push myself up on my knees when a deep, familiar voice said, "Don't get up just yet, miss."

I turned my head to the left and saw the base of a man's matchlock musket and black leather boots. The last thing I remember was being picked up by solid, warm arms. I squirmed in protest, but a pair of kind green eyes looked down at me, silently letting me know I was safe. I fluttered my heavy eyelids a few times, but their weight gradually forced my eyes shut, and my body went limp.

Chapter Fifteen

A Maid Without a Mistress

"Our men were destroyed with cruel diseases as swellings, fluxes, burning fevers, and by wars, and some were departed suddenly, but for the most part they died of mere famine. There were never Englishmen left in a foreign country in such misery as we were in this new discovered Virginia." – Sir George Percy, 1607

November 5, 1608

"Anne... Anne," I heard Jack whisper. I felt his hand on my shoulder as I woke up from what must have been a long nap. My head was spinning, but I managed to open my eyes slowly. I blinked several times. Jack, Sir Forrest, and the Company's doctor stood over me.

My face contorted from the bright light outside the door. "Where am I?"

Jack put one hand to his mouth, reached out, and grabbed my hand.

"She's had quite a shock," I heard a man say. "But she will be fine. What she needs most now is rest."

A mumble of voices and shadows clouded my vision. My head throbbed and something felt stuck to it. I raised my hand and felt a cloth wound tightly around my head. I moved my fingers around the wrapping until I gently grazed a large egg-size bump protruding underneath the fabric. I winced at the touch of it. It was tender, and sticky blood and dirt remained on my fingers after coming into contact with it.

"That's quite a bump you have there, pretty impressive," Jack laughed.

I frowned and he stood to leave the room. "Sorry, I know you need some rest."

My head filled with confusion, and I started to sit up, but the room began to feel like it was spinning again. I didn't want to be alone. "No, please stay!" I cried.

Jack returned to my side and helped me lie back down. "The doctor told me to make sure you didn't get up. You hit your head on a rock when you were dragged. Don't you remember?" He crinkled his nose, "The doctor said there was a lot of blood, but he put a rag on it and wrapped a cloth around it."

I put my hand up to feel the bulky bandage. Jack winced. "That must have been some rock."

"Dragged? Rock?" I asked, confused. Then, gradually, memories of being dragged against coarse sand and the feeling of my head meeting a hard rock came to my mind, along with flashes of a man's hand around my ankle, the taste of sweat, blood, and dark penetrating eyes.

I gasped and sat up again.

"Stop doing that!" Jack said. "You're going to get yourself hurt and me in trouble."

My head throbbed with pain, and I let it slowly back down onto the pillow. "What happened?" I asked.

Jack sighed and looked down. "You were almost kidnapped, Anne. You don't remember anything? Lucky for you, Mr. Layton was a watchman and saw the man drag you back. He didn't want to shoot you accidentally, so he went around the gate to get a better aim. The man went down with only two shots." Jack raised his hands and pretended to shoot across the room. "Bam, bam! A part of me wishes I could have seen it."

"Mr. Layton?"

"Yes, Mr. Layton. He is one of the carpenters I work with. He's also the one that helped dig the trench along your cabin during the storm. Lucky for you, he was on guard."

His familiar deep voice replayed in my mind. "That's how I recognized him."

"He brought you back here. Everyone was worried about you. Captain Smith visited last night, and I think Mr. Layton must have come three times already."

I was so confused, it hurt to think. "Did he?" I asked.

"It's not every day an Englishwoman takes on a Pamunkey man," Jack said with a smile. "How did you do it?"

My memory was still cloudy. "I think I bit him," I said.

"Bit him? Oh boy—wait until I write to Anthony about what you did. I can't believe it; you actually bit him?"

I chuckled, which hurt my head more. "I guess I did."

Jack only laughed louder but stayed by my side until I fell asleep.

November 11, 1608

After a few days, my head started to feel better and I was ready to resume my chores. The thought of going to the river terrified me, but I knew it had to be done. Mistress still lay in bed; for a time, she seemed to have recovered, then her fever returned.

I forced myself to go down to the water again. At first, Jack was permitted to go with me, but soon his master was getting angry at the time it took, and I was told to go by myself with the other men. The men stayed close by; I wasn't sure if it was for my sake or because they knew the guards were more alert when I was there. I was grateful for the company, even if they didn't talk to me.

Exhaustion set in from staying up late with Mistress all night. She'd thrown up several times and her fever had spiked. The copper pot I used to catch her vomit was full of blood and green bile. I tried several times to spoon her mouthfuls of soup, but she had only pushed it away and spilled it onto the floor.

She tossed and turned; her shift and hair were covered in sweat. I dipped a cloth into the remaining water and dabbed her forehead with it.

"I need to get more water," I whispered. She moaned but didn't open her eyes. Sir Forrest sat next to her and held her hand.

"I'll stay with her," he said.

I stood up and nodded, then grabbed the extra empty bucket.

It was earlier than I usually fetched water, but I needed more to cool her down. I looked left and right to see if anyone else was out. The sun hadn't risen yet but was near to it. I started to head toward the gate but passed by the craftsmen's quarters in case I caught sight of Jack and could ask him to go with me.

A man walked out of the cabin, but it wasn't Jack. My cheeks warmed when I recognized him.

His work shirt hung over brown breeches and opened into a V-shape in the front. He looked to be around ten years older than me, in his mid-twenties. His brown hair was unruly and slightly curled down to his chin, a nice contrast against his sea green eyes. Stubble covered his jawline and chin with a growing beard. He attempted to comb his hand through his unkempt hair and tucked his shirt when he saw me. He was more handsome than I remembered, and I blushed even more at the thought.

"Well met, Miss Burras," he said, dipping his head.

I bent my knees and dipped my head into a slight curtsy. "Well met, Mr. Layton."

"Do you need some assistance?"

"Yes, I was looking for Jack. Have you seen him? I wanted him to escort me to the water this morning."

"I believe he is still asleep. Shall I wake him?"

With one hand, I fidgeted with my apron, twirled the pot I held with the other, and looked down at my feet. I was discouraged and too embarrassed to say I was scared to go by myself.

"If I may," Mr. Layton said, "I need to get some water for a project I am working on and would love to be of service."

My heart skipped a beat, and I bit my lip. I was worried about how it would look, but I desperately needed the water.

"It may not be proper, sir," I said quietly.

Mr. Layton strained to hear what I was saying and was startled when he realized what I meant by that. "Oh, yes, I see. Guards will watch us the whole time so that we won't be alone." He was right, but it felt odd to be alone, just the two of us.

My cheeks flushed again, and I tried not to meet his eye. "I suppose you're right."

Without another word, we walked toward the gate and down to the water.

When we got to the river, Mr. Layton asked for my bucket and proceeded to filter the water for me. I didn't know what to say; I could do it myself, but the kind gesture took me back. He carried my bucket for me back to the fort.

Two sentry men nodded as we made our way back through the gate.

We stood together quietly once inside. The sun started breaking over the trees, and the air felt crisp. He handed me back my bucket, and our hands briefly touched. I felt a tingle run up my arm, and heat rose to my cheeks. I took a deep breath and looked down. I hoped he hadn't noticed my red cheeks.

"Good day, miss," he said.

I gave him another short curtsy. "Good day, Mr. Layton, and thank you."

Heat rushed to my cheeks again, and I tried not to smile too wide as I walked back. I didn't want anyone to assume something untoward had happened if they saw me.

I paused at the door of our cabin and gasped when I saw Sir Forrest lying across Mistress Forrest, sobbing.

I dropped the bucket, and water sloshed onto the dirt floor. "What's wrong?"

"She's gone," he said. He slowly sat up, still holding her hand.

All color was gone from her face. Her hair was matted with sweat, and her once-furrowed brow was calm. Her skin looked almost yellow, but her face looked peaceful.

In shock, I put one hand to my heart and one to my mouth. The image of Mr. Layton flashed in my head, and guilt boiled up inside me. If I had been brave enough to go to the water alone, I would have been here to help her. A tear ran down my cheek. "I shouldn't have left her."

Sir Forrest reached over and took my hand. "This is not your fault, you know. You were doing what you were supposed to be doing. You have been a great help to her, more than you know," he said, as a tear dripped down his cheek. "Besides, if anyone is to be blamed, it should be me. I should have never brought her. I should have known it wasn't safe."

"We both know she wouldn't have let you. She would have stowed away with the luggage if she had to."

He quietly laughed and smiled down at her face. "You're right, my dear. She would have."

Chapter Sixteen
WHAT SHALL WE DO NOW?

"When the words come, they are merely empty shells
without the music. They live as they are sung, for
the words are the body and the music the spirit." –
Hildegard Von Bingen

November 11, 1608

Mistress was not the only one to leave us that day. Two other men were buried inside the fort as well. They didn't wait long to bury the bodies. They started to dig Mistress's grave when they heard of her passing.

We walked towards the center of the fort with a small group of men. Mistress's body was carried by two men towards the place where they were digging the three graves.

Sir Forrest turned to Captain Smith. "Why are these graves dug inside the fort?" he demanded.

Captain Smith took off his hat and bowed his head toward the graves, not meeting the eye of Sir Forrest. "We can't let the natives know how many men we have lost and are still losing."

I heard the skeleton of a man next to me with long brown hair and a scraggly beard whisper, "They could get rid of us in one afternoon if they wanted to."

His words made me shiver. I felt like a trapped mouse in a cage, waiting to be killed or starved to death.

The men around me kept their eyes to the ground and I thought of what type of funeral Mistress would have had in England. There would have been a large procession of people following her casket. We would have been dressed in black mourning clothes and returned to Sir Forrest's home for a wake; a giant feast with drinking, dancing, and prayers for Mistress said by a priest throughout the night.

When men died here, they usually buried them naked in the dirt, without a coffin, but Mistress was afforded more dignity and respect due to her being married to Sir Forrest. I dressed her in her favorite green satin dress and pinned an emerald broach to her bodice. Her body was placed in a coffin crafted by Mr. Layton and Captain Smith and a few other men joined us in a moment of silence.

Sir Forrest seemed composed; he looked dignified in his best matching shorts and shirt and a bright blue suit. Metal pins lined his shoulders and chest. I had darned his stockings earlier that day, shined his shoes, and laid out his clothes. My heart ached for him, and I felt awful that I couldn't do more.

Captain Smith said a few words at her grave, before the men filled it with dirt. They gradually left but Sir Forrest and I stood for several minutes before he broke the silence.

Sir Forrest turned to me and took hold of my hand. "Anne." His voice choked as he tried holding back his tears. "Anne, I fear you have no other alternative but to marry."

"Marry? But sir!" I stepped back and let go of his hand. "Not to me, my dear. Things are different now. You are no longer a lady's maid. Another ship may not come or leave for months. It's not proper for you to stay here without a mistress to tend to. You can't be here alone; you saw what almost became of you a few weeks ago. You need protection." He regained his composure and added, "I shall give you a few days to decide. I know it isn't easy to rush these things." He patted my hand. "Until then, I will stay in a different cabin, and have tasked Jack to stay and watch over you in our cabin until you're wed. Some men here already have a wife in England, but many do not. You shall have the lot to choose from."

I hung my head low as the realization of what he was saying set in. I tried to think of something to say, something to contradict what he was asking me to do. An idea came to my mind, "I have no dowry or prospects."

"Do not worry about the dowry, my dear. I will take care of all of that."

I gasped. "Sir, that is more than kind of you. I don't know what to say."

"Think nothing of it, my dear. You have been so good to Mistress Forrest, and I promised your aunt I would look after you. I'm sure any man would be happy to have you."

His kindness surprised me, but the pressure of finding a husband was too much. My chest felt tight, and it was difficult to breathe. I was trying to mourn Mistress Forrest, and now this? I didn't know what to do.

Sir Forrest's words broke me from my thoughts. "We will surely find you a good match with one of the men here. What about Mr. Layton? He is a nice enough fellow and has helped you twice now."

An image of Mr. Layton flashed through my mind—his strong arms as they carried our heavy buckets of water. A nervous excitement ran through me, but doubt quickly set in. Would he want to marry someone like me? A maid without a real dowry?

My head felt like it was spinning, and I ached for Mama and Papa, or at least the ability to ask them for advice. "What if Jack stayed in the cabin with me until the boat went back to England?"

Sir Forrest gave me a pitiful look. "I wish he could, Anne, but that may not be possible for months, and I don't think his superiors would allow it. You need someone to watch over you. Look what happened when you tried to get water from the river alone. It isn't safe and the men would frown upon it."

I knew I had no other acceptable choice. I laced my trembling hands together, bowed my head, and nodded.

"Yes, sir, I think you are right. I don't have any other choice but to marry."

The verbal agreement made my stomach churn. We sat there in silence. My heart swirled with emotions. I wanted to return to the cabin but didn't know what to do or say. I didn't want to leave him like this, and I knew if I went back to the cabin, I would be alone, so I stayed by his side for a few extra minutes.

I looked down at the fresh dirt piled on top of Mistress's grave and an even stronger feeling of loneliness waved over me. A sob escaped my lips and Sir Forrest reached out and patted my hand.

"There, there, my dear. It can't be all that bad. Many people grow to love each other after they wed; I know I did. My first marriage was chosen for me. Although we did not know each other, we grew into a beautiful friendship and were very fond of each other. I would have been happy in my first marriage had my wife not died in childbirth with Peter. I was, however, fortunate to find love again in my second marriage."

Sir Forrest wiped his nose with his handkerchief and dabbed his eyes.

I kept my head down to give him some privacy and tried to swallow back my tears and think of how Sir Forrest felt. "What are you going to do now, sir?" I dared to ask.

He sighed, resigned to having to return to London without Mistress. "I suppose I will return home on the earliest available ship and report my findings to the London Company. Unfortunately, one might not be available for several months. I want to be the one to tell Peter. I don't want him to read about losing his stepmother in some letter."

I looked down at the makeshift crosses stuck in the row of graves and nodded in agreement.

We returned to the cabin, and I went straight to my room to lie on my bed. I threw off my coif hat but didn't bother to change out of my red kirtle or even take off my dirty shoes. I lay down with my hands on my stomach, looking up at the thatched roof. Too many thoughts went through my head to rest fully.

How terrible to lose not only one wife but two, I thought. I prayed Sir Forrest would be able to find peace and be home with Peter soon. I also prayed that I would know what to do and whom to marry.

I pulled out Mama's letter she'd sent me in London and reread it. I had known Rebecca Leigh since childhood and that her parents had planned an arranged marriage for her to William Jones years ago. I closed my eyes and rested the letter on my chest. I wondered if Rebecca was happy with an arranged marriage. I always dreamed about marrying for love like Mama and Papa, but that dream was gone. Would I be satisfied if Sir Forrest arranged a marriage for me? Of all the options I had, Mr. Layton was the best. I wasn't sure about love, but I liked him and knew him to be honest and hardworking. Plus, he did save me from being kidnapped.

I flipped onto my belly, pushed a strand of hair behind my ear, rested my elbows on my pillow, and looked at the letter again. "What should I do, Mama?" I asked, as if the letter could somehow answer for her. I closed my eyes and prayed it would be a good match, whoever it was.

Chapter Seventeen

TO MARRY OR NOT TO MARRY?

"Let me not to the marriage of true minds admit impediments: love is not love which alters when its alteration finds or bends with the remover to remove; oh! No! It is an ever-fixed mark." – William Shakespeare

November 11, 1608

The crisp fall air and crunchy leaves reminded me of autumn in England. I wished I was there so Mama and Papa could tell me what to do. I needed to figure out how to find a husband and fast. Jack moved in later that night, and Sir Forrest moved three cabins down. Looking for my own husband somehow felt wrong; I always pictured Papa arranging one for me or meeting someone in the village at home.

"Here is the last of it," Jack said as he brought in his only supplies.

"That didn't take you long, did it?" I asked, seeing that he had even fewer provisions than I did. He settled in and then asked me with a scrunched-up nose, "What now?"

I shrugged. "I suppose you stay here until I get married."

"Yes, but marry—marry who?"

I shook my head in despair. "I don't know. Do you think I should write to Mama and Papa?"

Jack's right eyebrow twisted in an arch, and his lip twitched upward in defeat. "And send it on what ship? Even if there were a ship, would they even receive your letter before you marry?"

Tears filled my eyes. "You're right. I don't know what to do, Jack."

He put his leather bag with his clothes on the hard dirt floor, making a swirl of dust rise. Then he sat on the wooden stool next to me at the table and put his arm around me.

All the feelings that had flooded my mind earlier manifested at once, and I let it all out with a burst. "There aren't ships coming and going, so I can't go home, and there isn't even a woman here to help me get properly ready for a wedding. No nice dress, no flowers, no grand feast, no Mama or Ellen as a bridesmaid."

Jack didn't say anything, just watched me and nodded his head.

The tears kept coming, and he lent me his handkerchief to blow my nose before continuing. "Sir Forrest said he could arrange things and even pay for my dowry. I feel foolish and so confused without Papa and Mama. I know girls my age are getting married at home, but am I ready? Would anyone want to marry me?"

Jack put his hand down and turned to face me. "Look at me, Anne." I hesitated and blew my nose again into the handkerchief, then gradually looked up into his blue eyes. They reminded me so much of Papa I almost had to look away. "Anyone would be lucky to marry you. You're kind, hardworking, smart, and funny. Plus, you are the only woman here." He nudged me and laughed.

"Ho ho," I said with a smirk.

He smiled, then his eyes grew serious. "I think Sir Forrest is right. You don't have much choice in the matter. Mama and Papa would want you to do the proper thing. What about Mr. Layton for a husband?"

I was too afraid and embarrassed to say that Sir Forrest had already suggested this and that I was considering it.

"He's a good man, and he likes you," Jack added. "From what we know of him, he's a hard worker with prospects here. I think he is a wise choice."

I agreed but wasn't sure if Mr. Layton would.

"Think about what this means!" Jack continued. "Captain Smith said those who stayed could secure one hundred acres of land. Imagine that! If we stay, you and Mr. Layton will get one hundred acres each, and I would get a hundred acres; then Mama, Papa, Anthony, and Ellen could come, and they could get a hundred acres. We would all be together again."

His words hit me like a wave against the shore. I had never thought of that before, but he was right. If we had to stay, we could make something of it. Mama and Papa, Anthony and Ellen could come.

Hope started growing in my chest, and a feeling of peace flooded me. Things may have worked out differently than I'd planned, but they were working out how they should.

"As the man of the house here," Jack said, puffing out his chest, "I will talk with Mr. Layton on your behalf."

"Oh, really? Why, thank you, sir." I bent low in an exaggerated bow and giggled. "How very manly of you, indeed." And I threw my pillow at him.

"If you don't want to marry him, I can spread the word around the tradesmen's quarters for you." He winked.

I shook my head and laughed. "I'm sure you could." My lips managed to form a small smile. "I'm glad you're here, Jack."

He put his arm around me again. "I am too. It's going to be all right. You'll see."

I nodded my head. "I think Mr. Layton would be a fine choice."

Jack whistled and grinned. "Imagine—my sister, the first Englishwoman to marry in the New World. I can't wait until Papa and Mama hear about this."

I laughed. "Now go before I change my mind!"

I gulped, and my hands began to shake as I watched Jack open the door and turn right to walk toward the craftsmen's accommodations to find Sir Forrest and Mr. Layton. I bit my nails and hoped I was doing the right thing.

November 13, 1608

"Well met, Miss Burras," Mr. Layton said when I ran into him on the walkway to the church.

He removed his gray wool cap and held it before his chest, revealing his long curly brown hair that wrapped ever so slightly below his ears. His eyes met mine, they had a sparkle to them, and they looked full of kindness. He gave me an all-too-knowing look of loss and heartache.

"Well met, Mr. Layton," I said timidly, trying not to blush too much.

Had Jack already talked to him? What did he say? I was too embarrassed and afraid to ask; instead, I didn't say anything and looked down.

"I have spoken with Sir Forrest and your brother, Jack, and know your predicament and would like to help. I don't wish to offend or presume, but I offer you my hand in marriage. It isn't much, but what I have is yours. I will do my best to work hard and make you happy."

So many thoughts ran through my head, and for the first time, I thought of what Mr. Layton might be feeling. Was this something he wanted to do or something he felt obligated to do?

I bit my lip, grateful that he was telling me more about himself, but I was unsure what to say, so I dipped my head and said, "Thank you, Mr. Layton."

Mr. Layton gave me a shy smile and a nod. "I want you to know, Anne, that I enjoy spending time with you. I moved here to get away from my past. I married my first wife when we were both very young. We were happy together." He paused and took a slow deep breath, then reached and grabbed what looked to be a small purple rock from his pocket. I wanted to ask him about it, but I didn't want to come across as rude. He didn't seem to notice and went on speaking. "She and our twin babies passed away a few years ago."

An image of my sweet brother Nicholas with his bouncing brown curls and Mary, the spitting image of Mama, burned in my mind, and my eyes filled with tears. My heart broke for him; I knew the pain of losing someone close to you. I wanted him to know he was not alone in his grief.

"Oh, Mr. Layton, I'm so sorry for your loss," I said.

"Thank you." He smiled sadly. "Fortunately, my son Thomas survived. I wanted to keep him, but the boy needed a mother. I couldn't take him to work with me each day and I couldn't leave him unattended at home."

He shifted his weight and turned his cap in his hand again. When the opportunity came to work in Jamestown and send money back, I took it. I want him well taken care of."

I nodded my head in understanding and encouraged him to go on.

"At first, I planned on working out my three years here, then heading back to England and working there. Now that they have offered us land and, with you, a chance of a family, I would rather he come to us when the time is right." He paused, then added, "Life is different here, but I wish to make something out of it and start anew."

His honesty was refreshing, and I suddenly wanted to know more about him and his life before Jamestown. He could help me have a good life in this place and a family and land of our own. I would be married to an honest, hardworking, caring man. The prospect gave me hope and made me grateful for another chance, free from service life and possible spinsterhood.

"I can't tell you how much I appreciate all you have done for me, my brother, and the Forrest family, Mr. Layton. Seeing how we hardly know each other, I know the situation is not ideal, but your actions have shown me—and Jack has said—that you are a good and trustworthy man. I accept your proposal and will try my best to be a good wife to you."

I hoped for a promising future for both of us.

"Then we shall both try our best. You may call me John if you like. May I call you Anne?"

"Yes, you may call me Anne." A pink blush spread over my fair cheeks.

Chapter Eighteen
THE FIRST ENGLISH MARRIAGE IN THE NEW WORLD

"A friend shall be known in time of need." – 1035 A.D.

November 21, 1608

Before the sun came up, I convinced Jack to go to the river with me to collect an extra bucket of water. He carried it back to the cabin for me to rinse off with. I stood behind the cabin and poured it over my hair and body while keeping my shift on. Jack stood outside as guard with his back to me to ensure no one was looking. I hadn't bathed since London, and although the water was freezing cold, it felt fantastic to be so clean. I used the soap I made from lye and ash and scrubbed my filthy skin until the dirty water ran clean over my body.

When I finished, I raced back into the cabin, changed into a new shift, and slipped my brown kirtle dress over it. The whole experience was exhilarating, and I finished changing before the rest of the town woke up. My wedding was the next day, and I didn't want to start a marriage feeling dirty and smelly.

Jack helped start a fire for me, and I put a pot of water in the hearth to boil soup for breakfast. A soft tap on the door surprised me.

"May I come in, please?" I heard a familiar voice say. I mouthed "It's Mr. Layton" to Jack and nodded for him to open the door. I quickly wiped my hands on my apron and pushed back a hair that had escaped my coif. *Ugh, my hair again,* I thought.

"Mr. Layton, please come in," Jack said, opening his arms to welcome him.

My stomach felt like butterflies, and I took a deep breath and gave him a small curtsy. "Good day, Mr. Layton."

He took off his cap and dipped his head. "Good day, Miss Burras. I mean, Anne."

He stared at me and slowly twirled his hat in his hands. Jack snickered. "Is there something we can help you with, Mr. Layton?"

Mr. Layton looked surprised. "Oh, yes! I have something for Anne."

For me? I was curious.

Mr. Layton—John—stepped back outside and returned carrying a large trunk. His arms stretched out wide, and his eyes were barely visible under its size. He turned sideways to fit through the door.

He set the heavy object down gently with a thump, and I gasped. A hope chest like Mama's stood before my eyes. I gently brushed my fingers over it and traced the carved initials: A.L.

I looked up and caught him looking at me. "A.L?" I asked.

"Forgive me for being presumptuous; as of tomorrow, your name will be Anne Layton, and I thought it would be nice to have an early wedding present while you prepared."

My fingers gently caressed the initials on the chest again. I glanced at John again and felt heat rush to my cheeks. "It is so beautiful. Thank you." Tears welled up in my eyes. "My Mama has one at home, and I have always wanted one."

"After what you have been through, I thought it might cheer you up and give you something to call your own," John said humbly.

I couldn't believe it. A chest like Mama's, now with my initials. I put my hand to my chest and sighed. It was as if Mama herself was there with me and approved of our marriage.

I let a tear fall, and John came closer and asked if I was all right. "I'm just happy," I said with a smile, and I really was.

I wrote Mama a letter, even though I knew she wouldn't receive it until the next ship went out.

November 22, 1608

Dear Mama,

I was married by Reverend Hunt to Mr. Layton today, November 22nd, during your favorite season of the year, with leaves still visible on the ground. The air was cold, but I felt a warmth in my heart.

It felt odd not to have you here to share the day and tend to me as I got ready like most brides have their mothers do.

Since Mistress Forrest's passing, I have been the only English-woman here. It is incredibly lonely and isolating, but Mr. Layton is kind to me and a good man. He is a carpenter like Jack, but the two couldn't be more different. Jack still acts silly and runs around with the other boys, while Mr. Layton is serious and, at times, stoic—but kind. Both are hard workers, and Mr. Layton wants badly to make me happy.

I also have Pocahontas for a friend. She comes often to play in the fort with the boys and to bring food.

She and a few others from her tribe joined us in our celebration. They brought deer and corn to contribute to the feast. She even gave me a beautiful necklace made of oyster shells as a wedding present. There are plans to eat and celebrate for two days! I wish you were all here to celebrate with us.

I ache for you and Ellen. I wore golden asters shaped into a wreath in my hair; they were the closest thing I could find to daisies here.

Jack walked me down the aisle of the church. It has been in such disarray from the fire that happened before our arrival, but the men worked together to restore what they could to make the wedding look nice. Benches were set out, and part of the roof was rethatched.

It felt like hundreds of eyes were on me, not one female. The reverend pronounced us the first man and woman of the New World! Could you believe that Mama—me? The first English bride in the new world?

John is a good man, Mama. Did I mention that his first name is John? Mr. John Layton. He has been kind to us and will be a good match for me.

I miss you and pray for you daily. Please give my love to Papa and Anthony and a kiss to Ellen and Grandfather.

Love always,
Anne

PART THREE

OUR LIFE IN JAMESTOWN

Chapter Nineteen
THE FLEET

"Expectation is the root of all heartache." – William Shakespeare

August 22, 1609

"Ships! I see four ships ahead!" shouted the boy on lookout duty.

The ships appeared in Chesapeake Bay one at a time. The first bore the name *Blessing* on its side, the next *Lion*, then *Falcon*, and finally, *Unity*. It took two full days for them to disembark all the people and unload the supplies; when they did, we eagerly went out to greet them.

"Oh, blessed day!" I said with delight to John. "The ships must be full of supplies, workers, and even some women!"

The realization brought joy to my heart as I touched my newly growing belly. I would not have to be alone when the baby came. We were told more ships were supposed to arrive. We had planted corn and vegetables in our garden, but I worried it wouldn't be enough for us to eat, let alone more settlers.

"Stay close, Anne," John said, gently placing his hand on my lower back.

"But isn't this the best news? Women and children and supplies; we won't be alone!" I said, as a tear rolled down my cheek.

"I am overjoyed at the prospect, my love." John patted me on the arm. "However, I don't think the natives will be. Tension has been growing among the men—and I don't see the newcomers bringing down many provisions from the boats."

"But surely they bring more provisions and men for protection?" I cried. "We survived one winter; why shouldn't we be able to survive another?"

"I hope so. Still, we should be cautious; there may be Spanish spies among them."

The mention of Spanish spies sent a chill through my bones. I had heard previous accounts of the Spaniards hiring men to report our numbers and conditions. The constant reminder that they were only a few weeks' journey away in Florida made my skin crawl even more.

My heart sank as I watched the passengers disembark the ships. *Where were the supplies?* So many men and women, with so little; how could we possibly feed them all?

John's right, I thought.

My thoughts were interrupted by a middle-aged woman with dark hair and an upturned nose, her arm linked closely with her well-to-do husband's. His heavy metal-pinned jerkin with fine blue silk looked dashing against her cream satin dress. She was beautiful and poised. A stark contrast to the men I was used to at the fort.

"Excuse me, miss," she said politely, in a clipped London accent. "My name is Mrs. Roberts, and this is my husband, Lord Roberts."

Lord Roberts gave me and John a curt bow and said, "Well met."

"Well met, Mrs. Roberts, Lord Roberts. My name is Mrs. Lay—"

"Layton; yes, we know," Mrs. Roberts cut in. "I asked one of the men about you when I saw you. I had heard rumors that a young maid and her mistress were here with all these men but did not hear of your mistress's passing until just now. Why, it is shameless, if you ask me, that Sir Forrest would force you to stay here after his wife's death. However, did you manage here among all these m en?"

She looked between John and me then smirked. "My, you have been busy."

John's face turned beet red. His muscles tightened underneath my arm, and his nostrils flared. The audacity of that woman! I didn't even know her.

I put on a fake smile and tried to ignore her insults.

"What a beautiful day to arrive," I said. "How was your trip?"

"Long and miserable," came her reply.

Lord Roberts was obviously embarrassed by his wife's comments and tried to recover quickly. His hair was a shade or two lighter than his wife's, and he slicked it back under a regal black hat with blue plume feathers protruding from its side. "Do not mind my wife, Mr. and Mrs. Layton. I believe she left her manners at home in London and is dreadfully tired of being on such a long journey."

"We know the feeling, sir," I said with a smile, trying to lighten the mood. John merely nodded his head in agreement, still put off by what Mrs. Roberts had said.

"I see that you are to have a child," Mr. Roberts said in my direction. "Congratulations to you both." He pointed to a young maid holding a baby in one arm and the hand of an older toddler. "Those are our children, little Lizzy and Ezra with their nursemaid." Mr. Roberts proudly smiled. "Children bring such happiness."

"And such misery," Mrs. Roberts mumbled under her breath.

John and I looked at each other in surprise. Before we could say another word, a woman who looked a few years older than me with bouncy blonde curls stepped off the ship, arm in arm with a stern-looking man who held the hand of a little boy with blond hair like his mother's.

"Ah, look here!" Mrs. Roberts said. "There is my sister, Mrs. Flowerdew. Is she not the prettiest thing?" She waved her sister over. "Temperance! Oh, Temperance!"

Mrs. Flowerdew's cheeks flared bright red upon hearing her first name called in the crowd.

"This is the famous Mrs. Layton, whom we have heard so much about," Mrs. Roberts said, as if I was some spectacle.

"Well met, Mr. and Mrs. Layton," Mrs. Flowerdew said with a kind smile, ignoring her sister's comments.

"Well met," we replied.

I curtsied. "I can't tell you how happy I am to have other women here, and to see children again," I smiled down at her small son.

She sighed and her shoulders relaxed. "We are grateful to finally arrive." She leaned over and picked up her son. "This is little George. He just turned three. I think he endured it better than the rest of us."

My hand reached out and squeezed his chubby arm. "Nice to meet you, George."

Mrs. Flowerdew looked around and gave me a genuine smile before looking down at me, noticing my expanded middle. "We are happy to be here and meet your little one when the time comes."

My smile grew, and I placed my hand on my belly again, feeling hopeful that I could make a friend for the first time in a long while.

September 2, 1609

The same day I met Mrs. Flowerdew, I also received a long-awaited letter that arrived with the ship.

Dear Anne,

How are you and Jack faring? I still can't believe you are in Virginia! I tell all my friends that my brother and sister are in the New World, but half of them don't believe me. Please write me a letter with the next ship so I can show it to them.

Mama told me she wrote to you of my intent to marry Sarah Dixon in her last letter before you left London. I did ask her to marry me, and you know what? She said yes, but to my grief, her father said no. He wouldn't let his oldest daughter marry someone without the means to support her. I don't know what else to do. I asked her to run away with me, but she said no; she wouldn't go against her father's wishes. I don't blame her, but I can't stand to stay here and watch her marry another.

Papa said we'd be better off selling the house and what is left of Grandfather's business. He said it in jest, but I think he might be right. We could buy our passage with the money, and I could get away from here. Maybe buy land there or invest a little in the company. At least then we'd all be together again. I miss you; we miss you!

Mama is doing better now; she struggled for a while. However, not two days went by after you left that she realized there was no one there to tend to Ellen, and that she herself needed to step back into her role as Mama. It took some time, but I saw glimpses of what Mama was like when we were children. She seems more like herself every day. Ellen is growing like a weed. She is four now! Can you believe it? She looks more and more like Mama. You must be nearly sixteen now! I bet I'm still taller than you, though.

We pray for you and Jack every day. Please keep us in your prayers for guidance on what to do next.
Yours sincerely,
Anthony

Oh, Anthony! I thought as I held the letter close to my heart. It had been so long since I heard from him, and I knew how much he loved Sarah. Not being able to marry her must have crushed him.

I hated that it took so long to send and receive letters. It dawned on me that I had a stack of letters I wanted to send but never had the chance to, even my letter to Mama about getting married—and now I could include that I was with child. I couldn't wait for the first boat that would return to London so I could send it along.

I reread the letter and prayed that Papa's words weren't just teasing. Now that Jack and I were staying in Jamestown, I prayed he would sell the house and business and join us. I wished I could send him a letter every day begging them to come.

Chapter Twenty
FRIENDSHIP

"A friend is one that knows you as you are, understands where you have been, accepts what you have become, and still, gently allows you to grow." –
William Shakespeare

September 14, 1609

Two more ships, the *Diamond* and the *Swallow,* arrived a few days after the first four ships. It was exhilarating seeing so many more English women there.

It almost made me forget the pit I once felt in my stomach for the longing of friends.

One night, John paced the floor with worry about the lack of provisions that had accompanied the ships.

"Anne, no good can come from this. There are just too many mouths to feed. We already lack the required provisions. I don't know how all these people are going to survive the winter with what we have here. What were they thinking? I worry there will be more death."

I gasped. "Do you really think it will come to that?"

John looked down at the floor, took off his blue cap, and twisted it in front of him. "I'm not sure."

My skin crawled at his words, and I shuttered. "What are we to do John?"

"Stay close to the fort. Tend to the garden we started as often as possible. I have a feeling it won't last long."

John's words haunted me, and I couldn't sleep. My growing belly made it even more uncomfortable, and it took me longer than before to go about my day.

He didn't mention the rations again. I'm not sure if it was because he didn't want to worry me or because he thought it was of no use to worry about it.

I tried to make do with what we had, a small crop of potatoes, radishes and cabbage I planted in front of our cabin. I kept myself busy with chores and visiting my new friend Temperance. We saw each other nearly every day after her arrival. We collected water, gathered firewood, sewed, and cleaned our linens together. It was so comforting having a friend to talk to, and I loved seeing her play with her little George. My heart yearned for the day when my sweet little one would arrive. George brought so much joy and hope with him. I liked to squeeze his cute little rosy cheeks and chubby legs.

Occasionally, her sister Mrs. Roberts would join us. On one such occasion, she arrived unannounced while Temperance and I sat in my cabin mending stockings. We welcomed her in, and she let her daughter play on the floor with little George. I smiled at them and chuckled as George pretended to ride his wooden toy horse.

"He's such a sweet little boy, Temperance," I said. "How lucky he is to have a mother such as you."

"Thank you," she replied. "You will be an excellent mother." I touched my growing belly and smiled.

Mrs. Roberts made a clicking sound with her tongue and stuck up her nose. "Childbirth is an awful business. Only the strong survive it."

My eyes grew wide, and I bit my lower lip. "I have heard of such. Is it really that dangerous?"

Mrs. Roberts scoffed, and Temperance rolled her eyes at her sister. "Don't pay her any mind, Anne. You will be fine. You're one of the strongest women I know."

Her words, though comforting, still didn't take the sting away from Mrs. Roberts's condemning ones. A tear skirted down my face, and I looked down at my darning.

Temperance placed a hand on mine and scowled at her sister. "I see the way you are with little George; you are a natural. We will be here to help you through the process."

My hand squeezed hers back. "Thank you." I looked back again at little George and Mrs. Roberts's daughter and took a deep breath. *It will be worth it,* I thought.

Temperance must have sensed that I was bothered. "Is there anything else the matter? You look lost in thought."

"I suppose seeing little George made me think of Sir Forrest's son, Peter. It must have broken his heart when Sir Forrest told him that his other mother had died."

Temperance's eyebrows scrunched together in surprise. "Another mother?"

"Yes, his mother died in childbirth, and Mistress Forrest was his stepmother."

She sighed and shook her head. "That's awful."

"I agree; it's horrible to have to go through such a loss at such a young age."

Temperance grew quiet for a minute and went back to her stitches. She looked up at me and her lashes fluttered. "Was it terribly hard?" She frowned.

My eyes flashed. "Was what terribly hard?"

"Coming here, losing her and being the only woman, being forced to marry? All of it." She picked up a toy horse George had dropped and handed it back to him.

"It's not what I expected," I said, sighing and wiping my nose with my sleeve.

"I suppose all of it was hard in the beginning. It was hard to leave home and, surprisingly, even harder to leave England. I felt so scared and odd being one of only two women. Then, when Mistress died, I didn't know what to do. Sir Forrest suggested I marry, and I honestly didn't have a choice."

"But you did have a choice," Temperance said. "Hundreds of choices."

She pointed to the men walking outside the cabin and laughed. She had a contagious laugh, light and airy, that made you want to join her.

I sniffled and smiled. "I guess you're right. John had been so kind to me and the Forrest family. My brother also knew him and said he was honest and hard-working. He even saved my life once."

Temperance gave me one of her big smiles that lit up her whole face and said, "Sounds romantic."

"I suppose it was." I hadn't thought of it like that before. I was traumatized by Mistress dying and leaving me alone, but Temperance was right; I was fortunate to be married to such a good man.

Temperance touched my hand. "It's all right to be scared, Anne. I was too. Bringing a child into this world can be dangerous, but I will be with you. I'm here now. And even though Lydia can be a stick in the mud, she was great when I had my baby. We will help you through it."

I felt my chin start to quiver and I bit down hard on my bottom lip to keep from crying, but the tears stubbornly found their way down my cheeks. I gulped and gave her a sideways smile. My hand reached out and squeezed hers.

"Thank you," was all I could manage to say, and I turned back toward my mending. The weight of emotions I felt inside of me was too heavy to share, as if the dam I built around my heart might burst and I could never get back control if I let her see.

October 1, 1609

By the end of September, another ship had arrived, the *Virginia*, totaling seven ships that had recently arrived on our shores. Two more ships were still missing, the *Catch* and the *Sea Venture*.

I couldn't help but feel a pang of worry in my heart after what John had said. I prayed that he was wrong and that, somehow, they had more provisions on their boat. If not, how long would we all last?

Jamestown started to fill up fast. The once-empty cabins were bursting to the brim, and I had to wait in line several times at the newly built well.

While in line, I heard the two women in front of me in line gossiping.

A tall, thin woman with auburn hair and a baby on her hip made a *tsk* sound as she looked around. "So little supplies, so many mouths to feed. They promised we would have enough."

The woman next to her was a few inches shorter, also with red hair—possibly her sister. She nodded in agreement. "My husband said the Company will figure out a way to solve our problems.

Captain Smith traded with the natives last winter. I heard they practically worshiped him. I'm sure he can make them do it again."

I rolled my eyes to myself. Captain Smith couldn't make anyone do anything, certainly not Chief Powhatan. Their conversation, however, did make me think about the provision supply and Pocahontas. I hadn't seen her since the new ships arrived. I prayed she was doing well and that her disappearance was not a foreseeable sign of trouble with the natives.

Later that day, I brought lunch to John at his carpenter's post. He usually came home for lunch, just a few minutes' walk, but was so burdened with getting materials ready for the new cabins that he didn't have time to come home to eat. While I was walking, I saw Sir Ratcliffe stumble out of one of the initial cabins that they'd turned into a tavern.

I had met Sir Ratcliffe before with a few other leading council members for Jamestown. He was even at my wedding, but I didn't trust him as I did Captain Smith. He was tall, with a pointy black beard, broad shoulders, and an enormous belly. When he looked at me with his sinister brown eyes, it gave me chills, so I tended to keep my distance. I tried to ignore him, but it was hard not to hear his loud slurred voice as he yelled at the captain of the *Diamond*.

"My lord," the captain pleaded, "I'm trying to tell you that they should have arrived here by now. If they don't arrive soon, we won't survive, our provisions are already scarce."

Sir Ratcliffe staggered a bit, and slouched the alcohol he had in his hand onto the dirt floor. "Why not just pull more provisions down from the ships?"

"Sir, you are not hearing me correctly," the captain said in an angry huff. "They loaded the majority of the fleet's provisions onto the Sea Venture. As well as the leaders, the doctor, and new reverend. We don't have any left."

Sir Ratcliffe's expression changed as if hearing the captain for the first time. "What? None left?!" he yelled.

"No Sir." the captain responded in a quieter tone. He looked around and realized a crowd was starting to form. Several men and women had heard the noise and stood gawking at the two men. His eye caught mine, and I returned to collect the water, trying to act like I didn't see him. "Quiet your voice Sir, or you will frighten the people," he said in hushed tones.

"We have a few provisions but not much is left. They may last us a few more weeks, a month if we are lucky. Let's pray the *Sea Venture* arrives soon; if not, we must look for food elsewhere." I quickly filled my buckets and returned to the cabin to tell John what I had heard.

I set the buckets down and bent over to catch my breath. John quickly ran to me and placed a hand on my belly. "Is it the baby?" he asked with worry.

I took another deep breath. "No, it's our provisions."

He stood up and scratched his thick beard. "What do you mean, our provisions?"

"You were right. A captain from the new ship said they didn't have much left. That most of it was placed on the missing ship."

John's eyes grew wide. "I was afraid of this; we may need to try to trade for food again. I knew the men were foolish not to plant more crops. Their only concern is to find gold for King James, forgetting that gold would do them no good if they were dead. The same thing happened before you arrived."

Bile rose in my throat as the memory of what Jamestown looked like when I arrived flashed through my mind. I shivered and gripped my stomach. "We can't let that happen again. We can't let that happen to our baby."

John saw the panic in my eyes and words and tried to shift the conversation. "Everything will be all right, Anne. I promise you."

Just then, Jack ran in. His eyes seemed frozen and full of fear. "Did you hear the news?"

"What news?" John asked.

"I overheard Sir Ratcliff say, plain as day, that we don't have enough rations. The captain of the *Diamond* said two ships must have been trapped in the storm, the *Sea Venture* and the *Catch*. The *Sea Venture* carried a majority of the supplies and most of our leaders."

John shook his head. "That's what I was afraid of. Too many people came at once."

Jack nodded his head. "I also heard some say that the *Diamond* had the plague on it, and two other ships threw thirty-two dead bodies overboard from yellow fever while they were at sea."

I gasped and cupped my hand over my mouth. I'd heard about the supplies but not the plague and yellow fever. *Here?*

I looked over at John. His hands visibly shook as he tried to stay calm. The anger and hurt at the word "plague" were written into his creased forehead and trembling, clenched hands as he no doubt remembered the loss of his dear wife and children. He again pulled his purple stone from his pocket and started rubbing it. It calmed him when he did.

My heart raced, and I placed my free hand into John's. I tried to shift the focus of the conversation, for all our sakes.

"Have you met any new friends from the ships?" I asked Jack.

His eyes widened. "Yes! There are so many boys my age—and did you see some of the pretty girls, too?"

There was my Jack, the social butterfly, lighting up around people.

"I talked with Temperance," I said, "and she volunteered to help me when my time comes to have the baby. Now I don't have to deliver the baby alone."

"That's wonderful," Jack said.

John visibly relaxed next to me too. I didn't know he had worried so much about me and the baby. I wondered what it was like with his other children. Would he love this child the same as the others? It broke my heart to think of all he had been through. "Yes," John said, patting my arm when I slipped it through his. "Nothing would make me happier than knowing you and the baby are safe."

I cringed. He was right. I hadn't realized how much I had felt the burden of delivering the child alone.

Chapter Twenty-One
VIRGINIA

"She openeth her mouth with wisdom; and in her tongue is the law of kindness. She looketh well to the ways of her household. And eateth not the bread of idleness. Her children arise up, and call her blessed; her husband also, and he praiseth her." – Proverbs 31:26–28

October 7, 1609

The pain started in my lower belly and quickly moved to my back. It had happened intermittently over the past two days, then usually went away when I sat or lay down.

This time, it wrapped around me so tightly that I had to bend down on my knees while working in the garden planted a few months earlier. It wasn't much, but we hoped it would give us a good harvest. The cramping only lasted a minute, so I breathed through it until it stopped and returned to work. By the afternoon, the pain increased to the point where it didn't go away when I squatted down, and it came every few minutes. My heart raced; I didn't know what to do.

I looked around the field for Temperance but caught the eye of Lydia Roberts instead. Another surge of pain wrapped around from behind, and I squatted down where I was to make it go away. She looked at my pleading face and dropped the ear of corn she plucked into the basket and walked over to me. "Mrs. Layton, I believe your baby is on its way."

My body winced in pain. She knelt beside me and held my hand as I breathed through another round of birth pangs. When it stopped, she helped me up and patted me on the hand. "Come along, the pain will pass once the baby is here. These things may take time. Let's get you back to your cabin."

My eyes welled up with tears, and I nodded my head. I was surprised by her kindness but gladly welcomed the help. As we walked to the other side of the field, Temperance stood up and wiped her sweaty brow. George pointed a chubby finger in our direction. "Mama, it's Anne," he said. I was in no mood to wave but looked at her with pleading eyes. She was on my other side in a minute, helping me walk back to my cabin.

"George, can you help Mama and run ahead of us and grab a warm blanket from our cabin, then meet me at Anne's, please?"

His little head bobbed up and down, eager to help. "Yes, Mama," he said as he ran off toward their cabin.

"Let's get you home, Anne," Temperance said.

My heart melted with relief over having these two women at my sides. Another pain hit, and I rested on them to push through it.

"I can't do this!" I cried as we approached the cabin.

"Yes, you can!" Temperance replied. "And you will!" She squatted down in front of me. Her blue eyes penetrated mine.

I nodded silently, then stood again to walk, only to fall two minutes later. A rustling sound came from the bushes nearby, causing us all to jump back in fear.

"Anne!"

I nearly collapsed from relief when I heard John call my name and come rushing over.

"They told me the baby was coming and you might need help. I came as quickly as I could."

Another pain came on, and down I went. John looked at Temperance and Mrs. Roberts. "How long has she been like this?"

"Off and on all day," Mrs. Roberts said, "but the last few hours have been more often and consistent. I think this baby is coming soon, Mr. Layton. We need to get her back home."

John nodded, picked me up, cradled me in his arms, and rushed me back to the cabin.

"Best leave us to tend to her," Mrs. Roberts said. "This is no place for a man."

Stunned by it all, John could only nod in agreement and shut the door. I let out a scream, and he raced back in.

"Outside, Mr. Layton. She will be fine."

He didn't come back in, but I could hear him walking up and down in front of our cabin. George brought the blanket over, and Lydia poked her head out to John and asked him to help George return home and stay with Mr. Flowerdew.

I could hear John outside when he returned because he made a loud scuffing sound in the dirt while he paced in front of our cabin.

After what felt like hours of more pain, I felt like giving up. Then the pains started to become unbearable and closer together. I saw Temperance and Mrs. Roberts glance at each other with pity. As they looked over my head at each other, and I could tell they both knew the time was approaching.

Temperance untied some of the rope from the bucket handle and asked me to bite down on it. The pain wrapped around me again, and I cried out. Seconds later, things shifted, and I suddenly felt an urge to push.

"I think the baby is coming!" I yelled.

Mrs. Roberts sat before me, and Temperance helped hold me in a squatting position.

"Then push, Anne," Mrs. Roberts said.

I pushed for several minutes, but there was still no baby. "Keep pushing, Anne; you can do it. I can see the top of its head."

That gave me an extra burst of strength, and I pushed with all my might. After two more efforts, the baby emerged. I heard a soft cry, followed by a strong wail. I couldn't believe it. The baby was finally here!

Temperance laughed and kissed me on my head. Mrs. Roberts held up a beautiful baby to my chest. "It's a girl," she cried.

"A girl?" I said with a giant smile. I took her warm wet body into my arms and fell in love with her at first sight.

"She's perfect." Temperance squeezed my shoulder.

"She is," Mrs. Roberts agreed. "You were amazing, Anne. Simply amazing."

"I couldn't have done it without the two of you," I said. "How can I ever thank you, Mrs. Roberts?"

"You could start by calling me Lydia," Mrs. Roberts said.

That made us all chuckle, and we all looked down at my sweet baby girl.

They were right: she was perfect. One look at her, and my world stopped. Her blue eyes mimicked the sea on a dark stormy day. They reminded me so much of my little sister Ellen's, whom I hadn't seen in so many years. It was as if Ellen were looking back at me. Her tiny fingers and toes took my breath away. I counted each one, feeling the soft touch of her skin against mine. I was utterly entranced by her tiny fingernails, soft downy-like hair with beautiful brown curls, rose-pink cheeks, squished-up nose, and dark blue eyes staring back at me. Words could not express my immense love for her and the desire to protect her from the hardships of this world. I was truly humbled and in awe of her and motherhood.

How do women do this multiple times? I wondered. But I knew I would do it all over again in a heartbeat for her. *I have a baby girl,* I thought, with joy more profound than I even knew possible.

I could hear John pacing back and forth in front of our cabin. I imagined him twirling his purple rock in his hand for comfort and praying for all to go well.

Lydia poked her head out the door, "You are a father again, Mr. Layton."

John's face brightened when he saw me. He took off his cap and held it in front of him as he walked to my side and kissed me on the forehead.

"You were wonderful, Anne. Is it...?"

"A girl? Yes."

His smile widened as he took hold of her little hand with his finger. "How wonderful!"

"Truly? You are not disappointed that it isn't a boy?"

"How could I be disappointed? We have enough men here at Jamestown. I am just happy you are both well."

The light from the glass window reflected on John's hair as he tucked it behind his ear. He looked down at me, and our eyes met. We had grown closer together, so much had happened. The way his soft gaze lingered on me felt like a warm blanket wrapped around me. For the first time, I realized that I loved him and that he loved me.

My silence must have startled him because his brows creased together, and he frowned. "You are well, are you not?"

His question brought my mind back into focus. "Yes, I'm sorry. We are both well." I confirmed as a tear rolled down my cheek. "Indeed, I couldn't be happier."

"Neither could I," he said. "Now, what shall we call her?"

"Virginia," I said with a smile.

"Virginia," John repeated. "How fitting."

Her blue eyes looked up at both of us, and we melted into each other's arms.

Chapter Twenty-Two
A Season of Change

"Nothing is sweeter than love, nothing higher, nothing stronger, nothing larger, nothing more joyful, nothing fuller, and nothing better in heaven nor on earth." – Thomas A. Kempis

October 15, 1609

My arms felt warm and complete when I held Virginia. I gently touched her cheek with my finger and pushed her soft brown hair from her face. Jack came to visit the day she was born and reminded me that Ellen had dark hair too when she was born, but it later lightened to blonde. I wondered if Virginia's hair would change color as well.

It hadn't been much longer than a week, but I already couldn't picture life without her. My heart ached to hold her when someone else was, and I loved hearing the funny sounds she made while sleeping.

My initial recovery was swift and uneventful, which I was thankful for. A week later, though, I started to feel nauseated and threw up most of the night. It took a few days to stop vomiting, and despite the quick recovery from Virginia's birth, I was weak after losing so much fluid. John and Temperance helped care for Virginia as I recovered.

Virginia could still nurse, but I felt exhausted from the combination of post-labor recovery and being so ill. I couldn't keep anything down; my head felt fuzzy, and my arms and legs were limp. John spoon fed me soup, and Temperance stayed up with Virginia and gave her sugar water when she was fussy. She was starting to gain weight, so I wasn't worried.

Food was being rationed out more sparingly after the new arrivals. I worried about the rumors floating around town that we wouldn't have enough.

Captain Smith had told us that those who did not work would not eat. So many lay sick that it was hard to tell what was ailing them: dirty water, not enough food, disease, or lack of desire? Something needed to be done.

Fall had been bitterly cold, and we worried winter would be much worse. Our food was sparse; we harvested what we could before the freeze. Most of the crops were destroyed or picked over by the natives.

The rivers that once were full of rainwater were now receding, leaving black marshlands in their wake. A salty, muddy residue was all that was left to drink from. The stench of wastewater from the settlers washed up against the shore. Men were continually sick from dysentery and dehydration.

It was in the middle of this predicament that Jack ran to our cabin, frantic and breathing heavily. "It's Captain Smith! He's back but badly wounded."

"Back?" I echoed, sitting in bed. "What do you mean, back and wounded? What happened?"

John tried to calm me and help me lie back down. He gave Jack a frustrated look.

"Anne is still recovering from being sick, Jack. Can we discuss this outside?" he said through gritted teeth.

"No, please, I want to hear what he has to say." John shook his head but let Jack continue.

"He told Sir Ratcliffe that he would take a skivvy and a few men upriver to Powhatan and ask for more help and supplies before we all starved to death," Jack said.

Even in my weak state, I jolted upright in my bed. "Starve?" "We don't have enough provisions, Anne, and now Captain Smith is badly wounded."

"Badly wounded, what happened?"

Jack shrugged his shoulders, "He was shot in the leg. Not sure by who."

"Shot!" John yelled.

Jack nodded. "A few men just brought him to the square. He is talking to Sir Newport now. A crowd has gathered. I am going to go hear what he has to say."

"I'm coming too," John said. "Me too," I chimed in.

John sat at the side of my bed. "Anne, you can't. You are still weak from the birth and from being ill, my dear."

"I feel well enough, and I want to hear what Captain Smith has to say too. This might be the last time we see him."

John and Jack looked at each other as if asking the other what to do.

"I'm going," I said, "and that's that."

Jack shrugged. "I don't think we could argue with her, John. It won't do any good."

"I have to agree with you there," John said, patting Jack on the shoulder. "If she is strong enough to argue with you, she is strong enough to go."

The two of them snickered together. "Will she ever learn?" John laughed with Jack.

I walked through the crowd toward Captain Smith with Jack and John right behind me. I clutched Virginia to my chest when I saw Captain Smith lying on the dirt, surrounded by a group of people.

"What happened?" I asked a man next to me. "He's been shot, miss," he said.

"Shot! Shot by whom? The natives?"

The man shook his head. "Not by whom, by what? The gun powder in the boat exploded."

"They said it was an accident, miss," a man with a long beard and tattered cream shirt said. His gray doublet jacket hung over his gaunt frame. "But I think it was no accident. Not by the look of him."

As I pushed through the crowd of men, I saw blood oozing from Captain Smith's leg. My stomach turned, and I had to cover my mouth to avoid vomiting. Half his leg was burned off or singed, the skin wide open and flopping around. I had to look away for a minute to compose myself before turning back.

A woman beside me gasped. "Poor Captain Smith! What is to become of him?"

"My boat," Captain Smith said with a moan. "Someone tried to sabotage the skivvy and ignited the gunpowder."

The crowd gasped, and the men began to argue among themselves.

"This is treason!" Sir Ratcliffe shouted, shaking a raised fist. "Someone will pay for this!" the men began to cry. Their petition was silenced when Captain Smith spoke again.

"We are not in shape enough to last this winter. I need to return to tell the king. If I stay here with this leg, I will most likely die, and what would that do for the rest of you? Let us take up one of the ships and return for additional supplies and help. We will take four vessels, the *Diamond*, *Lion*, *Falcon*, and *Unity*, back with us; that way, we may be able to return with more supplies."

"Here, here!" shouted some of the men.

"Is it true?" A man with shaggy brown hair and several missing teeth shouted next to me.

"Is what true, man?" Sir Ratcliffe asked.

"Smith, is it true that Chief Powhatan shot and killed the remaining Roanoke people?"

A gasp escaped my lips, and shouts were heard from the other men.

"Do you think he is the one who did this to you?" the same man asked.

"Men, men, listen to me!" Captain Smith pleaded, trying to breathe through the pain. "There have been reports that the Roanoke people joined with the Hatteras people on Croatoan Island and then made their way up here. Powhatan himself told me that he had his men kill them and the tribe they were staying with. Do not underestimate the Powhatan forces nor their great chief." He put his hands on his chest and took several deep breaths, trying to recover before going on. "I'm not sure if Powhatan said those things about the Roanoke people to trick us and stop us in our search or if it really happened."

He then grabbed Sir Ratcliffe's arm and pulled him in close. I was near enough to hear his whispers. "Do not underestimate Powhatan! Please do what you can to get these people food. Promise me you will take care of these people."

Sir Ratcliffe froze and didn't say a word. "Promise me!" Captain Smith demanded.

"I promise," Sir Ratcliffe said, growing pale in the face.

I placed my hand over my mouth to keep from gasping. Sweat dripped down Sir Ratcliffe's already-wet brow. Fear was in his eyes, and I didn't feel I could trust him.

He shifted his eyes toward two skinny young men with tattered clothing barely hanging off their backs. "You two! Help Captain Smith onto the ship. He is going back to England. I will stay and watch over these people." He shook his fist into the air as if swearing an oath. "We will find food, and we will survive."

Captain Smith dropped his head back to the ground and closed his eyes, satisfied that at least Sir Ratcliff would do what was in his power to help the people. Sir Ratcliffe gave a slight nod, and Captain Smith was carried away by the two men onto the ship.

We watched as our only links to London slowly edged up the James River. I longed to be on that boat, yet I felt pulled to stay, and my heart felt torn between the two lands I had grown to love.

As the group of us onlookers turned around to leave the dock, I saw a set of eyes hidden in the underbrush of the woods and let out a sharp exhale. John stilled and followed my pointing finger.

"In there. I saw someone watching us."

John looked around again and wrapped his arms around Virginia and me. I could almost feel his heart beating through his embrace. "Let's get out of here."

My heart raced. Too afraid to run and make any sudden movements we kept a quick but not alarming pace towards the fort.

Within a few yards of the gate, I heard multiple swishing sounds as if someone was slicing at the air with a sword, then a piercing scream came from a woman a few feet behind me.

"We're being attacked!" someone else shouted.

People pushed and shoved past us. I didn't bother to look around. I wrapped my arms tighter around Virginia, and John tightened his around me, and we ran toward the fort as if our lives depended on it—because they did.

Inside, John, huffing and out of breath, looked me over and placed his strong hands on my shoulders. "Are you hurt?"

Dazed and terrified by what had just happened, I knit my brows together and looked down at Virginia, safe and sound in my arms. "No, I don't think so."

Shots and screams were heard as people surged into the fort. Four men carried two bodies shot full of arrows. I gasped and turned my head into John's chest to not see. The men had either died or would die soon from their wounds.

"Two more men are still out there!" a man with a thick German accent shouted. "They were shot full of arrows; there is no way they would survive. We couldn't get to them."

A woman screamed when she saw that one of the men was her husband.

Panic rose in my lungs when I realized I didn't see Jack. "Jack!" I yelled. "Jack!"

"Over here," he cried, waving frantically in our direction.

I turned and looked back at the woman on her knees next to her husband's corpse and felt immediate guilt. That could have been me and John. Bile rose in my throat, and my heart raced. *How are we going to survive this?*

Chapter Twenty-Three
TO STAY OR TO LEAVE?

"Now all of us at James Town are beginning to feel that sharp prick of hunger, which no man truly describes but he which hath tasted the bitterness thereof." – Sir George Percy

November 25, 1609

"*F*ifty men!" Governor Ratcliffe's assistant shouted. "Fifty men are needed for Point Comfort this winter."

A few of the five hundred plus settlers came out to hear the commotion.

Concerns were growing over Captain Smith leaving and the situation with the natives escalating, and the ever-present fear of Spanish invasion lingered on everyone's lips.

"I think we should go," John whispered in my ear.

My heart raced. Memories of the attack by the river flashed into my mind, and I held Virginia close to my chest.

I turned and whispered back. People around us were doing the same, whispering, worrying, and debating about the safest course to take. Shocked, scared, tired faces, all trying to do the same thing: survive.

"But wouldn't it be more dangerous to go there, away from the protection of the fort?" I asked.

"Sweetheart, I fear if we stay here, we will be more likely to be attacked or starve from within. Look at all these people."

I followed his gaze left and right and quickly realized he was correct. Hundreds of people surrounded us without crops or the means to feed them all. John had survived with the first group that made it to Jamestown. He knew firsthand what people would do when there wasn't enough food. The man hanging from the gallows came to mind. It was rumored that he had eaten the corpse of his dead friend.

The thought sent a chill throughout my body. "You're right; I think we should go."

John raised his hand high without further discussion and offered, "We will go! I am a craftsman, and so is my young brother-in-law here. My wife can tend to us and the other men while we are there."

"Ah," said the governor's assistant, "Mr. and Mrs. Layton, young Mr. Burras, very well. Thank you for volunteering. See, it is safe. Even a woman and her young babe are going."

Even though I agreed to it, my eyes widened at his comment. Were we truly making the right choice?

"I'm going to talk to Temperance," I told John. He nodded. I looked around for Temperance and ran to her side as soon as I spotted her in the crowd. She and her husband, William, stood in the back.

"Temperance!" I waved. "Good day, Anne," she said.

"Good day," I said and curtsied to her and William.

"Are you and your family planning on coming to Point Comfort?" I asked with a hopeful smile.

"No, Anne," Temperance said in a concerned quiet voice as she hefted little George to her hip. "William thinks we should stay here. Lydia and her family are staying, too, and refuse to leave. We don't have much of a choice."

I could see that she wanted to go to Point Comfort with us. My heart pumped fast, and I bit my lip to not speak out of turn, but I couldn't help myself. "They said there isn't enough food if we stay here," I blurted out.

William tapped his foot, impatient with me and Temperance for not siding with him. "Governor Ratcliffe assures us that Chief Powhatan will trade food with us for our glass beads and pans. He said Chief Powhatan would do anything to collect riches from the English."

It's a lie! I told myself. I shook my head, and my hands began to shake with worry. "It isn't true," I cried. "The Powhatans are angry with us. We said we would leave and not take over their hunting areas, yet more and more people have arrived. I saw a man watching us in the brush when we said goodbye to Captain Smith with my own eyes. They know our numbers are growing; they won't want to feed us. I don't think they will trade, and if they do, will it be enough?"

"My point exactly," William protested. "You saw what they did to those men, and that was just a handful of them. Imagine what they could do to you without the protection of the fort? I will not put my family in danger."

"But they would be in danger *here!*"

William's face turned red, and he puffed out his cheeks in frustration. He pointed his index finger at my face. "Sir Ratcliffe said we would be protected here."

"William!" Temperance said in shock as she grabbed his arm to try to calm him down.

I shook my head at that point, not caring if I did make him angry. The only thing I cared about was keeping Temperance and George safe.

"The only person who could have helped us with the natives is Captain Smith, who is gone. Sir Ratcliffe has just made them angry," I said.

I knew I shouldn't have spoken out of turn, but I was genuinely worried for my friend. Temperance's blue eyes flooded with tears.

She looked terrified. I was too. I knew winter was just around the corner, and already our meals were being rationed. I had the same worries. What if we were foolish to break off from the rest of the group?

"Please." I tilted my head up toward William. His stern face and smug smile intimidated me on a good day, but I wasn't about to leave without saying my piece. I knew if I did, that I'd regret it. "If you stay, your family will starve."

He looked at them, then at me, and his eyes glossed with sadness. "Anne, if you leave, you may as well count yourselves killed by the natives."

He put his hand on the small of Temperance's back. "Come along now, Temperance; there is nothing more to hear."

"No, please," I cried, reaching for Temperance's red linen sleeve.

"I'm sorry, Anne," she said as tears ran down her rosy cheeks.

My chest felt heavy, and I wanted to cry and scream all at the same time. *Please listen to me!* I wanted to yell. I didn't know what would happen at Point Comfort, but it was better than staying here and starving to death.

"Please, Lord," I prayed, "please help us be together again someday. Please watch over Temperance and little George, and the rest of the people. Please."

I ran to her and gave her and George a big hug. Virginia nestled between the three of us.

"Please take care," I told her.

"You as well," she said with a smile and quivering lip, showing off a dimple in her chin. "Here, take this," she added, wrapping a light blue shawl around my shoulders. She smiled through tears. "Something you can remember me by until we see each other again."

I nodded and offered her a tight-lipped smile, holding back my tears. My heart wrenched as I saw her walk away.

"Farewell, my friend," I said as I waved goodbye.

Temperance's voice cracked as she wiped away her tears. "Farewell, and may God be with you."

"And you," I yelled as she made her way through the crowd.

Chapter Twenty-Four
POINT COMFORT

"Lastly and chiefly, the way to prosper and obtain
good success is to make yourselves all of one mind
for the good of your country..." – Virginia Company
Instructions, 1606

November 27, 1609

About sixty of us volunteered to go to Point Comfort. Tension was high, and people seemed on high alert. Women briskly walked by without saying hello, and families and friends fought over who should or should not go.

Jack, John, and I quickly gathered what little belongings we could and met by the docks with the others. I ripped the extra blanket left by Sir Forrest in half and scooped up Virginia with it after I swaddled her in linen first.

Mr. James Davis, a short man with thinning brown hair peppered with white, a large pointy nose, and a trimmed beard, waited for us at the docks. He wore a dark blue vest over a white work shirt and detachable sleeves to match. The assignment to watch over our little group was given by the London Company, and Mr. Davis took the appointment very seriously. He stood, quill and pen in hand, to mark every single one of us, and tapped his clean black shoes impatiently as we waited to board.

"Name?" he curtly asked.

"John Layton, and this be my wife, Anne, our daughter, Virginia, and my brother-in-law, Jack Burras."

Mr. Davis scrolled down his list of names and looked us over. "Yes, Mr. And Mrs. Layton, I remember when you volunteered. Very brave of you considering your family's situation," he said, pointing with his quill at Virginia.

I flinched and hugged her tighter to my chest.

Jack and John both pulled a face and John clenched his fists. "Brave and wise, I'd say," Jack said.

I knew that John did not appreciate Mr. Davis's sentiment but was too polite to say anything. Mr. Davis slightly nodded his chin and puckered his lips but said nothing in return.

He rechecked his list. "Second skivvy on the right," he said before asking the name of the people behind us.

Jack huffed. "He has some nerve."

"Jack, don't," I said as I shushed Virginia back to sleep. "It will only make matters worse. People are scared and still aren't sure what to do,"

We walked toward our skivvy, and John helped me climb into the boat. I hadn't been on a boat since I arrived in Jamestown, and it teetered back and forth. A stream of icy cold water poured over my ankles like knives against my kirtle and stockings. I let out a small yelp, which made Virginia cry. Immediately, I felt John's hand covering my mouth. I looked at him, startled, but as he put his finger over his lips and looked around, I saw the fear in his eyes and realized my foolishness. There could be natives watching us, and we didn't want to draw attention to ourselves or let them know we were leaving.

I wobbled for a moment and was afraid I would fall with Virginia in my arms, but a kind older gentleman reached out a hand to help steady me.

The older man nodded in agreement. "He's right, miss. Please do what you can to keep you and the little one quiet. I'm in charge of this here skivvy, and I will do my best to get us there safely, but we are counting on you not to draw attention to ourselves."

I gulped and nodded. John's fingers slowly moved away from my mouth. They tasted like dirt and salt, and memories of almost being kidnapped flashed back to my mind. My eyes widened; they flicked to John's, and he mouthed the words, "I'm sorry." His eyes looked remorseful and worried, and I knew he meant it.

We set out before the other boats and made it halfway down the James River when the old man commanded in a gruff whisper, "Slow down your rowing, men. The natives' fish in these waters. We don't want to make too many ripples and let them know we are here."

I shivered again and held my breath. If we were caught, we would be sitting ducks, waiting to be shot full of arrows.

John sensed my anxiety and wrapped his arms around Virginia and me. "It's going to be all right, Anne. We'll make it."

I nodded and tightened the blanket around Virginia, who thankfully had fallen asleep.

November 27, 1609

The fort was situated in a beautiful location. It was small and not inviting, but the trees surrounding it were vast and reminded me of home. After dropping their colorful leaves onto the forest floor, their limbs looked bare.

Timbers lined the small fort, which was built right up against the water. A tower was erected to keep watch for Spanish ships. Our job was to let Jamestown Fort know immediately if a vessel was spotted so that they could prepare the cannons and other weapons to ward off an attack.

"Word reached our ears," one man whispered, "that the day the new supply ship arrived in June, a Spanish vessel was on its way to attack. They fled when they saw the British ship, thinking England must have sent reinforcements."

"What if another one comes, but this time, we don't have big ships to frighten them away with?" asked another man with a long, scraggly gray-and-brown beard and several missing teeth. "Enough of that talk," John whispered. "There be women and children onboard."

The men stopped talking and looked in our direction. Having them all stare at me felt awkward, and I quickly looked away. I could see John fiddle with his purple rock again.

We soon landed. Our wake made chunks of icy water slosh against the muddy shores. My skirt felt nearly frozen. I couldn't wait to start the fire and get dry. Virginia fussed and cried against the cold wind but fell back asleep when I nestled her closer. I hoped she was warm enough. I took the pale blue shawl I was wearing and tucked it between the blanket and her face. Temperance had given it to me, and somehow, it made me feel as if she was right there with me.

February 23, 1610

Winter passed slowly and seemed to never end. I kept busy with so much to do between tending to Virginia, cleaning, cooking, and trying to maintain the clothing and supplies we had. Another woman came to Point Comfort along with her husband and two children. I enjoyed her company but missed my friends at Jamestown.

Chunks of ice floated down the James River, and snow covered the ground.

"A man from the nearby Kecoughtan tribe said this is the coldest winter he's seen in many years," John said.

"I believe it," I replied, holding Virginia close to my chest. "I'm grateful we have enough food. I just hope we can stay warm enough."

"We'll be warm enough. I copied the Kecoughtan and made a hole in our roof, so the smoke has a place to go. If we light a fire inside, we will be all right."

I leaned over and kissed him on the cheek. "What was that for?" he asked with a smile.

"For taking care of us and for not being too prideful to try something new."

John kissed me back. His face glowed, and he gave me a lopsided grin.

I playfully pushed him. "What?" I asked, trying to get behind the meaning of his smile.

"Nothing. I am just happy, that's all." He laughed. I smiled back. "Me too." And I kissed him again.

Jack coughed to remind us that he was still there. "Enough you too or I may lose my breakfast."

He stayed with us in our makeshift cabin in case we were raided by natives. Jack and John worked tirelessly to carve out stakes and materials for the lookout and traded what they could for food.

"Look what I got!" Jack said with a big smile one day, showing me an armful of corn before placing it on the table John had made.

"Wonderful. What did you trade for it?"

"Some glass beads I exchanged with a glassmaker in Jamestown. The locals go crazy for them."

"Do you have any more?" I asked. "A few."

"Try to get venison next time," I said with a wink. "And could you please go fishing with John tomorrow and try to find more blue crab and trout?"

"Yes, ma'am," Jack said. He squished Virginia's rosy cheeks and tossed around one of the blue glass beads from his pocket.

Jack stood almost a head taller than me; at fourteen he looked more and more like Anthony. I shook my head and laughed at his antics. *Still the same old Jack.*

Chapter Twenty-Five
THE SEA VENTURE

"A bird in the hand is worth two in the bush." –
Proverb

April 13, 1610

There was a shift in the air. The harsh winter wind had stopped, and a refreshing light breeze had taken its place. Tiny pink and white buds had formed and were now in bloom on the ash and maple trees. My anticipation and hesitation to return to Jamestown weighed heavy on me. I longed to see Temperance and George again and prayed they fared as well as we did. We'd been fortunate to have plenty to eat between the crabs and fish. The water was much cleaner, and there seemed to be less illness than when we lived in Jamestown fort.

A few weeks after spring began to set in, shouts were heard from the lookout.

"Ship!" a man yelled.

When I looked toward the river, I saw the small outline of a mast in the distance. I had to look twice to see that there was not one ship but two—but I wouldn't call them ships, exactly.

They were more like makeshift boats made from the wood and materials of one ship.

Panic rose in my chest when I thought it could be the Spanish. With Virginia strapped to my back, I ran to the cabins to tell others what I had seen and warned them to hide. I'd heard horror stories of what the Spanish would do to women, and I didn't want Virginia or me anywhere near there. It would be better to take my chances in the woods.

Everyone scrambled to gather their loved ones and supplies. A loud commotion erupted. Men screamed for help and frantically grabbed what they could to run for the woods.

"Halt!" came a voice from the watchtower. "They are English! They bear King James's flag!"

"English?" a man shouted, as perplexed as the rest of us.

John ran to the house, grabbed his gun, and left to warn the others.

"'Tis our ship, my lord," the guard called again. "'Tis English!"

Curious, I walked out with Virginia to see an English flag— or what was left of one.

"John," I said, shocked, "this cannot be. Look at the name written on the side of one of the boats: the *Sea Venture*. It is! It must be. Look, there they are!"

Men and women waved at us frantically off the riggings of the deck. "Ahoy, there!"

As the boats approached, a few leaders got off and rowed to us in a small skiff. Everyone else stayed aboard. As they got closer, I recognized one of the men.

"That's Captain Newport!" I said to John, practically jumping up and down.

Mr. Davis squinted at the ship with concern, then a smile crept into the corners of his mouth.

"Mrs. Layton is right," he said, brushing back his thick black hair. "It *is* Captain Newport." And he walked to the shore's edge to greet the skiff.

"Well met, Captain Newport," he said.

"Well met, sir," Captain Newport replied. "And you are?"

Mr. Davis rolled back his shoulders and puffed out his chest. "I'm Mr. Davis, Sir. I was tasked to stand as a lookout for the Spanish this winter."

"I see," Captain Newport responded.

"Sir?" Mr. Davis stuttered as he tried to find the right words. "What are you doing on those...ships?"

His last word sounded questionable; judging by the state of the two ships, I couldn't blame him.

"We were sent with the *Catch* with all the supplies for the new settlers, but got caught in the storm. The *Catch* went under, but we were fortunate enough to drift to Bermuda after the storm," Captain Newport replied. "We were shipwrecked there for several months. These two ships are what we could make out of our ship that wrecked. We figured if we could get them to sail it would be worth a try to reach Jamestown."

My head tilted to the side as I looked at the ships. One leaned slightly to the side. A mast was placed in the center of each ship, and clothing or fabric from the previous ship and outfits formed the sails. *How did they make it here from Bermuda in those?*

"We were planning on heading back to Jamestown once spring hit," Mr. Davis said. "Since it's nearly spring, we will travel back with you."

"Formidable plan, sir," Captain Newport answered. "We will sail the rest of the way come morning. For now, have the men and women gather their belongings and close the cabins."

"Very well, sir." Mr. Davis shook hands with Captain Newport. "I will need to leave some men behind to stay on watch for the spring and organize a few things, but we can be ready by next week. I'm sure your return to Jamestown will be a welcome one.

April 16, 1610

"Tomorrow!" I said as I packed our things. "I can't believe we are leaving tomorrow."

"I'm excited as well, my dear," John said, "but truth be told, I'm not sure what we will find. There were far too many people and a decreasing amount of food when we left. I fear there will be many lives lost."

A painful lump sank into my chest, and I sat down. "I was so caught up in seeing Temperance and little George that I nearly forgot about the state we left them in. How could I be so heartless?"

"You aren't heartless, my love; you are human. It's only natural to want to see your friends. Let's keep praying that they figured out how to get food. I heard Governor Ratcliffe was taking a group of men with him to trade for food the day we left. Let us hope he was able to."

I nodded and bit my lip to stop myself from crying. "You're right," I said. "All we can do now is pray."

Chapter Twenty-Six
THE STARVING PERIOD

"All was fish that came to net to satisfy cruel hunger,
as to eat boots, shoes, or any other leather some could
come by. And now famine beginning to look ghastly
and pale in every face that nothing was spared to
maintain life and to do those things which seem in-
credible, as to dig up dead corpses out of graves and
to eat them." – Sir George Percy

April 17, 1610

Forty-five of us joined the *Sea Venture's* two ships with our skiffs and headed to Jamestown. About fifteen men were chosen to stay behind to guard Point Comfort. I breathed a sigh of relief that John wasn't among them.

"I can't believe we are going back," I said. "What do you think it will be like when we get there?"

John was silent for a moment, as if his thoughts were somewhere in the past instead of the present. "I fear it will not be as we hoped. I want to stay optimistic, but I just don't know."

I looked over at Jack holding Virginia, his blue eyes penetrating mine with fear.

John noticed and quickly added, "Whatever happens, stay together. Everything will work out."

I felt my insides turn and tried not to let the others see how worried I felt. John placed his arm around my shoulders and gave me a knowing squeeze.

The James River was full again, beautiful and glowing, with the sun outstretched on top of it. The sycamores were full of thick green leaves, a gorgeous contrast to the red oak trees' fiery leaves laced across the landscape. The air was fresh and sweet. Could anything be more beautiful?

Our skiff boat landed at the dock first, then the two make-shift ships. I wanted to jump out and run to my friends, but something froze me in place. Arrowheads protruded out of the fort's woodwork at all angles, and the smell of dead flesh reached my nose. It seemed to touch us all at once. We instinctively covered our noses from the stench.

"Stay here with Virginia," John said, with panic in his eyes. "Whatever you do, do not get off this boat until we men return. Do you understand?"

"Yes, of course," I said. "Be safe!"

The men returned within an hour, pale as ghosts, some green and yellow in the face.

"John?" I asked. "What is it? Did the Powhatan people attack?"

I pleaded in my heart that they hadn't.

John was silent for what seemed an eternity and tried to mouth what he found several times but could not find the words. "John." I took his hand, wrapped my fingers around his, and peered into his soft wide eyes. His pupils were large and frightening. "John?" I cried.

My heart thumped in my chest. I'd never seen him like this.

His face was pale, and there was fear in his eyes. "There...there be no words to describe it," was all he could muster. "I would have stayed to help, but we wanted everyone on the ship to know we were not under attack. Anne, I, I..." he stammered off.

"Help who, John? What is it?"

"They're almost all gone," he choked out.

"Gone? What do you mean, gone?"

"Dead, most of them. The ones who remain look as if they wish they were dead, with sunken eyes, bones for skin, and flesh nearly falling off." There was terror in his eyes. He stood hugging his chest and swaying, almost as if he was rocking himself. "It is like walking among the dead in there: bodies heaped in piles, a living person sometimes mixed with them. There seems to be a mere handful of them left. Just like it was my first winter here— but this time with women and children."

Every muscle in my body tensed at his words. I wanted to cry and run at the same time. My heart raced when I thought of Temperance and Lydia.

"I have to find them."

John grabbed my arms and pulled me back. "No, Anne. You don't want to see that. They are probably gone." His eyes pleaded with me to understand.

"I have to try, John!" Tears ran down my cheeks. "Temperance and Lydia. Little George."

"Then I will go with you."

We walked past my brother and a girl on the opposite side of the boat.

"Please watch Virginia," I said, handing her over to Jack as we passed. He wasn't so little anymore; I knew he would protect her at all costs.

"Prepare yourself, my dear," John warned. "It's worse than we could have imagined."

I nodded. He grabbed my hand as we faced the fort. Every step felt like I had weights on my feet. I inched my way out of the ship and onto the dock. The hopes of having been met there by my dear friends shattered. The smell was overwhelming, as were the cries and moans I heard as we approached the gate. A few men lay face-down in the mud with arrows protruding from their backs.

Inside the fort, a few people lay or sat on the ground, some dead, some nearly dead, and others too weak to bury the ones who had already passed. Their flesh rotted away as they lay in the spring sun.

"Temperance?" I called, frantically peering into the decaying corpses and deteriorating faces to find my friends. "Lydia?"

Some people jumped out at us, begging for food. Most crouched down behind barrels or homes, hiding away their shame—or worse, in such a frame of mind that they thought we were a figment of their imaginations and weren't there at all. I searched the sisters' cabin but found nothing but dilapidated buildings, wood taken away from the frames presumably for firewood, tables thrown over, blankets tattered, and mud and human waste everywhere. What had happened?

"Anne?" a faint voice whispered. "Anne, is that really you?" A woman with sunken eyes walked out from one of the cabins. Her hair was matted and clung to her head. She stood in front of me as if she were a ghost. Her clothes draped against her body, and her cheekbones protruded. Seeing her made me want to gag and cry all at once until I recognized her voice.

"Temperance?" I cried, running to her. "Temperance!" I stopped, afraid that an embrace would break her. "What happened to you? Where are the others?"

"Dead," she cried. "I might as well be dead too."

"Please don't say such things. What happened?" She shook as I embraced her. "Do sit down. Here, let me fetch you some food or water."

"There is none," she said as she sank down beside me onto a nearby bench. "That is the problem. Don't you see? We have none; we ran out of provisions months ago. Sir Ratcliffe set off to teach the Powhatan a lesson and burned down some of their villages. They retaliated. They wanted to kill us off, so they forced us to stay inside the fort until we starved. If anyone left for food or even fresh water, they were shot through with an arrow. The water we used made us even more sick. We ate all the horses, dogs, and pigs, even the belts and shoes off our feet. Anything to survive. Oh, Anne! Some, some—" She sobbed into my shoulder, unable to say the words. "Some even resorted to cannibalism. They would eat the bodies of the dead. Oh, Anne!"

"And Lydia?" I pleaded. "Little George?"

"Gone. Months ago. All of them, gone." She melted into my shoulder, her whole body shaking. "I feel as if I am the cursed one who had to stay. I'd rather die than be stuck here alone."

She sobbed violently in my arms. We sat there for what felt like hours. All I could do was hold her and rock her back and forth until she finally fell asleep from sheer exhaustion.

Chapter Twenty-Seven
TURNING POINT

"There were never Englishmen left in a foreign country in such misery as we were in this newly discovered Virginia." – George Percy

April 30, 1610

"Ladies, it's time," John said with his arm around me, guiding Temperance and me onto the boat.

After two weeks of burying the dead and trying to turn things around at the fort, Captain Newport and the other leaders decided it would be best to abandon the fort and return to England. The plan was to make our way north, where the French had established a colony known as New France. From there, we were to separate into groups and get on ships to London.

My heart was flooded with emotions as I turned back one last time to look at the fort. It was my home. I'd made my first real friends in years and had my Virginia there, but nothing could keep us. Only sixty-five of the five hundred and fifty left in Jamestown survived! Temperance was one of them, but her husband, dear Lydia, and little George were all gone.

Temperance and I slowly crept onto the ship along with the Jamestown survivors. It had taken all my powers of persuasion to get Temperance on the boat and leave the bodies of her loved ones behind.

It was strange, but even being on the river felt different. I had felt so much hope when we were returning to Jamestown from Fort Comfort, but the sunshine and excitement were gone and fear, disappointment and sorrow had taken their place. It seemed as if even the river was crying, with blue waves slowly inching out toward the banks, not fully rising to their true potential.

All our hard work, my dream of Mama, Papa, Anthony, and little Ellen running around our land, was gone.

The mood was somber, and besides a few sniffles, coughs, and cries of children and those still not in their right mind, the deck was eerily quiet.

"Anne, take a deep breath," John kept saying, his guiding hand on the small of my back. "We must make a new life for ourselves in England instead. We could go back to Durham. Most of my family is gone now, but I know the old carpenter there and could work for him. Then we could finally get Thomas back and raise him as our own. Then Virginia will have her big brother."

"You're right, John," I said with a sigh of relief, thinking that we could finally be in a place where we felt safe and could be with family again—Mama and Papa and sweet little Thomas, whom I had never met.

I turned to Jack, who had been standing in a daze. "What will you do?"

"I—I don't know. Return to Norfolk, open a shop near Mama and Papa. I just can't believe it. I—"

His words were cut off by shouts from the watch. "Ship! Ship ahead! Everyone, take cover!"

"It must be the Spanish!" a woman screamed. "They are here to finish us off."

Panic ensued. Women and children frantically huddled together. My heart leaped into my throat, and my mind raced. I grabbed Virginia from John and started to make my way down below the deck. Before I hit the stairs, a man shouted, "It be English!"

"He is right, sir," a guard shouted. "I see the King's flag!"

"English!" a woman said. "We're saved."

"Or we are doomed," said another. "They will force us to go back!"

"No!" a man screamed. "Please! Please don't make me go back. I can't go back!"

He was so emaciated that his clothing hung on his frame. His teeth had all but fallen out, and his eyes were hollow from lack of food. His breeches were only held up by a thin rope tied around his waist, and he wore no shoes, presumably from chewing on the leather for sustenance.

"What does this mean?" I asked John.

"I'm not sure, but it means we must return."

The ship got closer, and a small skiff was let down and rowed toward us. A man with a handsome navy-blue jerkin and a large black hat stood up in the skiff as it approached the ship. Captain Newport walked up to him and welcomed him aboard.

"What is the meaning of this?" the man asked. "Send these people back at once!"

"I cannot do that," Captain Newport said. "We are from the Sea Venture. We were shipwrecked for months in Bermuda. When we finally arrived at Jamestown, we found it in ruin. Only sixty or so men, women, and children out of the five hundred and fifty survived. The other people on board are from Point Comfort and other lookout points in the area. We are going to Newfoundland in the north to wait for a ship to return to England."

"Nonsense. Who is in charge here?"

"Sir Ratcliffe, but the people have told us he was skinned alive by the natives, and they besieged the fort. We must get them back to safety."

"I am the new leader now," the man said. "My name is Sir Thomas West, and King James appointed me the new governor here to replace Sir Ratcliffe. Seeing how he is already dead, there will be little dispute. I command you to return these ships to Jamestown at once."

There was silence for several seconds. Then Captain Newport ordered his men to turn us around, back the way we came, toward Jamestown, possibly even toward our deaths.

Bile rose to my mouth, and I vomited over the side of the deck. John gently rubbed my back.

"What does this mean?" I asked, terrified of his response. "It means all will be well. By the looks of it, Sir West has more than enough provisions for us, and we can finally start moving forward as a colony."

I didn't know what to think. I was terrified of returning to Jamestown but happy that our work, sacrifices, and losses— Temperance's losses—would not have been for nothing.

As we re-entered the Chesapeake, my heart felt a flutter. From the corner of my eye, I saw my brother Jack talking to the young girl he had met on the ship earlier. Her father was the reverend appointed on the *Sea Venture*. When speaking to them, they'd both seemed eager to return to England after being shipwrecked in Bermuda for so long. The pair of youths seemed well-matched, his brown hair and blue eyes and her soft brown eyes and dark hair. Jack even wrapped his coat around her to help her stay warm in the spring breeze.

I couldn't help but smile at Jack and the sweet brunette. I looked down at Virginia asleep in my arms, with John on one side of me and Temperance on the other. Whatever the next adventures of our journey held, at least we'd have each other.

PART FOUR

AN OLD FRIEND

Chapter Twenty-Eight
BUILDING A HOME

"Marriage hath in it less of beauty but more of safety, than the single life; it hath more care, but less danger, it is more merry, and more sad; it is fuller of sorrows, and fuller of joys; it lies under more burdens, but it is supported by all the strengths of love and charity, and those burdens are delightful." – Jeremy Taylor

March 7, 1613

The return trip to Jamestown and the years that followed were both thrilling and terrifying. Our problems weren't over; we still returned to an area occupied by hundreds of thousands of natives who were not pleased that we were there, especially because we brought along two hundred more English men. However, things felt different. This time, we had enough food, provisions, and firearms to protect ourselves.

Sir Thomas West became our leader and was officially set apart as governor of Jamestown. He laid strict rules to plant Company crops and individual gardens in and without the fort.

He brought several pounds of gunpowder, extra cannons, chickens, pigs, leather, pots, pans, flour, sugar, and wine.

We did our best with the supplies we had left after returning to Jamestown. One year passed and the Company came down hard on rationing, giving us just enough to get by. Sir Ratcliffe had caused great trouble with the natives, but Governor Thomas West was worse. King James gave him strict orders to end the conflict once and for all and show the Powhatan that we meant to stay.

He returned to London several times, some trips lasting for months, some for years. Each time, a deputy acting governor was chosen in his absence. On one such occasion, Sir Thomas Gates was selected to act in his stead. Something about him unnerved me. His eyes lit up when he talked about "controlling the savages" as he called them. It wasn't how Captain Smith had done things and I knew nothing good could come of it.

John tried to come home for supper as often as possible, but sometimes the company gave him more work than he anticipated, and he had to stay late.

One evening, I looked out the glass window of our cabin and saw a cloud of dirt surrounding a tall brunette. I laughed to myself; I knew it was John the minute I saw him. I was familiar with that dust cloud and saw it on days when John had a hard day at work.

I took the pot off the fire and went out to greet him and check on the girls playing ring toss on the ground. Sweet Alice joined our family two years ago and Virginia wanted to play with her every minute of the day.

I stepped over the two circles they'd drawn in the dirt with a stick and waved hello.

The girls looked up from their game and ran to follow me. "Papa!" they shouted.

John leaned over and swooped them up into his arms and gave me a kiss on my cheek. "And how are my girls?" he asked.

"We are doing well; the girls are keeping me on my toes," I said and smiled.

Virginia caught John's face with her two little hands to get his full attention. "Mama taught us how to make minced pie today."

"Oh, did she? I can't wait to eat it."

I placed my hand on my belly. "If this one is a girl, I could open a shop in our cabin and sell minced pies in a few years."

John bent down and kissed my belly. "If this one is a girl, I will eat a whole minced pie myself."

The girls flew into fits of laughter, and I directed them to go back to their game so I could get some time alone with John.

"How was your day?" I asked.

He crinkled his nose and the corner of his mouth turned down.

I mirrored his worried face. "That bad?"

He placed his hand on the small of my back and led me around the cabin to be out of earshot of the girls and the neighbors.

John had made us a larger cabin a mile or two south of the fort. We were surrounded by plenty of neighbors and traded for goods we couldn't make ourselves. It felt calmer than living directly inside the fort, but we still had the protection of the Company while we waited for the rights of our land promised to the first settlers.

"What is it?" I asked.

John sighed. "More villages were burned down today. William and Joseph asked me to go with them, but I refuse to go out with the men and kill for fun!"

John slumped down against the fence and emptied his boots. Dirt, rocks, and even small wood chips slid out when he tipped them upside down. The rest of his body was covered in sawdust. I wrapped his hands in cloth. They were cracked and blistered from hard work.

"You're a good man, John," I said, leaning over my growing belly to kiss his cheek.

He gave me a quick smile back and sighed. "Sorry to share such disheartening news."

Then his face went rigid. "In all seriousness, we need to keep our girls close by. I'm worried that Powhatan will seek revenge."

"You're right," I said as I moved to sit next to him. "Something needs to be done; violence will bring more violence. I wish Pocahontas and Captain Smith were here. Things were so much more peaceful between the settlers and Powhatan then. When is all the warring going to stop? Haven't we already been through enough heartache as a people? Why do we encourage more violence and retaliation?"

"I don't know, my love. I agree, the fighting should stop before it destroys both of our people."

John stood up and turned to walk into our cabin. I wanted to say more on the subject but knew John was tired, and we needed to eat. After our minced pie, we put Virginia and Alice to bed, and I ventured the topic again.

"Any word about the Moral and Martial Laws I have heard so many rumors about?"

John's hands clenched into fists. "The Moral and Martial Laws are to be implemented as soon as possible. We are to have a meeting at the church house tomorrow about it. Anne, it doesn't feel right; I don't think any good will come of it. The Company means to restrict and improve behavior within the colony, but I fear innocent people will be punished or killed."

Killed? There was talk of the strict set of laws created to help the colony, but no one said anything about being killed for not following them.

John must have seen the worried look on my face and took my hands in his. "We will find out more tomorrow, my dear. For now, let's get some rest."

I nodded but couldn't sleep that night. The baby seemed to have his or her days and nights mixed up and kicked me most of the evening.

"All right, little one," John whispered to my belly as I tossed and turned "That's enough, you hear? Time to let your mama sleep."

I laughed and tried to push all my worries aside and thought about the new baby about to join our family instead.

March 8, 1613

The air felt crisp and chilly; the house smelled of smoke from the fire we let go out. I yawned and moaned as I stretched when the sun came up. I felt exhausted from lack of sleep; my belly grew more every day, and I could never quite get comfortable.

My list of never-ending tasks waited for me, and I needed to get breakfast ready before the girls woke up and I'd have to tend to them.

I retrieved water from the new well, cleaned out our chamber pots, made breakfast, and helped dress Virginia and Alice, then weeded the garden in preparation for spring until I heard the large church bell ring. It summoned us to the meeting with Sir Dale, the new Deputy Governor in charge, while Sir Thomas Gates went back to England for a time.

I slipped a woolen shawl over my shoulders and tucked it into my kirtle. I wrapped two small matching shawls over the girls, and we walked as a family to the fort, where we met John, who was already at work.

The fort seemed eerily quiet as people crowded into the new church building, waiting for instructions. I held Virginia's hand as we walked toward the center beside John, who carried Alice. People still felt the pain of that awful winter three years ago. The images I'd seen and heard that day haunted me. Temperance never fully regained her cheerful self; however , a few months after our return, she married Sir

George Yardley, who'd lost his wife shortly after returning to Jamestown. He had been left with three young children of his own and they often played with my children. I wondered if Temperance would be at the meeting with Sir Yardley.

We made our way into the newly built church and looked for a place to sit.

"Gather in as tight as you can," Reverend Whitaker said from the pulpit. "Thank you all for coming. As many of you know, attacks from the savages have become more prevalent, and with our ever-increasing numbers, theft and violence have become more of a daily occurrence. Our beloved governor has devised a plan to combat the latter and make Jamestown more profitable in return. I now turn the time over to Acting Deputy Governor Dale."

"Ahem." Sir Dale made a loud noise to get the crowd's attention. "Order: order is what's lacking in this settlement. The London Company gave me a strict command to turn this place around. Not only are we fighting an enemy without the fort, but we are fighting an enemy within. Crime and disorder have arisen, and I intend to squelch them."

A shiver of fear washed over me. How did he "intend to squelch" things?

"I have a list of thirty-seven new laws that everyone must abide by. I will tack them up inside the church for you to view. We will meet as a group twice a day for prayers and pledge allegiance to the Company. Those who do not comply will be severely punished."

There was that word again— "punished." Hadn't we already been punished enough? I didn't know how much more the settlers could take between the starving times, illness, and attacks.

"Each person over twelve will be given a specific task. Some settlers will be ordered to plant, harvest, cook, clean, grow tobacco, build supplies, or store goods. Others will be asked to repair ships, hunt, fight off the natives, dig, or build. If we work together, we can make a thriving settlement. You will be tasked with your jobs by the end of the week."

Murmurs of voices and complaints rose in the crowd. John squeezed my hand, and I squeezed it back.

The heaviness of the meeting weighed on me. Things were already strict, even for those in the surrounding areas; now, we had to walk down for prayer twice daily and report for particular jobs. How would I have enough time to finish the jobs I already had to do at home? It wouldn't be so bad in the spring, but it would be miserable when the insufferable, humid summer air started in a few months.

I shifted in my seat, annoyed and uncomfortable. My back was stiff from not sleeping well the night before. I readjusted my brown kirtle to place the center opening in the front instead of twisting to the side, which was no easy task with my growing belly.

After another yawn, I sighed and looked around. Stern, tired faces looked back at me. I wondered what they were thinking. The Company promised us this would be to our benefit, but I wasn't sure it was worth the cost.

Chapter Twenty-Nine
CAPTIVITY

"For feature, countenance, and proportion, (Pocahontas) much exceedeth any of the rest of his people, but for wit and spirit, the only nonpareil of his country." – George Sandy

April 6, 1613

I was assigned the job of mending the workers' stockings. Due to my experience as a lady's maid, I became proficient at using a running stitch to darn a sock. The worst part was that it took up most of my afternoon when I could have worked in the house or tended to the girls. I tried to make the most of it and taught Virginia how to handle the darning needle and thread. Alice tried to untangle Virginia's messy web, but the unraveled yarn rolled across the floor instead. She scowled and I had to cover my laugh with my fan.

"Mama," Virginia said, tugging on my skirt. "Can you play with me?"

"Not right now, dear one. I need to finish my needlework for the Company." Her little face began to pout, so I added, "Why don't you take your sister and look at the new doll Temperance made for Elizabeth?"

"Yesss, Mama," she said with a lisp, bouncing out of the house with Alice in tow.

Just then, Temperance came running in.

"Aunt Temperance, can you play with us?" Virginia asked, perking up.

"Sorry," Temperance replied, "not now, dear. I need to speak to your mother." Temperance pulled me out of the cabin, away from listening ears.

"What is it?" I asked. "You're scaring me."

"Did you hear the news?"

"What news?" I suddenly found myself out of breath.

"It's Pocahontas. Captain Argall kidnapped her."

"Kidnapped?" A feeling of disgust washed over me; my heart went out to my old friend. "Is she well?"

"Yes. They have just arrived at the fort. She is in the governor's home meeting the old governor, Sir Thomas Gates."

I looked to the right and left to make sure no one was listening. "Temperance," I whispered, "I am afraid the Powhatan will retaliate tenfold."

"I agree," she said quietly. "My husband thinks the same but is too afraid to say anything. Oh, please don't tell anyone I told you!"

"I won't. I promise." I clasped her hand. "Thank you for telling me about Pocahontas, Temperance. I must try to see her!"

Her eyes grew wide with concern," I was worried you'd say that. It's dangerous Anne. I don't think they'd let you."

"Will you please watch the girls? I won't be gone long, I promise!"

"Anne, wait!" I could hear the concern in Temperance's voice as she called after me, but nothing she said would stop me. I walked by the old chapel in which John, and I were married and ran my fingers across the wooden beam posts. So much had happened since then, and even though we spent time in it every Sunday, I still liked to reflect on my memories there. I loved to look out the western windows facing the harbor. The palisades blocked much of it, but I could feel a sense of its grandeur and hear the birds flying above.

Behind the chapel on the east side was Captain Argall's cabin. A guard stood outside it, but I managed to get close. I gasped when I heard a woman in broken English ask to be released. I strained to hear more.

"My father will see to my release; you will see." Pocahontas? I knew that voice anywhere.

I peered through the small window and caught a glimpse of her sitting in a chair. Her dark hair was bluntly cut and swung above her shoulders. She had several tattoos around her arms and three others drawn in small lines from her bottom lip to her chin. It had been years since I last saw her, and I almost didn't recognize her.

"We will see about that, Princess," a gruff voice said. "He needs to return our weapons and our people before that happens."

She stood up straight and folded her arms. "He will. You will see."

I was so engrossed in what was happening that I didn't hear or see the guard until he stood before me. He stood at least a head taller than me, and his broad shoulders were intimidating.

He glared at me, and his mouth was set in a hard line. "What do you think you are doing?"

I flinched and stepped back. "I—I..." The words seemed stuck in the back of my throat. "That's Pocahontas. She is my friend. May I visit with her, please?"

"She's nothing but a filthy savage." He spat. The phlegm barely missed my shoe. "Besides, she won't talk to anyone, and she is not allowed to have visitors."

"She is not a savage," I replied. "She is my friend!"

"No!" the guard yelled, seizing me by the arm. "Get out of here, woman!"

He shoved me down, despite my obvious pregnancy, and I fell hard on my knees onto the solid ground below. I scrambled to my feet and tried one more time.

"Pocahontas," I cried, "it's me, Anne!"

A muffled cry broke back. "Anne?"

I took a few steps in her direction, then felt hard hands push my shoulders back and I fell to the ground again. I groaned and clasped my large belly. Dazed and surprised, I slowly pulled myself up to my hands and knees, then stumbled as I stood up. My hand went instinctively again to my unborn child. My knees felt wet and sticky as they clung to my shift. My back ached, and it was hard to breathe. My eyes opened wide in shock as I stared at the guard.

His light brown eyes, fierce and intent, paid me no regard other than to shout, "Serves you right!"

I stumbled again as I walked home, and I prayed that my baby wasn't harmed.

My mind forced my feet onward. Each step felt excruciating once the sharp cramps started to pull at the lower part of my abdomen. My hands scooped under my large belly to support the weight of it. I slowly peeled my linen skirt away from my bloody knee and reached a shaking hand to my throbbing head.

Temperance took one look at me and ran down the street to help. She placed her arm under me for support.

"Anne, are you well?"

One look at her and tears welled up in my eyes. The truth fell from my lips in rapid succession, mingled with tears and gasps of air. "The guard. He wouldn't let me see her. Pushed me down. Hit me."

"Oh, Anne!" she cried. "Let's get you home!"

She knew not to ask me more questions and waited for me to get the words out in my own time. Fortunately, our cabin was close to hers, and she helped me into bed.

Her eyes brushed over me, and she frowned. "You need to rest. I'm going to go get John."

I grabbed her arm before she could get up. "Please don't! I'm so ashamed. What if I lose the baby?"

Her mouth briefly opened as if she would tell me otherwise, but then her eyebrows scrunched together, and she held my hand. "You have nothing to be ashamed of. This was not your fault. We need to place a formal complaint to the governor."

My eyes grew wide. "No! It was his bodyguard. He told me to leave, but I didn't listen. Nothing will be done."

She grabbed a cloth near my bed, soaked it in water to clean off my face, then looked down at me. "Either way, I will ask John to file a complaint."

Pain pulsated through my stomach, and I curled into a ball on the bed.

Temperance threw the rag back down into the copper water basin. "That's it. I'm getting John."

Within moments, John was at our bedroom door and sitting next to me on the bed. His mouth snapped shut and hardened into a firm line.

"Who did this to you?"

I looked away and shook my head. I didn't want John to get in trouble for me disobeying the guard.

Temperance stood behind him in our doorway. "Captain Argall's guard did it."

John turned back slowly in surprise. "Why were you with Captain Argall's guard?"

I scrunched my nose and took a deep breath. "They took Pocahontas, and I had to see her."

John placed his hand on mine and pushed wet, dirty hair back from my brow. He clenched his jaw to try to control his anger. "I know what she means to you, but Anne, that was foolish. You know how Captain Argall is, and his guards are even worse."

"I know," I managed to say between sobs.

"That doesn't mean what he did to you is okay. I will put a formal complaint in, but I'm not sure if the governor will listen or care much."

He picked up the wet rag again and dabbed my forehead. "Men like that have no respect for women or life. They shouldn't treat people this way, especially a woman."

John cupped his hand over my cheek, and I turned my face into it and sobbed. He was right, but I knew deep down there was nothing he or anyone could do about it. Women had been treated like this or worse for years. It broke my heart for my daughters.

I looked down and gently rubbed my belly. In a way, I wished this baby was a boy so he wouldn't have to be faced with such mockery and shame.

I was grateful John was there, but it made me miss my mother all the same. How tender she used to be, how safe I used to feel in her arms. I pulled out a letter I had tucked under my pillow from her, held it to my heart and cried.

August 13, 1613

Dear Mama,

Congratulations—you have another granddaughter! We named her Katherine, with a K, after Lady Catherine. Without her, John and I may never have met. I never would have imagined that her connection to Sir Forrest would bring me here.

We chose to spell Katherine with a K for John's mother, Kimberly, who passed away several years ago.

Katherine has dark auburn hair that sparkles in the sun like strawberries in summer. She has green eyes with a hint of blue and chubby thighs you want to squeeze. She is a joy, and the girls are smitten. She came a bit sooner than we expected, but all went well.

I can't tell you enough that I ache for you to be here and wished you were at the birth with me. It may seem odd for a nearly twenty-year-old to still pine for her mama, but I do. I wish you, Papa, Anthony, and Ellen could all join us. I'd suggest coming in the autumn or spring; summers are dreadfully hot here. The mosquitos and flies dot the land almost as much as tall trees and shrubs.

Do say you will come. Please give my best to the family and kiss Grandfather for me.

Love always,

Anne

Chapter Thirty
MATOAKA

"Why do you take by force what you could obtain by love?" – Chief Wahunsenachawh Powhatan

March 19, 1614

She sat under the shade of a thatched roof near the town square, dressed as an Englishwoman with a white bodice embroidered with flowers, her skirt the popular shade of red for warmth against her skin. A woman of seventeen years, no longer the young girl doing cartwheels down the road or racing the other children. Her once short hair had become thick and long, wrapped up inside an English coif cap. Although she was dressed like one of us, I recognized her instantly.

Between her lips and her chin were three thin vertical black lines. I wasn't too surprised. Jack told me that he saw it often on Powhatan women. Her brother, Rusirur, told us a long time ago that when girls turned into women, they were given a tattoo under their bottom lip, down to their chin. They also grew out their hair, and many had multiple tattoos on their arms and legs.

I wondered if Pocahontas had more, but I didn't ask.

Her eyes were still the same shade of chestnut brown. She looked sad, and I hesitated to take her from her thoughts.

It had been almost a year since she was tricked into getting into the boat by Captain Argall, her release arranged in exchange for prisoners, weapons, and tools her father had taken. Chief Powhatan returned the prisoners but only some of the tools and weapons.

I walked over to her, the dry dirt raising a cloud of dust around my feet. Katherine lay asleep in my arms. Her curly auburn hair peeked out from underneath her tiny coif cap.

"Pocahontas," I cried out.

"Anne?" She turned. "Anne, is that you?"

"Yes, dear friend. It is me."

"Well met, Anne," she said politely.

"Well met," I replied with a slight bob of my head. Being so formal with someone I had known for years was odd, but it had been ages since I had seen her, and things were so different now. The corners of her mouth turned into a slight smile. "I heard you outside the governor's door," she said. "Thank you for coming. It was foolish but brave."

I nodded, images of a fearless young girl popping into my head. "You would have done the same."

"Probably," she said with a nudge, "but I think I would have learned the first time the guard said no."

A small chuckle left my mouth. She knew I was stubborn. I laughed again, then tried to change subjects.

"I heard they took you upriver to the Henricus area. Were they kind to you?"

I found myself hoping her answers would make me feel better about her situation.

"They were kind," she said. "Reverend Whitaker and his wife took me in, and they helped me improve my English, even my reading and writing. I would have loved to see you again, but I didn't travel back to the fort."

"Why are you here now?" I asked.

We sat silently for several minutes. Katherine stirred and twirled a strand of hair that had fallen out of my cap with her little fingers as she nursed. The silence was almost too much, and I was about to speak when I heard her whisper.

"Things are about to change," she finally said. "What things?" I asked.

"My name is Matoaka." Her voice was so soft and calm that it was barely audible. It startled me.

My tongue rolled softly off the roof of my mouth as I whispered. "Matoaka." The word seemed too sacred to say aloud. "What does it mean?"

"It means 'little snow feather.' It is my name. My real name." Bewildered, I asked the obvious question. "I thought Pocahontas was your name?"

"It is my name." She took a deep breath. "My people believe that names have more than just meanings; they are a way to the soul. My father was worried that if the English knew my real name, they would have control over me, so he told them my nickname, Pocahontas. I was just a child of ten when I met John Smith and the English. Pocahontas means 'playful one.'"

"That you were." I gave her a nudge and smiled.

"Yes, I was." She smiled, as if remembering her childhood. She smiled, then her face grew serious. "Pray tell, what of

Captain Smith? Have you any news? I heard he is alive."

I nodded, "Yes, word came back to us that he survived, and the doctor was able to save his leg; although he now walks with a limp."

Her smile faded into a serene and determined expression as she contemplated the news.

She twirled a strand of hair around her finger and changed the subject. "I will be getting a new name soon."

"What do you mean by a new name?" I was intrigued. Was this part of their custom, a ritual, perhaps? I looked at her and wondered what she truly felt behind those inquisitive brown eyes. The light seemed to leave them, but her demeanor and self-control took me back. How could she remain so calm after what happened to her?

"It has been almost a full turn of the sun, and my father still refuses to return the tools and weapons requested by the governor and Captain Argall. Captain Argall took me to him, hoping I could make him change his mind."

"I still don't understand. Why did you get on Captain Argall's ship in the first place, and why is he returning you?"

"It was a trick." The tears of hurt and frustration gently rolled down her cheek. "I went to visit my friends in the village of the Patowmacks. My dear friend is the wife of Lopassas, a brother to the chief there. They said the English were nearby and that she wanted to see the English ship."

Her hands trembled in her lap. My insides winced, seeing the struggle it must have been to retell what happened to her, and instinctively, I reached out and held her hand, nodding for her to proceed.

"At the time, I was leery. I had not seen the English since I was told that John Smith was dead three or four years ago. I was told never to trust them. I could sense that something was wrong. Lopassas said his wife could only investigate the ship if I went too. She started crying, so I obliged. When we reached the ship, Captain Argall greeted us and invited us aboard for dinner. Trying to keep the peace, I agreed to go. The dinner was cordial. It was late afterward, so he invited us to stay over, as per the custom of the English.

"They told me to rest in the gunner's room. When I woke up the next day, they refused to let me leave, said I was to be set free only upon my father returning their stolen tools, guns, and prisoners."

"What of your friends? Did they take them as well?" I asked, shaking my head. I couldn't believe that Captain Argall could be so cruel.

"They knew but feigned shock, pretending not to be in on the scheme. But I knew my friend knew. I could see it in her eyes and in the reward of a copper pot tucked under her arm as she walked off the ship."

"I have made several trips to different tribes on behalf of my father and was sent to their village for several weeks at a time. The villages consider it a great honor. I'm sure Lopassas will spread falsehoods that he and his wife were ambushed and blame it all on the Englishmen."

My heart ached for Pocahontas. I didn't know what to say aside from "I am so sorry." Tears poured down my cheeks like rain. I tried to revert to our previous conversation—anything to bring her out of this depressed state.

"What about your new name?" I asked.

"My new name?" She was lost in her thoughts. "Oh, yes. I'm not sure. I will be baptized by Reverend Whitaker, who will give me my new name. He said I could pick the Christian name I wanted to go by. I am thinking of Rebecca."

Rebecca. I liked the sound of it, and it suited her.

"I am also to be given a new life with John Rolfe. He has been kind to me, and since my husband, Kocoum, died in battle the year I was taken, I decided to marry again. With my people, women choose who they wish to marry. It's not unusual for women and children to be taken by other tribes. We adjust, and we make a new life where we are. I wish to marry John Rolfe. He lost his wife and child coming here and knows my pain."

"*Married?* You were married?" My eyes widened in disbelief, but I was not completely shocked. Pocahontas was beautiful, intelligent, kind, and the daughter of a chief. Of course, she would be married by now.

"Yes, to Kocoum, one of my father's top bodyguards. He was a good man. We were married three years ago, when I was fourteen. News of his death reached me weeks before I climbed onto Captain Argall's ship."

"That must have been very hard," I said. "I'm sorry for your loss."

"It was. In my culture, one must mourn the loss of a loved one and then move forward in life. Kocoum will always be in my heart, but now I must try anew. I know what this marriage would mean between my people and yours. I could help end the fighting; we could have peace and be friends."

"Oh, Pocahontas, the loss of your husband, the betrayal of your friends, all in one year. That must have been so difficult."

"My old life is over. I must make a different path for myself." Katherine started to wake, and I rocked her gently back to sleep. Pocahontas smiled down at her and gently wiped a soft auburn curl from her face.

"She is beautiful," she said.

"Thank you." I smiled. My heart ached for Pocahontas, and I reached out to hug her.

"You are so strong," I whispered to her.

She pulled her arms back and again looked me straight in the eye. "So are you, Anne. I hope you know that." Her eyes searched mine.

I was shocked. "Me!"

"I know some of the things you have seen and had to bear. You yourself left your homeland and had to make a new life here. You were among the first Englishwomen I knew, and I came to respect you. I consider you a dear friend and hope you will rejoice with me and pray for my new life with John."

"I would be honored," I said, confidence and courage filling my heart. "My prayers and heart will always be with you."

"And mine with you," was her reply.

Chapter Thirty-One
Mrs. Rolfe

"It is Pocahontas to whom my hearty and best
thoughts are, and have been a long time so entangled,
and enthralled in so intricate a labyrinth that I [could
not] unwind myself thereout." – John Rolfe

April 9, 1614

It was a warm and breezy day in early April when everyone gathered to witness the first marriage between a Powhatan woman
and an Englishman. Reverend Whitaker stood at
the front of the church, looking through papers, making sure he
was ready for the big event. Jack sat next to John and me with our
girls.

"Isn't this exciting?" I asked John and Jack, bouncing Katherine
in my arms, hoping she would fall asleep.

"It is," Jack said sincerely.

"It's shocking that Mr. Rolfe would choose Pocahontas for a
bride," John said. "She is a native, after all."

"But a baptized native," I added. "Maybe that is why Reverend Whitaker and the governor gave their consent? Mr. Rolfe did write them a letter to ask their permission."

"Yes, but why would her father give his?" John asked. "Maybe because he wanted all this fighting to end as well,"

Jack replied. "And we can finally have peace between our two people."

"I hope you're right," John said.

"Me too," I added as I looked around the church. "I heard some of her family is to attend."

"Mama, when will she be here?" Virginia asked, interrupting our conversation. Her laurel wreath of bluebell flowers we found in the field earlier that day matched her blue eyes.

"Soon, sweet girl, soon," I said, lightly tapping her on her cute, upturned nose.

A few minutes later, Alice pulled on Virginia's sleeve. "They're coming! They're coming!"

I expected to turn around and see Pocahontas, Mr. Rolfe, and the reverend, but instead met the dark, penetrating eyes of Pocahontas's uncle, Opechancanough. I gasped and held my breath as he slowly walked past with three men and two other women.

He hated the English, and I felt a shiver run through me as he entered the door. His head was shaven on the left, scraped by muscle shells or plucked, while the hair on the right side draped long past his shoulders. His face was painted white. He wore a tall headpiece, taller than the rest, symbolizing his status. His deer-skin skirt had beads strapped together to make a colorful belt around his waist. His moccasins mirrored the pattern of beads on the strings. As he walked, he carried a large stick. His bronze jewelry made a loud clanking sound, followed by an even more deafening stomp from his feet.

The pressure and confidence of his walk made me jump. Puffs of dirt drifted up under his feet. I felt he could attack and kill us with his gaze alone. The men clung to the muskets and knives at their sides, ready, if necessary, but one glance from the reverend told them to take their hands off their weapons.

John quickly put his arm around me and the girls. After everyone was seated, Mr. Rolfe walked in wearing a handsome matching gray doublet and breeches. His stockings looked white and crisp, and his black hat was ornamented with a gray feather.

Pocahontas followed shortly after into the room. "She looks beautiful," I said.

"I like the flowers on her dress and coif," Virginia said.

I nodded in agreement and smiled at the beautiful bride and groom.

"Remember when we married here?" I quietly asked John. "How can I forget?" He smiled.

Reverend Whitaker read their wedding vows. The congregation cheered. People celebrated for three days! More of Pocahontas's people joined us, and we feasted on grouse, venison, corn, squash, blue crab, pease pudding, minced pies, bread, and cheese.

"I'm so full," Jack said after the first day. "I don't think I've ever eaten this well before."

"Me neither," John agreed, patting his swollen belly, causing each of us to laugh.

"Come dance with us, Uncle Jack," Virginia said, pulling Jack out of his chair.

I smiled as I watched Jack dance with Virginia and Alice, making them feel like they were the only girls in the whole world. "What a day," I said to John, resting my head on his shoulder. "I wish we could have this much joy every day."

"Me too, my dear, me too." John leaned down and kissed me sweetly on my forehead.

Chapter Thirty-Two
LONGING FOR HOME

"A tale is but half told when only one person tells it."
– The Saga of Grettir the Strong

January 14, 1617

*D*ear Anthony,

It seems like ages since I last wrote.

My sweet baby Margaret was born last spring. It was an arduous labor and birth, and we almost lost her, but she is a tough little thing and pushed through it, despite being the smallest of all my babes. It took several months for me to recover; childbirth is not for the faint of heart. I was blessed with the help of John, Jack, and my friend Temperance. I wish you could meet her. Margaret has a full head of dark brown hair, like Ellen and Virginia when they were born, which will likely lighten to blonde like the others. It feels downy-soft and smells sweeter than any flower. She also has her papa's eyes and my button nose. The girls adore her, and Alice refuses to put her down. Katherine still fights for the title of youngest and pines for my attention. She likes to sit by me while I nurse and tell her stories.

Virginia is seven, Alice is almost six, and Katherine is three. They are growing like weeds!

I imagine you've heard from Jack by now. He was married to Reverend Buckley's daughter, Bridget Buckley. She was a passenger on the Sea Venture so long ago. Jack worked for years to save enough money to marry her, and her father finally consented. It's odd thinking of him as a grown man, but he is. He is as tall if not taller than you, if you can believe it! Bridget is expecting their first child. I keep telling him if it is a girl, he should name her Lizzy after Mama. You would really like Bridget. She is kind but keeps Jack in his place. I don't think I've ever seen him so smitten.

How are you faring? Does Mama have any matchmaking plans for you in the future, or do you have your eyes set on a certain someone?

Moods in the fort have been solemn lately. When Sir Thomas Dale was the acting governor for Sir West, he issued a strict code for Jamestown, which he deemed "Moral and Martial Law." A mandated meeting is required twice daily where prayers are said, and all are forced to pledge their allegiance to King James. If we don't show up for prayer, we are severely punished. We try our best to comply, but sometimes I fear the strictness of the leaders.

You may have heard that Pocahontas, now Rebecca or Mrs. Rolfe, left with her husband and their son, Thomas, for London to improve relations between the English and Powhatan. I am sending this letter to you on their ship. I will miss her terribly. She and Mr. Rolfe created a tobacco farm a few minutes from Jamestown, and John and I occasionally visit

them. Have you heard any news about them? What I wouldn't give to be at court when she is presented to King James and Queen Anne. I imagine they would be quite taken with her; everyone here is. If you hear of anything, please write to me about it. Your letter may not arrive until they do but I'd still like to read about it from you, nonetheless.

Jack and John continue to grow in their carpentry business together, and soon we will have enough saved to expand the one hundred acres each they will give us. It's so hard to wait until then.

I promise to send more letters now that Jamestown has become more profitable, sending goods back to England. The largest export these days is tobacco. They have found ways to help it thrive here. I see men's stalks of it drying out in the storage hall, where they often keep dried meats and corn. Once the tobacco stalks are cut, they usually dry them outside for a few days, then hang them from the rafters and store them in barrels to transport. The whole process is fascinating, even down to the soil preparation. Rebecca taught us to bury dead fish in the soil to help nourish the plants. Could you imagine Mama planting a dead fish in our garden to help it grow?

How is Mama doing? She seemed well from her letters, but I could see her withholding something so as not to upset me. What of Ellen? She is going on thirteen now, nearly the same age I was when I left home. Please send her my love and tell me how she fares.

Oh, Anthony, I wish you all could join us! I long to see Ellen. I'm sure I will hardly recognize her when I do. I still long for the day when we can all be together again.

Yours,

Anne

Chapter Thirty-Three
TAKEN TOO YOUNG

"All must die, but 'tis enough that my child liveth."
– Pocahontas

April 3, 1617

Chief Powhatan sent an embassy of men and women to greet Pocahontas—now Rebecca—at the dock when the Rolfes returned from London. Dozens of us English gathered there as well with excitement and anticipation to welcome her, Mr. Rolfe, and little Thomas back to Virginia.

I walked down to the docks with Margaret in my arms and Katherine near my side, while John walked with Alice and Virginia behind me. My heart felt like it would burst with joy at the thought of spending time with my dear friend. After the fanfare died, I planned to pepper her with questions about England, and I couldn't wait to hug her and little Thomas.

"Mama, when is Rebecca coming?" Alice asked, as she repeatedly tugged on my arm. A small, adorable dimple appeared in the middle of her chubby cheek.

"Soon, I hope," I said, trying to soothe the girls and myself.

The ship drew closer, and four older boys jumped into the water to assist in tying the lines. With water up to their chests, they grabbed the giant rope, lifted it over their shoulders, walked it back, and tied it to the pier to keep the ship from drifting away from the dock.

I scrunched up my face and placed my hand above my eyebrows for a better view. My eyes grew wide when I saw the Powhatan people who had accompanied Rebecca and Mr. Rolfe to England. I turned my head in worry and stood on tiptoe to whisper in John's ear. "Are their faces painted white?"

He squinted to get a better look, then draped his arm around me and pulled me close. "They are." He turned to lock eyes with me. "Someone has died," he said. "And from what I can tell, it must be someone of great importance for them all to be painted white."

Memories of Rebecca's face painted white when her cousin died came to my mind.

The Powhatan men and women near must have noticed too; one of the women screamed. I looked over to see her on her knees, crying and chanting. The only word I could make out was "Okee," whom I knew to be their prominent god.

My heart sank, and my stomach turned into knots; I knew something must be terribly wrong.

I inhaled sharply as they lowered the gangplank, and Captain Newport and Mr. Rolfe descended onto the pier.

Mr. Rolfe's face looked pale and solemn. He ran a hand through his wavy flaxen hair. Captain Newport put a hand on Mr. Rolfe's shoulder, then took off his old black hat with green plume feathers and looked down before he faced the crowd.

The once noisy shore grew eerily silent. Captain Newport closed his eyes then looked up again to address the mass of onlookers.

I took another deep breath and strained my ears to listen.

His voice was deep and firm. "It is with my deepest regret that I inform you that Mrs. Rolfe has passed away."

"No!" I heard myself cry in disbelief. The air felt like it had been sucked out of my chest, and my legs went limp. I might have fallen if it wasn't for John's arm around me.

Rebecca gone? It couldn't be! I'd just seen her a few months ago. I'd just talked with her, laughed with her, held her hand as we discussed our lives, watched our children play together, dreamed together. *How can she be gone?* Didn't she recently entertain the king and queen? She couldn't be gone.

My chin started to quake, and my eyes filled up with tears that ran down my cheeks. My friend, gone! It was too much. I felt like my heart had been taken out of me.

Men and women from both cultures started to cry and scream out. Several Powhatan men started beating their walking sticks on the ground, and voices from both parties rose with hurtful accusations.

Everything seemed to echo in my ears, and my eyes saw spots. None of it seemed real. As I looked around the crowd, the reality of the situation set in. I started to panic.

I instinctively pulled my older girls in closer to protect them from my hurt, protect them from the crowds, protect them from the horrible things of the world. I wanted to hold them in my arms forever and never let go.

Captain Newport clenched his hands into fists and his nostrils flared. He stepped forward and stood up tall, showing off his large stature, and shook a fist in the air. "We did everything we could for her." He took a deep breath and paused before continuing. "When we were leaving port, she suddenly became ill on the ship. We turned around and stayed in the village of Gravesend for three days, hoping she would recover and travel back with us, but she never did. Her health took a turn for the worse, then she was gone. We wanted to bring her body home and bury her here but did not want to contaminate the crew and passengers, so we buried her at a cemetery next to the church in Gravesend."

At his news, the wailing grew louder and more robust. I looked at the Powhatan women crying on their knees, and my heart went out to them. I knew that burial was an important part of their mourning process. Would one of their holy men, a shaman, pray over her spirit tonight as she journeyed to the hereafter, while our reverend prayed that she would return to Jesus? My heart ached for them, for all of us at her loss.

"And what of Master Thomas?" an Englishman with a shaggy gray beard and tattered clothing shouted.

Captain Newport looked down at his hat, then back up again. "He took ill as well."

The crowd gasped. "Not Master Thomas, too!" a blonde woman beside me cried.

It looked like Captain Newport was trying to speak again, but I couldn't hear him over the noise from the crowd. People began to shout and push each other. An Englishwoman fell and tripped over one of the wailing women, and a Powhatan man raised his staff to hit her. A hand shot up before he could, and the crowd gasped as a musket fired into the air, sending chills down my arms.

Everyone paused and made way for a tall, slender man with a dark gray doublet and matching breeches as he and two guards pushed through the crowd.

He stood next to Captain Newport and Mr. Rolfe and pounded a musket into the wooden planks of the dock. "Order, order!" he shouted.

"It's Sir Samuel Argall," John whispered. "The lieutenant governor for Sir Thomas West."

It made sense that he was there, but why hadn't he made himself known before? Maybe he was waiting for things to get out of hand to restore order and show off his power. Or it could be that he wanted to remain in the back until Mr. and Mrs. Rolfe arrived, and then present himself. Either way, it was odd, and I wondered if Powhatan knew that this was the man responsible for Pocahontas's kidnapping.

My eyes frantically darted to the Powhatan who were present. Besides a few sterns looks from men on the ship, no one seemed to recognize Sir Argall.

The crowd started talking and whispering to each other again until Sir Argall shot another round of musket fire into the air.

"Here, here," he shouted. "Let the man finish!" He nodded to Captain Newport to continue.

"Thomas is well and yet alive. He was gravely ill, so Mr. Rolfe thought it best to leave him with his brother and sister-in-law in London until he recovers."

Mr. Rolfe kept his head low, and his eyes locked on the ground. His cheeks colored, and shame swept across his brow. Not only had he lost his first wife and daughter, but now he had lost his second wife and son.

I put my hand up to my chest; my heart longed to comfort him, to send him our love and let him know he was not alone.

Captain Newport moved closer to Mr. Rolfe and said something in his ear.

Mr. Rolfe shook his head.

"Mr. Rolfe would appreciate the time to mourn appropriately without being bombarded with questions. Please, it has been a long and challenging journey. Let me and my men disembark and recuperate. Lieutenant Governor Argall will fill you all in at the next town council."

There were more gasps, and wagging tongues started to whisper about why Thomas should or should not have been left in England, but gradually the crowd dispersed, leaving a few who stayed to mourn.

I felt a pull on my skirt and looked down to see sweet Alice with a questioning look in her eye. Guilt swept over me as I realized I'd almost forgotten my children were there with me.

"Mama, where is Rebecca?" she asked. "Where did she pass to?" Her sweet innocence caught me off guard and melted my heart.

I didn't know what to say. John bent down to match her height and put his hand to his heart. I bit my lip to keep back my sobs. "She went to live with the angels in heaven, my love," John said.

"Is she with your brother and sister now?" Virginia looked up at me innocently.

My chin started to quiver again, and I couldn't help but let the tears fall. "Yes, sweetheart," I said, trying to catch my breath. John looked over and caught my eye, knowing that I couldn't bear to say more. "Many will feel her loss, but oh, what a celebration there must be for her there with friends and loved ones who passed before."

"Like when we die and get to see my twin brother and sister in heaven. Right, Papa?" Virginia asked.

John's eyes welled up with tears. "Yes, my darling, like when you get to see your brother and sister in heaven."

John stood up and squeezed my hand while giving me an understanding frown. His bright green eyes looked full of concern and sorrow. "I'm so sorry, Anne. I know how much she meant to you."

I gulped back the tears and blew my nose into my handkerchief. "She was my first friend here. I can't believe she is gone."

"I know." He nodded, then embraced me. "Do you want to go home now?"

I looked around me. Spring was beginning; and although the day had been tragic, the soft pink sky looked peaceful and calm. "I'd like to stay a few more minutes alone if you don't mind."

"Of course," he said, and took sleeping Margaret from my arms and grabbed Katherine's hand. "Come now, girls, let's let Mama have a few minutes to herself." He turned back to me with a sad smile. "We will be at my workshop when you are ready."

"Thank you," I mouthed. I sat down and stayed there for several minutes gazing out at the harbor. A few white and black herons flew overhead, forming a circle. Their squawks and cries disarmed me.

How was it that life could keep going on when another had just ended?

A crunching sound slowly approached from my right, and I looked up to see Temperance. She gently laid her hand on my shoulder.

"May I sit with you?" she asked.

I nodded and patted the space beside me. "Where are the children?" I asked her.

"Matthew and Georgiana are with my neighbor, and little Edward is with my mother-in-law."

I nodded. I knew things were difficult for Temperance after she lost her first husband and George. It comforted me to know that she was settled and happily married to a widower with three children of his own. I prayed that Mr. Rolfe would find such happiness one day.

Temperance blew at one of her soft blonde curls that came out of her coif. "I'm so sorry for your loss, Anne. I know how fond you were of Mrs. Rolfe."

I stared back into her blue eyes, which sparkled with new life, and I gently squeezed her hand and let the tears fall. "Thank you. I can't believe she is gone. She was there for me when I had no one else but Jack. I know it sounds strange, but even if she wasn't nearby, I felt safer knowing she was still out there somewhere and that she would return. I keep thinking of poor Thomas and Mr.

Rolfe. Their lives won't ever be the same without her. And her family and friends... what must they think?"

Temperance hugged me and let me cry on her shoulder. "I know. She was a good woman and will be truly missed. I'm so sorry, Anne."

I sniffled and took out a handkerchief from my napkin to blow my nose and wipe away my tears. I let my body lean back and felt the soft grass between piles of sand. My hand cupped around them and let each blade pass through my fingers like snow drifting to the ground.

We sat quietly for a few minutes, soaking in the world around us, just two friends experiencing the joys and sorrows of life together.

Chapter Thirty-Four
LIFE AFTER DEATH

"Blessed are you, Lord, who makes a calm after the storm." – 13th-century Proverb

October 16, 1617

Summer gradually faded into autumn, my favorite time of the year. The constant humming of mosquitos and crickets seemed to lessen, and leaves turned into a majestic sunset of oranges and yellows. More ships arrived full of anxious new-comers ready to try their luck at making their fortune.

Our once-little town was growing and busting at the seams. More families moved away from the fort to plantations and farms. Some early settlers were given one hundred acres of land of their own.

John and I had just earned ours, but John felt hesitant to leave his carpentry business until he earned enough money to buy more land. He spent a few hours every week with Mr. Rolfe, learning how to farm and harvest tobacco so that we could do the same.

"Thank you for coming," Mr. Rolfe said one afternoon as he shook John's hand. His smile melted my heart. I had worried that teaching John the trade would burden Mr. Rolfe, but it seemed he also enjoyed the company.

I went with John the first time he visited, and memories flooded my mind of spending time there with Rebecca. My lips pulled into a tight smile on our first visit. It was comforting to see Mr. Rolfe, but it felt strange to be there without her. It was quiet and lacked the usual charm about the place.

Mr. Rolfe grew quieter and kept to himself; I could tell he missed her terribly. He stayed on his plantation with a few other workers, some of whom were relatives of Rebecca. I gazed curiously at them and wondered how they felt about the situation.

Since Rebecca's death, conflicts had risen between the natives and settlers once more. Sir Argall was gruesome regarding revenge, and a tit-for-tat war had ensued. Natives burned down crops, and Englishmen retaliated fourfold by plundering their villages.

John and I tried to stay close to home or town and avoided being out too far from the protection of the cannons and guns.

I shuddered when I heard stories of women taken from their homes and sold or traded by the natives to other tribes. With four girls of my own, my heart raced with worry that our family might be next.

October 23, 1617

My hand formed a line over my eyebrows, shielding the setting sun so I could see down the road and across the fields. "Girls! Come help me get supper ready!" I cupped my hands over my mouth and yelled, "Virginia, Alice, Katherine," with my back to my cabin so I didn't wake up Margaret.

Three little heads came bobbing down the road. "Coming, Mama," Virginia said.

"Please pick some carrots and pull out a head of cabbage for soup today."

"Yes, Mama," Alice called back. "I'll get the cabbage." "No, I want to pick the cabbage," Virginia said.

I snickered. "You both can pick a cabbage. Help Margaret pick one too. We need to salt and preserve more."

"Yay!" they cheered.

I giggled, then turned back to the house when I heard someone running toward me. *Jack*.

"Anne," he huffed, out of breath, a large grin on his face.

Surprised, I raised my eyebrows. "Jack, it's so good to see you. What are you doing here? Are you faring well?"

He nodded and hugged me. "I was in town picking up supplies and thought I'd drop by to see you and the girls."

I wiped my dirty hands across my white linen apron. "This is a nice surprise. Come on in; the girls will be delighted to see you. I was just about to put supper on the hearth."

He grinned again, and I laughed. "So, that is the real reason you are here."

He chuckled. "No. Well, it wouldn't hurt."

I hesitated, then asked, "Is everything well with Bridget and your new land?"

"Yes. She is doing well, and the land is a lot of work, but we have high hopes. We just acquired two indentured servants that have already started tilling the ground for a winter crop. We plan on a good harvest this year."

"That's wonderful." I beamed with pride as I looked at Jack and the man he had become.

"Uncle Jack!" the girls screamed as he approached the cabin. They nearly tackled him to the ground with their hugs. He roared with laughter, and my heart melted.

"Here, I have something for you," he said, pulling three molasses sweets from his pockets.

I put my hands on my hips. "Jack, you shouldn't have." His face reddened. "I wanted to."

"Thank you, Uncle Jack," each of the girls said, and they each planted a kiss on his cheeks before going back to pulling up plants from the garden.

I gestured for Jack to join me inside.

"I have something for you, too," he said as we sat down at the table.

I gave him an inquisitive look. "For me?" He handed me a letter. "Open it."

My eyes grew wide as I read its contents. "Mama and Papa are coming?" I shouted.

He nodded his head emphatically. "Anthony and Ellen too!"

I jumped up from the table and hugged him. "Ahh, I can't believe it!"

It seemed too good to be true. I pressed the letter to my chest, then pulled it out again to read.

June 17, 1617

Dear Jack and Anne,

I couldn't pass up the chance of sending a letter as soon as things were final.

There has been nothing but wagging tongues about Pocahontas and her Mr. Rolfe, dancing the night away and being entertained by King James and Queen Anne. She is known as the "court's fa-

vorite" in London. I still cannot believe how amazing it is that you are friends with her.

I wish you could have joined her on the visit, my dears. I have ached to see you these many years, and I intend to remedy that soon. It is time to count our losses and sell Grandfather's business. We have put in too many years and too much money for it not to give us a proper return on our investment. Between selling the assets that are left and, more importantly, the house, we should have enough to afford our passage and life there.

We could grow and sell tobacco like your dear friends, the Rolfes. It may be a while until all the affairs are accounted for and settled, but I shall try, my dears. May God be with you and your beautiful families. Please tell the girls Grandpapa cannot wait to meet them.

Papa

Part Five

Moral and Martial Law

Chapter Thirty-Five
NEW ARRIVALS

"About the latter end of August, a Dutch man
of Warr of the burden of a 160 tunes arrived at
Point-Comfort, the Comandor name Capt Jope, his
Pilott for the West Indies one Mr Marmaduke an
Englishman. ... *He brought not any thing but 20. and
odd* Negroes, w[hich] the Governor and Cape Mer-
chant bought for victual[s]." – John Rolfe

February 27, 1619

News of the successful tobacco shipments from Jamestown
must have spread around London because more and more
settlers arrived, primarily men. The
Company was finally starting to see a profit in its investment and
wanted it to grow even more.

The more people, the bigger the threat we became to the natives. Chief Powhatan died; some say of a broken heart from losing his favorite daughter. His brother Opitchapam took over as chief.

The English had matched the Powhatans' cruelty of killing even the women and children and burning down villages and crops. Fear was felt from outside and within the fort. Attacks grew increasingly, and Governor Berkley and the other leaders tightened the reins on us, handing out harsh discipline to anyone who would not obey their rules.

"This must stop," Governor Berkley said in our early-morning meeting at the church. "Chief Opitchapam must not be allowed to hurt our people again. He will know his place. I want your tactics to be swift and harsh if necessary. You must make a point: the settlers will not be moved."

John tensed. His tanned hands found mine, and I closed my eyes for a moment. When I did, images of the man hanging from the gallows when I first arrived flashed through my mind. I recoiled at the memory. I looked down at my hands, weary of the debate and struggle to thrive here as a community. I squeezed John's hand and prayed that all would be well.

August 27, 1619

After the harvest, I brought my pressed cider to town to trade for cloth. I made cider from the three apple trees we had planted a few years prior. This year was our first full harvest, and it made me proud to make the cider with our own fruit. The fruit itself was too sour to eat off the tree, but it was delicious as cider and could last all year.

I also learned how to make cheese with the leftover milk from the cow we shared with our neighbor. Working with others really made a difference. My heart skipped a beat as I thought about the contrast between when we first arrived and now. We were truly blessed.

"Virginia, Alice, Katherine, Margaret," I called out. "It's time to go. We'll stop by and see Papa on our way into the fort."

"Hooray!" little Margaret squealed. I gathered her in my arms and spun her around. Her chubby little finger twirled around one of her soft brown ringlets, making me think of my baby sister, Mary. Margaret's chestnut eyes reminded me of her, too. Although they were a different color, they still had that look of joy and innocence.

"Are you excited to see Papa?" I asked.

Margaret nodded her head enthusiastically. I smiled, knowing she would be happy to visit John at work. "Well, then, let us be off."

We were able to sell some of the cheese to a few families we passed on our way to the fort and a jug or two of cider. Once we arrived, the best part of the day was sitting by the shoreline with John for lunch—cheese and a slice of bread. As we sat, I noticed a new ship docking in the harbor—one I had never seen before, with the name the *White Lion* painted on its side. I gasped as people with skin the color of ebony walked off the dock with their hands and feet bound by ropes. Most of the passengers looked so sickly and thin that I was shocked they had survived the voyage at all!

"John, what are they doing to those poor people!" I cried. The sight of them made my heart hurt and ache for them.

John squinted his eyes and cupped his hand over his brow. He stood up and wiped dirt and grass off his breeches. "I am not sure what they are doing, but I say, there must be at least twenty of them."

A commotion broke out as people stopped to stare; they must have been wondering the same thing.

A man stood up and banged a large paddle on the deck several times for everyone to quiet down. "Now see here, we found these African people captives on a Portuguese ship on their way no doubt to serve as slaves for their people. We commandeered said ship; therefore, they are now ours to trade. Who would like more indentured servants? I will give them to you for a fair price. All I need is food and clean water for my men, and then we will return to Holland.

"Price? They should be able to choose if they are indentured servants," I said.

John shook his head, "Unfortunately, not always, my love" he said with a sigh.

"And Holland?" I asked. "If he is Dutch, why does he speak like an Englishman?" I whispered to John.

John shrugged his shoulders. "Maybe he is an English privateer; they can sometimes work for a Dutch employer."

"That would make sense, but those poor people!"

"They are not unlike many others here, me included, who work for the company or others to gain land and opportunity," John said.

I furrowed my brows at him, "Yes, but these people did not volunteer. Others have chosen for them."

John pressed his lips tightly together, "Yes, you are right my love."

A pull on my skirt drew my attention back to my girls. I felt awful, but seeing the ship and the people almost made me forget they were there. I glanced down to see Katherine looking up at me with curious blue eyes. "Mama, what is an indentured servant, and why do ropes pull those people?"

My eyes began to water, and I bit my lower lip. "An indentured servant is someone who volunteers to work for someone so they can earn their land."

"Is Papa an indentured servant?"

I squatted down to look Katherine in the eyes. "In a way he is my love, but not to a person, to the London company. And once he is done, he can own his shop and his land."

"Oh," Katherine replied as she scrunched up her nose. "Mama," she said, tugging again on my skirt, "he doesn't he have to wear a rope on his hands."

I looked up at John and felt my chin begin to quiver. "You're right, my darling girl; your Papa doesn't have to wear a rope around his hands."

Chapter Thirty-Six
SHORT SHIRT SHENANIGANS

"If discipline had not been restored, and quickly, I see
not how the utter subversion and ruin of the Colony
should have been prevented." – Ralph Hammond,
1615

September 16, 1620

Summer had been swelteringly hot, and I couldn't wait for the
temperatures to cool. A ship full of women had arrived on our
shores last spring. Ninety women were sent from England to marry
men here. Many were purchased beforehand with tobacco or cash
and matched with men they had never met. Each was guaranteed
to have a set of behaviors and skills, and each was vouched for
by clergy, family members, or prominent people in society. Their
numbers were staggering. Most were married off within a few
weeks.

As our numbers grew, so did the chores and restrictions from
the Company. My tasks for the Company varied and stretched over

weeks at a time. One day, I was given a new task that was more time-consuming than some. I wasn't told beforehand what I was to be doing but was asked to wait in line with four other women until someone provided us with instructions. Luckily, Temperance offered to watch the girls for the day while she darned socks from home.

"Anne Layton," said a man in a deep voice. He had dark brown hair, light brown eyes, and a double chin. "Please step forward."

"Yes."

"I heard your mending and sewing skills are commendable."

I blushed and bowed my head. "Thank you, sir. I was a lady's maid when I arrived here."

"Ah, yes, for Lady Forrest. I heard. Tragic what happened to her." He nodded, as if contemplating what to say next. "My name is Mr. Williams. I've been tasked with overseeing you and the other women. You will be making work shirts for the craftsmen. Two example shirts have already been made."

I looked over two white linen work shirts. They had a V-shaped collar with two long strings hanging down. Puffed sleeves bulged at the elbow, then tapered back toward the wrist.

"You must follow the pattern with precision and stay consistent with the design," Sir Williams said. "Is that understood?"

"Yes." The task was reasonable; I thought I could manage the pattern easily.

"Good. Here are your supplies." He handed me some fabric, a metal needle, and six long strings of white linen thread the length of the distance between my elbow and middle finger. "You may take one of the shirts with you as a sample. I expect you to make a shirt out of these. When you're done, come grab more supplies for another."

I gave him a questioning look. "Where is the other material?"

He sighed. "These are the supplies the Company is giving you. I expect the shirts to be done by the end of the week."

"But—"

"The end of the week," he repeated, then gestured for me to move out of line.

The four other women joined me in the tiny one-room work cabin. Each expressed disbelief and fear as they entered the room and examined their trifling supplies.

A young blonde woman carried her supplies and plopped down next to me. She had a thick London accent and bright green eyes.

"I'm Jane Harrington," she said with a smile. "Well met, Mrs. Harrington. I'm Anne Layton."

She laughed, hitting her forehead with her hand. "Harrington! I meant Wright. I'm not used to going by my married name."

"Did you just arrive on the…" My face flushed as I tried to think of a more polite name for it.

"Bride ship?" she asked. "Yes," I said sheepishly.

"I sure did, and I'm not ashamed of it. There were no prospects or money for me at home. My uncle had some connections, and now here I am. It's better than staying a spinster at home. You know how society treats unmarried women. Mr. Wright paid for my passage, and we were married two days ago."

My eyebrows rose in surprise, and I smiled at her. "Two days! Congratulations."

She blushed and tucked a wayward curl back into her coif. "Thank you."

"I'm from London, Cheap Town," she said, changing the subject. "Where are you from?"

"Norfolk." I smiled. No one had asked me where I was from in years.

"I see, a northern country bumpkin." She laughed. Her words cut deep, and I glowered at her. She looked down sheepishly at her hands resting on her supplies. "My apologies; sometimes I forget my place. We called anyone not from the city a country bumpkin and look at us now. We couldn't be more country bumpkin if we tried."

My mood lightened, and I shrugged my shoulders. She was right. I sighed and looked down at my lap.

"We sure have our work cut out for us, haven't we?" Jane whispered. "How do they expect us to make shirts out of these?" My first instinct was to complain alongside her, but Mr. Williams gave me a daring look. I kept my head tucked down and said nothing.

We sat in the hot cabin for hours, and I grimaced at the uncomfortably tight lace of my bodice. My belly started to show under my kirtle, and I wished I hadn't laced my stays so tight; they seemed to fit yesterday just fine, but today, they felt like they were pinching at my waist. The heat was unbearable, and I tried to loosen my bodice without anyone noticing. Some other women saw and gave me an all-too-knowing smile.

"I just don't get how they expect us to make a shirt out of so little material," Jane said as she lifted her second needle and thread. I nodded but didn't want to agree vocally. A few weeks before, I had seen a man tied to the stocks for days because he missed curfew. Another woman was dunked several times in the river when she didn't harvest enough tobacco. I didn't even want to think of what they'd do to us if we didn't fully comply.

After looking around the room, I saw similar concerns on the other women's faces.

Rip. I thought my ears were playing tricks on me. I glanced up at the stout brunette woman sitting across from me, but she focused on her work. Rip came the noise again. This time, I caught a glimpse of its source. The woman lifted her hand, and a thread hung from it.

"Where did you get that?" Jane asked her unabashedly. The woman looked up, startled. She glanced toward Sir

Williams sitting outside the door.

"If you must know," she said irritably, "I ran out of thread and took some from my shift. It's the only way to have enough material."

I looked down at her shift and saw its hem, jagged and frayed, obviously stripped of material.

"That's brilliant!" Jane exclaimed. I wasn't so sure.

Jane's face flushed with embarrassment. "I only have one extra shift," she admitted.

I nodded in understanding. "I don't have a third one either. My girls use up any spare clothing we have."

"That's enough," Sir Williams scolded, entering the cabin.

"Too much talking makes for idle work."

"Yes, sir," we said, leaning a small curtsy toward him. He left the room.

It was incredibly humid and hot for September. The air visibly irritated Sir Williams, so he stood as a guard outside instead of inside the cabin. I was grateful for the cabin's privacy and shade, but I was sweating and wished for a stronger breeze. The other women were hot, too, and tried to cool down with their fans.

What were we going to do? We didn't have enough thread to make the shirts.

Jane and I looked at each other. We were clearly out of place, with dirt and food smudged on our only outfits and hair falling out of our coifs. The other three women sat in finer attire, with clean stockings and hair pinned up in place. Each was wealthier than us, with more prominent husbands than we had.

"What are we going to do?" Jane asked.

"Just keep sewing," I mumbled. "We'll figure something out."

Before long, Mr. Williams returned to announce that out time was up for the day. My heart raced as I picked up my belongings to head home. I wasn't sure how I was going to finish the shirts on time without enough material, but at least I had made it through the day unscathed. Jane eyed me as we left, following me out the door with the others.

September 17, 1620

Jane grabbed another strand of thread and paused. She pushed her dark blonde hair back into her coif, and her lips formed an enormous smile with two prominent dimples. Her green eyes danced excitedly, reflecting a blueish-green hue.

"I have an idea," she whispered. She pulled a completed shirt from her basket and handed it to me. "What if we took a little thread from each of the bottoms of the shirts we already sewed? No one will notice if we undo the hem and pull some thread out."

My smile at her faded into a frown. "Jane, surely someone will notice. There must be a better option."

"Listen. My sister had her ear nailed to the pillory post for not being prompt to her job in the communal garden. The guard said it was her second time being late that week, so he nailed her ear to the post for a few hours to teach her and the others a lesson. If they would do that to her, what would they do to us for not finishing the shirts on time?"

She was right. We'd risk much more by not completing the shirts than by trying to stretch what thread we had among them. I took a deep breath and looked back at Jane. "You're right,"

I said. "Be careful, and don't let the other women see you."

We unraveled what we could from the completed shirt, avoiding making it look too obvious that we were taking some of the thread. We worked the rest of the day as if nothing had happened. Occasionally, we'd look up to see if the other women were watching us.

They looked just as intent as we did. Our hands trembled as we sewed. We held our breath in the hope that our plan would work and the Company wouldn't find out. I just wanted to get out of there.

"Time's up for today," Sir Williams announced. "Remember, tomorrow is your last day to have the shirts finished. I expect them to be done on time."

I sighed. "I'm worried," I told Jane. "What if they find out?" "They won't find out," she said. "They aren't seamstresses.

I don't think they will notice if some of the shirts are too short." I wasn't so sure she was right. A pang of nausea struck, and bile rose in my throat. Tomorrow was the day they would examine the shirts. I hoped Sir Williams wouldn't investigate the shirts too closely. I felt awful about not being honest with my work, but I didn't know what else to do about not having enough thread. I placed my hand on my belly and took a deep breath. I thought, *For now, this will have to do.*

Chapter Thirty-Seven
MR. AND MRS. WRIGHT

"Without friends no one would choose to live,
though he had all other goods." – Aristotle

September 20, 1620

"Time's up!" Sir Williams said. "Hand in your shirts. You should each have two completed, and I expect the sample shirts back."

Jane and I looked at each other and tried not to make eye contact with Sir Williams as we handed him our shirts. Margaret was with me, and I pretended to be distracted by her when Sir Williams said, "See, I knew you could make the shirts with the thread we gave you."

I gave him a wry smile as I dropped off my needles.

He counted the supplies, and his chubby fingers held up the linen shirts one at a time for quick examination before he threw them into the wicker basket with the rest. He looked down at his recordings, then back up at me. "Very well; you may leave."

I looked at Jane, who was trying to hold back the grin spreading across her face. The corner of her eyes crinkled as she

smiled at me. My heart pounded, and I tried not to bite my lip like I often did when I was nervous or hiding something. "Thank you, sir," I said, and I hurried home as fast as possible.

September 28, 1620

With each new set of shirts, I became more confident that no one would notice the shirts were two inches too short. The other women must have gone through half an under-shift to compensate for the missing thread.

Another week passed, and a second set of shirts came and went without being caught. I hated lying to John about what was happening, but I didn't want him to worry. Jane didn't seem concerned about Sir Williams, but she did seem lonely. She mentioned more than once how she missed her mother's cooking and her little brother and sisters, so I invited her and her husband to supper.

At the door, I greeted Jane and her husband. Jane carried a variation of dried fruit on a platter and smiled when she saw me.

"Anne, this is Mr. Wright," Jane said proudly.

A smile grew over my face, and I gave Mr. Wright a small curtsey while John shook his hand. "Well met, Mr. Wright. This is my husband, John, and my girls, Virginia, Alice, Katherine, and Margaret."

To the delight of my girls, he shook each of their hands individually.

"And how old are you, Miss Virginia?"

Virginia stood up nice and tall. "Almost eleven, sir."

"My! Eleven years old. You are practically a lady."

She giggled and turned her skirt to the side, her face beaming with pride.

"And you, Miss Alice? How old are you?"

Alice scrunched up her nose, showing off her adorable freckles. She stood on her tippy toes, trying to look as tall as Virginia. "I'm nine."

"I'd say you will be a lady like your sister soon enough."

She smiled at his compliment, and her dimple showed.

"I'm seven!" Katherine announced, too excited to wait to be asked.

"Oh ho!" Mr. Wright replied in surprise. "Seven? Well done!" he said, as if it was a great accomplishment.

Katherine beamed, soaking up the praise.

Mr. Wright then turned and squatted down to Margaret's height. "And you must be thirty-two."

Margaret giggled, hid behind my skirt, then held her hand up, revealing four fingers.

Mr. Wright smiled. "You're four?!" he exclaimed.

Margaret nodded emphatically and we all laughed.

"What a beautiful family you have, Mr. and Mrs. Layton."

"Thank you. Please, call us John and Anne."

Mr. Wright nodded. "John and Anne, then. Please call me Richard."

He seemed much older than I imagined, almost the same height as Jane and bald in the middle of his head, with a few brown hairs that he'd combed down the sides. His eyes were warm and kind, a dark shade of blue, and he donned a thick brown beard peppered with gray hair. Multiple scars spread across his face from what I assumed to be smallpox. The pox scars were not as prominent as I had seen in some; however, they were still visible and left slight indentations all over his face. Although his outer appearance had much to be desired, he seemed like a kind man by how he treated my girls, and Jane glowed whenever she was around him.

John placed a hand on the small of my back, breaking me away from my thoughts. "Where are my manners?" I gestured into the room. "Please do come in."

Supper was lovely. We ate minced meat pie, biscuits, and fresh lettuce from the garden. The children's eyes grew wide as they ate the treat Jane brought for them and savored each piece of fruit one by one.

"Thank you, Miss Jane," Virginia said, licking her fingers. Jane laughed. "You're welcome, Virginia. I'm glad you like them. My mama used to make them at home for me and my siblings."

Virginia's eyes grew wide with curiosity. "How many siblings do you have?"

"Seven," Jane said, tapping Virginia on the nose. "I am the oldest, like you."

After supper and plates were cleared, Jane told us stories of her home life with six younger siblings, two dogs, and five cats who proudly caught and laid dead mice at her front door each night. John and Mr. Wright joined in with tales of romping through forests as boys and pretending to fight off the Spanish. The girls giggled at their renditions and continuously asked for more. The girls entertained us with songs like "To Market, to Market" and "Ding Dong."

The sun began to set and filled the sky with majestic shades of pink.

"Off to bed with you now," I said.

After several minutes of sighing, the girls were soon fast asleep, and the four of us adults sat and talked on the porch as we watched the Virginia sky. It was gorgeous this time of year. I loved looking up at the setting sun and the rising kaleidoscope of stars at night. We sat on rocking chairs John had made for me, breathed in the fresh cool air, and heard the cicadas chirping loudly in the hawthorn trees. I felt like I was home.

John and Mr. Wright discussed the tobacco trade, woodcarving, and farming. Jane and I talked about London and life in Jamestown. It was a treat to hear the recent happenings and goings there, which seemed so foreign and far away to me here.

Chapter Thirty-Eight
THE LONDON COMPANY VERSUS ANNE LAYTON

"We cannot but resent, that forty thousand people should be impoverished to enrich little more than forty merchants." – Howard Zinn

October 6, 1620

Someone pounded loudly on our door before sunrise, jostling John and me out of bed. John reached for his shotgun and raced to the door.

"Stay back with the girls," he whispered to me. Through the door, he asked, "Who's there?"

"Sir Walker, with orders from the governor."

My face went pale. Was it an attack? Something in my heart knew why they were there. Then realization dawned on me. *They know what I did to the shirts.*

John turned, giving me a look of concern and confusion. My heart pounded inside my chest. *What have I done?*

John's hands bawled into fists, and a vein bulged in his neck. "What is the meaning of this?" he demanded.

"By order of the governor, Anne Layton is to come with us!" Sir Walker shouted.

"Anne?"

I glanced pleadingly at John and mouthed, "I'm sorry."

John's face twisted, and his eyes pleaded with me to say it wasn't true. He opened the door, and two men pulled me from behind him out the door.

Sir Walter stood in front of me, looking prouder than he had before. His face was stern and unreadable. He pulled out a letter with the governor's signet ring pushed into a red wax seal. "Anne Layton, by order of Governor Argall, you are to be

put into prison until he sees fit what to do with you."

I gasped. *Prison? Because I should have sewed the shirts longer? This must be some cruel trick, some misunderstanding.* His eyes bore into mine, and I knew he was not joking.

Craning my neck toward my family, I saw my four beautiful girls awake from the commotion, crying and screaming for Mama as the officers took me away. I wanted to reach out for them, but the officers shoved me harder, pushing me away from my home and onto the dirt path.

They walked with me the half mile toward the fort, passing multiple cabins as we went. I went without complaint, so they didn't need to drag or tie me. I passed my beloved chapel across from the newly built one and wept.

How did it come to this? Taken away for trying to make out what I could with what little I was given.

A thin guard, younger than me, opened the door to a cabin refurbished as a holding cell. The room was damp, and the floor was cold. The eastern window showed the sun rising. The orange and pink colors gave me hope but terrified me. What if this was my last sunrise?

The thought only lasted a moment, and then the cabin door opened and a woman with long blonde hair stuck to her wet cheeks was shoved in, screaming and pleading.

"Jane!" I cried.

Jane shook violently and grabbed my hand. She squeezed her eyes shut, and her lashes fluttered. She looked so young and innocent. All I wanted to do was protect her.

"What—" Her sobs cut off her words. I strained my ears to listen. "What are they going to do with us?" she cried.

Rain started to fall and beat hard against the prison walls and roof. It was coming in from all directions. The wind rose up and through our cell windows, and flashbacks of hurricanes and storms from previous autumns came to my mind. I couldn't help but shiver from the cold.

"I don't know." My voice trembled with fear. "I just don't know. But we will get through this, Jane. You'll see."

I wasn't sure if I believed my own words. My thoughts raced to John and my girls. What was going to happen to them?

I knelt and prayed with all my heart. "Please, God, help me overcome whatever punishment they give me. Forgive me for shortchanging the shirts and help me to live to raise my daughters."

Chapter Thirty-Nine
MORAL AND MARTIAL LAW
#34

"And further she [Isabelle Perry] sayeth that in the time of Sir Thomas Dales' Government, Ann Leyden and Jane Wright and other women were appointed to make shirts for the Colony servants and had six needles full of thread allowed for making of a shirt, which if they did not form, they had no allowance of diet." – Minutes of the Council and General Courts of Virginia, May 25, 1625; testimony of Isabelle Perry, several years after the fact

October 7, 1620

The rain kept pouring through the morning and seemed to seep up from the ground. The irony was that, because of it, they took us to the chapel to receive our punishment. The same building where I'd married John, the same building I'd christened my children in, and the one where they punished people unjustly

226

and claimed it was from God. The verdict and punishment were decided without a trial or someone to speak on our behalf.

"Please note," the guard boomed, "on this day, the twenty-fifth of September in the year of our Lord sixteen hundred and nineteen, that Anne Layton and Jane Wright are found guilty of disobeying direct orders of the London Company."

He held up a long work shirt. "See here; these are the shirts produced for the men. This is the length it is supposed to be. Now, compare this length to the length of the shirts produced by Mrs. Layton and Mrs. Wright." He smirked as he held up another shirt. "The latter is several inches shorter than the first. After questioning several witnesses who sewed with these two women, all confirmed that Mrs. Layton and Mrs. Wright unraveled the bottom layers of previous shirts to make their own."

A woman sitting in the pews gasped.

"We have here direct evidence that these women stole from the Company and used trickery and lies for their benefit, thus breaking Moral and Martial Law number 34."

The guard produced a large paper scroll detailing the Moral and Martial Laws and their appointed punishments. "What man or woman soever, launderer or laundress, appointed to wash the foul linen of any one laborer or soldier, or anyone else as it is their duties so to do, performing little or no other service for their allowance out of the store and daily provisions and supply of other necessaries unto the Colony, and shall from the said laborer or soldier, or anyone else of what quality whatsoever, either take anything for washing or withhold or steal from him any such linen committed to her to wash or change the same willingly and wittingly, with the purpose to give him worse, old and torn linen for his good, and proof shall be made thereof, she shall be whipped for the same and lie in prison till she makes restitution of such linen, withheld or c hanged."

The sentence from the magistrate came like a wave of terror across the room. "For not creating shirts under the direction of the London Company's explicit expectations and requirements, both of these women will receive ten lashes apiece, then recompense the Company by using their clothing to fix the shirts."

Mr. Wright stood up. "This is an outrage!"

I was shocked when I heard John's voice yell from the back, "Please, no! Mrs. Layton is with child! Whip me instead."

A commotion erupted in the chapel. People shouted among themselves.

I prayed my ears were playing tricks on me and that it wasn't my husband's voice from the back of the room. I turned around, and our eyes met. Tears of rage boiled up in John's eyes at the magistrate's declaration.

"Order, order!" called the magistrate, banging on the table, his large red robe dancing with each pound of his fist. "Restrain that man at once! For that outburst, sir, she shall receive five more lashings. Now take them to the streets."

Once again, hands were on me, shoving me outside the small church and toward the town square near the pillory post. Out of the corner of my eye, I saw John struggle to get free from one of the guards. In the square, they pushed Jane and me down on our knees, both still in our nightgowns. Jane cried hysterically. Tears fell from my own eyes. We both recoiled as the whip came down.

One. My body arched up in rebellion to the sharp leather beating across my back.

Two. I locked eyes with Jack as he struggled through the crowd of onlookers.

Three. I screamed as the governor's guards forced him back.

My arms reached for him, but he couldn't get to me.

Four, five, six. The whip came down relentlessly.

Seven, eight, nine, ten. Blood poured down my back and sweat dripped down my hair, then stuck to my face. I looked toward John as he broke free from the guard. His tears mirrored mine.

Eleven, twelve, thirteen. I curled into a ball to guard my unborn child. My body heaved up and down in convulsions from the pain. Blood oozed and dripped from my back, neck, and face, where the whip cruelly wrapped around.

Fourteen. Fifteen. Done.

"Those five were for you," the guard sneered cruelly in John's direction. "You better think twice before opposing the Company again."

A guard on each side picked me up by my arms and dragged me across the village square to my prison cell. I could hear women gasping and crying as they paraded me by. My head hung low. Hair flapped in my face and sweat, and tears dripped uncontrollably. Blood ran down my back and legs.

Jane emerged in the jail doorway after me, then was quickly thrown back into her cell. She was eerily quiet. Neither of us said a word. I sobbed softly on the floor in the corner of the room for what must have been an hour.

A loud screech from the prison doors made my heart race and the hairs on my arms stand on end. I curled further into my cocoon until a light hand touched my shoulder, and I jumped.

"John!" I cried.

He carefully placed his arms on my sides to not aggravate my wounds, letting me sob into his chest. Temperance stood by his side with matching tear stains and concern on her face, a bucket of water and rags in her hands.

The pain was fierce. Temperance gave me a stick to bite down on, which also muffled my screams. Little by little, they tended my wounds, brushing and pulling the torn fabric, dirt, and debris away from my ripped flesh with a cold, wet rag. Jack came to offer help and gasped when he saw me. I asked him to leave; I couldn't bear him to see me that way.

The burning and stinging sensations were so intense that I hardly noticed the cramping in my lower abdomen until it became unbearable. I clutched at my lower belly, pain welling in my eyes, forcing John and Temperance to stop the work on my back. Temperance gasped when she noticed the blood running down my leg and pooling beneath me. The color drained from John's face when he saw it too. Stabs of pain wrapped around my abdomen and back. John and Temperance gave me the space I asked for. The baby came soon after that, no larger than my palm, without breath. The boy I always longed for.

I scooped my baby into my arms and held him as if he were alive.

John fell to his knees beside me and sobbed. Temperance stood back to give the two of us room.

John wiped hair away from my face. His eyes flooded with tears, and I knew he felt the loss as much as I did.

I sniffled and kept my gaze on my little baby. Ten perfect fingers and ten perfect toes. What kind of life could he have had? Why did they take him from me?

I sat there for another hour until John and Temperance convinced me to let go.

The cold emptiness of my arms when they took him consumed me, and I fell to the floor and cried.

Chapter Forty
A Sentence Served

"Remember those in prison as if you were their fellow prisoners, and those who are mistreated as if you were yourselves suffering." – Hebrews 13

October 9, 1620

I woke suddenly from a dream to the sound of John's voice. A dream with vague pink and white lights, where I was surrounded by my girls.

"Anne, stay with us," John pleaded.

"The girls," I mumbled. "Where are my girls?" "Anne, wake up, my darling."

My eyes squeezed together, and my lashes fluttered. I slowly opened them to see John sitting next to me on the floor. His brown hair was disheveled, dirt was smeared on his face, and his eyes bore dark puffy circles beneath them.

"Are we still here?" I asked in a shaky voice.

He smoothed back my hair from my face. "Yes, my dear. They won't let you leave until you fix the shirts. It's utter madness!"

"What about Jane?"

He gave me a small smile. "She was released yesterday after she fixed the shirts that she sewed too short. She is sore but will heal."

"And the girls?"

"Temperance is watching them." He hesitated, then said, "The Company brought more supplies for you and Jane. They won't let anyone else do it. Most people are scared, but some women have come by to plead your case—but the Company will not budge. You must finish the shirts yourselves."

I didn't care about the shirts anymore. I looked away from John, not able to meet his eye. I let out a loud sob. "I'm so sorry I lost our son!"

"Anne, look at me." John cupped my cheeks with his hands and turned my head toward his. "You did not lose our son. The Company did that to you. I promise you this: I will get you and the girls out of here. They owe us one hundred acres each for being here for ten years, and when they grant it, you will never have to be under their scrutiny and inhumane rules again. Do you hear me? This was not your fault!" He slipped something smooth and cool into my palm. "I want you to have this."

I slowly opened my shaking fingers to reveal an intricate white and purple stone.

"It's so beautiful," I whispered. "Do you know what that is?"

"No."

"It's called John Stone. My son, Thomas, gave it to me when I left for Jamestown. He told me to hold it whenever I was scared and that it would help me be brave."

"Has it helped?" I asked.

"I thought it did, but it wasn't the stone that kept me brave. It was my thoughts of Thomas and my thoughts of you. You have kept me brave, Anne; you and the girls. Can't you see? You are the bravest person I know." He lightly wiped a tear off my cheek and pushed back my mud-streaked hair.

"Me?"

"Yes, you!" he said with a small laugh. "You have faced so much, yet you kept pushing through and moving forward. One day, you will be able to move forward from this as well." He smiled gently, his eyes looking into mine with understanding. "I've finished my service to the Company but wanted to save more money for us to acquire more land, but I think it best if we take it now and get out of this place. The girls need a place to run around, and we need to get away from the scrutiny of the Company. Everything will be all right. I'm here, and I'm going to take care of you."

He wiped another hair from my face and placed a cool cloth on my forehead.

February 9, 1621

Dear Anne,

Jack sent me a letter informing me of what was done to you by the London Company. Words cannot express my heartache and worry for you. We all pray for you and your quick recovery.

On a happier note, I have news! Unless Jack hasn't already spoiled it. At first, I was reluctant to tell you and thought I'd keep it a surprise, but it's too joyful not to share.

We are coming to Jamestown! All of us—that is Mama, Papa, Ellen and me. We are hoping to ship out once the weather warms up.

After years of trying, Papa was able to sell off the business and the house. He used the money to pay for passage to Jamestown. We should

be leaving here early spring once the weather warms up. I can't tell you the joy it will bring to all of us to be reunited again, dear sister.
   Until then,
   Anthony

Chapter Forty-One
A Season of Change

"Now in Jamestown they were all in combustion, the
strongest preparing once more to run away with the
pinnace for England." – William Symonds

August 21, 1621

"Jane," I called out, waving, as I walked with my family toward the market near the Jamestown fort.

"Anne!" Jane Wright waved back and curtsied. "Well met, John,
girls."

John gave a short bow, and all four girls replied, "Well met, miss,"
and gave Jane a polite curtsy.

John touched my arm, and I could feel his sweaty palm through
my shift. "Anne, I need to check a few things at the shop. I will
meet you in a few minutes. It was nice to see you again, Jane," he
said, removing his cap and putting it back on.

Jane curtsied. "And you, John."

My heart raced, and I wanted to follow him, but I knew he wanted to be alone. Whenever I mentioned visiting Jane and

Richard after the trial, John made excuses for why he couldn't. I think seeing them reminded him of that awful day. I didn't blame him for feeling that way; I knew he was hurt too. It was different for me, maybe because I didn't blame Jane, perhaps because I was still healing. I wasn't sure, but seeing her with color again and joy in her countenance healed my soul. I was delighted that she was happy.

"I thought you moved to Elizabeth City and own land there now," Jane said.

"Not yet," I said. "We hope to have our land given to us soon but haven't decided where. Jack lives in Burras Hill with his wife, Bridget Buckley, and their son and daughter, Jack Junior and Sarah. They live next to her parents, Reverend and Mrs. Buckley. They are only a thirty-minute boat ride to Jamestown and should be here soon." I peered at the river to search for them.

"What are you doing here?" I asked her. "I thought you and Richard moved to Henrico?" Jane nodded enthusiastically. "We did. We are here to send off our crop of tobacco to England. Oh, Anne, you and John should join us in Henrico. They have a university there for native children to learn English and Christianity, shops, and public buildings. They even raised a church and wooden palisade with watchtowers around the seven-mile perimeter of the town. In some way, I feel safer there than I do in Jamestown."

Her talk of Henrico gave me the chills. Something about that place unnerved me. Maybe it was the thought of Rebecca spending that first year there alone without any friends, trained by the Reverend and his wife.

I nodded and gave her an upturned smile. "Thank you for the invitation. We will think about it. I am content with our little cabin and eagerly wait for John to build us a home on our land."

I saw her place her hand on her lower belly, and when she did, I could see a definite bulge.

She met my wide-eyed gaze and smiled. "Yes, I'm pregnant!" I embraced her. "Oh, Jane, that is wonderful news!"

"The baby should come when winter starts." "Congratulations. Truly, I couldn't be happier for you." Jane's smile widened, and a tear rolled down her cheek,

"Thank you. That means a lot to me. And I couldn't be happier for you that your family is coming. What joyous news!"

"It is indeed. I can't tell you what it means to me, to all of us. We had best collect John and make our way down to the docks. I'm hoping they will arrive today; the news told us that a ship was coming up the James. They left England near the end of June, so I came by with hopes of being able to catch their ship as it disembarks. Meanwhile, I am selling extra crops from our garden. I have peas, carrots, radishes, and cabbage. Here, have a few." I placed some in her basket.

"Thank you; that's kind." She slipped the food further into her basket and rested her hand on her large belly. "That's wonderful news!"

I squeezed her hands. "It was so nice to see you, Jane. Do be careful, and may God be with you."

"Thank you, Anne, and you as well."

The girls and I waved our goodbyes, met John at his shop, then headed toward the docks.

Butterflies fluttered in my stomach, and my heart raced. I couldn't believe it was finally happening. I hadn't seen my family besides Jack in fourteen years! Fourteen years seemed staggering to me. Images of a skinny blonde girl with dirty fingernails and holes in her stockings flashed through my mind. Not much had changed. I was taller and more filled out as a mother of four. The most significant difference was on the inside. I was wiser, more grateful, and more aware of the world around me.

I placed my hand above my eyebrows to fight off the glare for a better look at the port. There, indeed, was a ship starting to dock. My heart skipped a beat. I felt giddy inside.

It might be them.

"Mama," Alice asked, "is that their ship?"

"I hope so, my dear. I hope so. We'll need to wait and see."

Within an hour, most of the passengers had disembarked. First denial and then hope rose in my chest as I recognized one of the passengers.

"Anthony!" I shouted.

A tall man with a thick brown beard, highlighted with red whiskers, wearing a green doublet and matching breeches, emerged from the boat. He escorted a younger woman off the ship with blonde curls wearing a brown circlet. Two more people appeared beside him, a middle-aged couple walking hand in hand—the woman with brown hair peppered gray and the man with white hair.

"Mama!" I yelled. "Papa! Anthony! Ellen!"

"Anne!" Anthony smiled. He picked me up and swung me around and around. "I can't believe it!"

We hugged, then pulled back to study each other's grown faces. I had to tilt my head back to look into his eyes because he was still a whole head taller than me. The corners of his mouth turned into a large grin and his bright blue eyes still shone with mischief and adventure.

Giggling, I pulled at his beard and laughed. "You still look the same, maybe a bit older but still my Anthony."

He pulled me in for another hug and so did Mama, Papa, and Ellen.

I couldn't believe they were finally here! My heart felt as if it would burst!

"Let me look at you," Mama said, tears pouring down her cheek. "You are no longer a child; you're a woman now. Fourteen years. Fourteen years since I have been able to look at you."

My tears matched her own, and we embraced again. I looked around again, then paused. "Grandfather?"

Papa sighed and looked down. "He wanted to come but was too frail to make the journey. We didn't want to leave without him, so we waited. He passed away a month before our journey. I suppose it was his way of telling us it was time to go."

I nodded and closed my eyes as I took in the news that I would never see Grandfather in this life again. It didn't come as a shock, but the news stung just the same.

The realization that John was standing beside me sank in, and I almost forgot that my family was beside me.

"Mama, Papa, this is my husband, John."

Mama pulled John in for a big hug, and Papa shook his hand, along with Ellen and Anthony. Five-year-old Margaret pulled at my sleeve.

"And who is this?" Mama asked with a smile.

"Magwet," Margaret said with a lisp, unable to pronounce her r's.

"Nice to meet you, Margaret. I'm your grandmother, and this is your grandfather." Mama bent down to address the other girls. "And you must be Virginia."

"Yes, Grandmother," Virginia said. She blushed and turned her head to the side.

"Alice."

Alice nodded profusely and gave her a big hug. "And last but not least, Katherine."

Katherine gave her a wide smile with two missing front teeth.

Mama took the girls in her arms and held them tight. When she backed away, Ellen stepped in and squatted beside the girls. "I'm your Aunt Ellen," she said.

"You're pretty," Alice blushed.

Ellen smiled and giggled. "Why, thank you, Alice. And so are you."

I couldn't keep my eyes off my little sister. She had grown up so much. Tears poured down my cheeks. "Last time I saw you, you were but a wee babe. Now look at you!" I cried.

Ellen stood up taller, her soft curls bouncing under her coif. Her blue eyes radiated, and a sweet dimple formed when she smiled. "I'm a woman now of sixteen."

"And still not taller than you," Anthony teased.

"Looks like someone hasn't changed much," I said, poking Anthony's arm.

He laughed and turned his attention to the girls. "I'm Uncle Anthony," he said with a bow. "Your favorite uncle, might I add."

"Nu-uh," Alice said. "Uncle Jack is our favorite uncle."

None of us could hold back our laughter. Anthony gave a low whistle.

"Some things never change," he said, giving me a wink. Oh, how I'd missed that wink!

I tugged at his beard. "Some things never change, huh? What about this?"

Brushing his whiskers back down, he said, "All right, some things change."

He went to pinch me on my cheek, but his hands froze, and he instead gently touched the minor scars from where the tips of the whip had reached. Small lines also edged down the side of my jaw and neck.

"Jack wrote to us about what happened, but I never imagined it would scar your face too."

Self-consciously, I pulled away from his touch and covered the right side of my face with my hands.

"It's nothing," I said. I wanted to change the subject.

Tears sprang to Papa's eyes, and he gently squeezed my hand.

I wiped happy tears from my eyes. "Now we just need to find Jack; he said he would meet us here if he could. He is only a quick boat ride across the river. Maybe we could send word for him."

"No need," Jack said, who approached us with his wife Bridget, holding their new baby, Sarah.

"Jack?" Mama reached for him in a warm embrace.

Jack waved a letter at me, "You're not the only one who received a letter that they were coming. Bridget and I have been waiting here all week for them to arrive. I had just finished with a client when I saw the boat disembark. Sorry, I missed the big welcome."

"Oh Jack!" Mama cried and engulfed him in a big hug! "That doesn't matter, son," Papa hugged him. "All that matters now is that we are together. We've waited for over ten years to be together. What are a few minutes?"

"A few minutes matters to me," Mama said with a laugh. "I have several years to catch up with these grandbabies of mine, and I don't want to wait another minute." She took Sarah from Bridget's arms and loaded her with kisses.

Pride welled up in my chest as I looked around at each member of my family. I couldn't believe we were together at last!

Chapter Forty-Two
MANNING THE FORT

"Even the bravest of us loathe war, and those who long for it are the most dangerous." – King Richard

March 21, 1622

Spending time with my family in Jamestown felt like a dream. Everyone had to pitch in and work hard, but I loved every minute of it. Mama, Papa, and Anthony stayed with

Jack and Bridget, while Ellen stayed with our family to help with the children and stay closer to Jamestown. We convinced Jack and Bridget to sell their land and buy land closer to John and me near Elizabeth City where we planned on moving soon.

John learned so much about tobacco from Mr. Rolfe that he was ready to try his own luck at growing it. Mr. Rolfe and his new wife, Jane Pierce, had a healthy baby girl, Elizabeth. I couldn't help but think of Rebecca when I looked at her sweet chubby cheeks and light brown hair that stuck right up and melted my heart.

"She is beautiful." I told Mr. And Mrs. Rolfe.

They both smiled and Mr. Rolfe wrapped an arm around his wife and nodded with pride.

Elizabeth wrapped her tiny fingers around mine. Something deep inside told me that Rebecca would have wanted him to re-marry and be happy.

So much had changed since Rebecca was with us. Each of the settlers grew gardens and many lived on land miles away from the fort.

Our garden was in front of our cabin, and I loved to go out to see everything growing. My winter crop was full of spinach, Swiss chard, arugula, carrots, peas, and camellia for tea. Every morning, I went out with the girls to tend to it. When the weather turned, we occasionally draped a blanket over it to protect it from the snow.

This winter wasn't as cold as others, so our crop was larger than usual, a welcome change with more people in our family to feed. I smelled the snowdrop flowers starting to bloom. The fragrance was sweet, but it also made me frown. This would be my last winter with this garden. I would miss this place. Three of my girls were born here, and they all learned to walk and talk here. Then the thought of land for them to run on next to the rest of our family warmed my heart. I could already close my eyes and picture the garden I would grow with Mama and Ellen in my new home—the colorful array of beets, broccoli, cabbage, turnips, and squash; flowers of every color: white lilies, daisies, soft blue cornflowers, and roses like we used to have in Mama's Garden. I sighed. I couldn't wait.

John met me outside that morning before walking to his shop. He sat on the porch, slipped on his leather boots, buckled them, then readjusted his stockings. His light brown hair now seemed peppered with gray.

He bent over and snapped off a pea pod to try. "The garden turned out well this season. The corn and spring garden will need to be planted soon."

I also bent over to snack on a pea pod; it was hard but not too rough. "I hope the seeds from last year will take." I knew how vital spring planting was. If it wasn't done right at the right time under the right soil conditions, we wouldn't have enough food in the fall.

John put a hand through his curls. "I do too, my love. What a blessing that relations have been better with the Powhatan lately. Two men from the fort went on a hunting trip with some men from the tribe."

"That is so comforting. Temperance said men and women come and trade openly, and she had a family from the village over for dinner last Sunday."

John raised his eyebrows. "That is good news. How are Temperance and Lord Yardley doing?"

I bit my lip. "I believe she is doing well. She is pregnant again and busy with the other children. I wish I could see her more; they are so busy, what with him helping the governor. I try to see her whenever I am in Jamestown."

John smiled. "I'm glad for them both. They seem to be well matched."

I nodded in agreement and kissed John on the cheek before he set off for work. "Good day, my love."

"You as well, and thank you for lunch. I'll be home by supper."

"You're welcome," I said and waved goodbye as he walked down the road.

March 22, 1622

Early in the morning, I walked outside to throw out the chamber pots and inspected the cabbage leaves for traces of mites or rabbits.

I was so focused on the plants that I screamed when I stood up and nearly ran into a man before I realized who it was.

"Jack! You nearly scared the daylights out of me."

Jack's brown hair clung to his forehead and ears. Sweat dripped down his face, even in the crisp March air. His blue eyes stared back at me in horror. His legs were shaking, and he was struggling to catch his breath.

The sight of him made my knees buckle. Something must be terribly wrong. "Jack, you look pale as a ghost. What in heaven's name is the matter? Where is the rest of the family? Did something happen?"

Jack's shoulders slumped, and he bent over, resting his hands on his legs to catch his breath.

John heard the commotion and came outside with his musket. "Oh, Jack, I'm glad it's you. I heard Anne scream; you're lucky I didn't shoot you." He looked at Jack's solemn expression and the condition of his appearance. "What's wrong?"

I shook my head and shrugged my shoulders.

"The Powhatan," Jack panted out. "They are going to attack today."

My eyebrows shot up, and my heart raced. "What?" Shock and terror ran through me, and I felt like I couldn't breathe.

"Chauco, a Powhatan boy, warned my neighbors Mr. Perry and Mr. Pace last night. He told me this morning that they planned to eliminate all the English settlers once and for all. I safeguarded my home as best as possible, then rowed out with everyone this morning. We need to leave for the fort now! Please don't worry about your belongings. Hurry, they plan to attack before noon."

"Ellen, wake up," I said, rushing inside and frantically shaking her awake.

"What is the mat —?" I put a finger to my mouth. The black parts of her eyes grew large, and she held back a scream.

"The Powhatan Confederacy is about to attack," I whispered. "We must leave for the fort's protection now! Please help me with the children."

She nodded but didn't say a word.

I searched the cabin, grabbed whatever food I could, and shoved it into my pocket as I yelled for the girls to wake up.

"Girls, get up! We need to leave. We are going to Jamestown."

Virginia sat up in bed and stretched. "Huh?"

Margaret wrinkled her nose and yawned. "Why are we going to Jamestown?"

No six-year-old should have to be afraid for her life, so I bit down hard on my cheek to keep from crying. "We're going on an adventure, darling. It's a surprise, but we better hurry, or we will miss out on the game."

"I love games," she said, hopping out of bed.

I looked at John, who seemed as frightened as I was. I raised my eyebrows at him and nodded my head toward Margaret.

John handed her a shawl. "Hurry now. We don't want to miss the game."

Virginia looked between the two of us. Being thirteen, she was well aware of the dangers we faced and stories of raids by the Powhatan. We didn't need to tell her twice that when we said we needed to leave, we meant it.

"Quickly now," Jack said in a hurried tone.

We grabbed what we could and ran out the door. "We're all here," I huffed out to Jack and John.

"Good." John turned to look at me. "I'm going to stay back and warn our neighbors."

I gripped his arm. "No, John. We need to stay together." His light brown eyes were full of compassion and sadness.

"Anne, if we don't warn them, no one will."

I nodded and let go of his arm. A tear ran down my cheek. "You'd better go fast. Promise me you will make it to the fort before noon!"

He gave me a slight smile. "I promise. I'll be right behind you."

Jack picked up Margaret so we could move faster. Ellen took Katherine by the hand, and I ran alongside Virginia and Alice. I could hear John knocking on doors behind us and yelling at our closest neighbors. "Wake up; the Powhatan are planning to attack. Flee to the fort!"

Soon, dozens of others were running behind us, carrying loved ones and what possessions they could.

We arrived at the fort within an hour. The sun shone through the stockades onto the James River. We shoved through the large fort gate like cattle into a stall. I raised my clammy hand to my mouth and pulled at my lip as I looked through the crowds of panicked faces for my family. I stood rigid until I heard Mama call my name. "Anne, Anne!"

"Phew." I had never been more relieved in all my life.

I counted every one of my family members. I counted the children twice. All were present except John.

"Papa, Anthony, Bridget. Thank God you're all here."

"Oh, Anne, we were so worried Jack wouldn't make it to you in time," Mama cried.

I turned and placed an arm on Jack's shoulder. "I am forever grateful he did."

My hands went back to squeezing my fingers and picking at my nails. I looked around again and clenched my jaw.

"Who are you looking for?" Bridget asked.

I bit my lip again. "John. He stayed behind to warn our neighbors. He said he'd be behind us, but I don't see him anywhere."

Bridget bounced Jack Junior in her arms and pushed her chestnut hair behind her shoulder. She shuffled Jack onto her other hip and gave me a slight smile. "I'm sure he will arrive soon."

I bit my cheek and forced a small smile of my own. I didn't want the girls to see me cry. "Could you please watch the girls briefly while I look for him?"

Bridget's eyes widened with fear, but she nodded her head. "Be quick, and please, Anne, don't leave the fort. He might have taken to the woods to hide if he isn't here soon."

Her words rang true. Maybe John was hiding in the woods and would meet us later, maybe he was with the men fighting or maybe he was injured or worse. My heart raced and my body felt frozen in place, unsure of what to do or where to look.

I quickly walked around the inside perimeter of the fort. Most people huddled inside the church, some in individual cabins. Groups of men stood at each bulwark with cannon supplies ready to fire. Others were lined up with muskets, prepared to fire at any movement in the trees.

It was past mid-morning, and I still couldn't find him. I took a deep breath and swallowed hard. My mouth felt parched from running that morning and not having water or breakfast. I decided it was best to return to my family and pray that John would join us soon.

"Anne!" Bridget shouted and waved me down when she saw me. They had moved toward the church with the rest of the women and children.

I looked around and went pale. "Where are Papa, Anthony, and Jack?"

Bridget looked down at the ground before her beautiful brown eyes met mine. "They decided to help defend the fort with the other men," she cried in sobs.

Instinctively, I wrapped my arms around her, Mama, and the children. My chin started to tremble. I was terrified, but I knew it wouldn't do any good to cry. "Look at me. We are going to make it through this. Jack warned us just in time. By the looks of it, there must be more than five hundred people here, and more are probably on their way. When I walked around, I saw men posted to shoot cannon fire and muskets at anyone attacking. The fort is lined with sentry lookouts."

Bridget sniffled, and Mama hugged her closely. "But there are thousands, maybe hundreds of thousands of people in the Powhatan Confederacy. We English only number twelve hundred total in the whole of Virginia. How can we ever defeat them?"

My eyes met Bridget's again. "We are going to make it through this. Do you hear me?"

She nodded, and I held her while she cried.

Chapter Forty-Three
THE CONFEDERACY ATTACKS

"A brave and cunning man." – James Horn

March 22, 1622

When the sun reached its peak of the day, sounds of musket fire and cannons shook the ground of the newly constructed church, which sat near the original. Its walls were made of wood now instead of mud, capped with a wall the width of one brick around the exterior. It was much larger than the last church, fifty feet long and twenty feet broad.

The pews were full, so we huddled together on the cold cobblestone floor. I placed my arms around Virginia and Alice to keep them warm and calm their fears.

Another roar and boom sounded in our ears, and Ellen sobbed. "What was that?" she cried, trembling.

Mama placed her arms around her shoulders and squeezed her. "It's a good sound. It means our men are protecting us."

Mama's calm demeanor still caught me off guard. Again, she was the Mama from my childhood. Time had taken its toll on her and us; her once beautiful locks were streaked with gray, and wrinkles lined her face. She was still beautiful, full of spirit and strength. The period of her great sadness seemed to me like a lifetime ago. She softly smiled as she looked around at me and my girls. I squared my shoulders; I wanted to be brave like her.

The thought of Papa, Jack, and Anthony out there made me sick. I wanted to run out of the church and pull them inside to await the day's horrors. And where was John? Had he made it back in time to join the others? What if he was still out there? A large cannon fire rang through the air and dust sprinkled down on us. I leaned over and huddled my girls closer to me.

More shots were fired, and a man outside the church uttered a muffled scream. I couldn't tell who it was, but it was English.

"Mama, I'm scared!" Katherine cried.

I wiped a tear from her cheek and opened my arms for her to sit on my lap. "I know, sweetheart. It will be over soon. Keep your hands over your ears. I'm here." I stroked her strawberry blonde hair and hummed "Triumphs of Oriana" to her. I wished Papa was here to play the tune on his lute to help soothe my girls. My heart ached for them, and a feeling of anger and frustration muddled with fear came over me.

"We are going to be all right, girls." I nodded reassuringly, as if doing so would help me overcome my own anxiety.

Another hour of fighting ensued, and then we heard a loud bang on the church door.

My eyes froze open. I quietly pleaded that whoever was at the door was English.

A woman near the door timidly lifted the locked latch. I breathed a sigh of relief after my eyes adjusted to the bright sun and saw three Englishmen standing tight-lipped and breathing hard.

Their expressions were difficult to read. All I could think about was John.

"The Powhatan Confederacy," a man with a shaggy dark brown beard huffed, "attacked, but we held them back. They fled back to the woods. We don't know if they will return. You may leave the church, but please don't leave the fort."

"What about our husbands?" a woman closer to the door cried out.

He looked down at his feet. "Some of our men are wounded." I noticed his hand twitch against a knife on his belt, covered in blood. *Dear God, bless; let it not be John!*

The man rubbed his right eye and then looked back at us. "Most have made it through but need their wounds tended to."

The women at the front of the chapel didn't waste time waiting for him to finish, and we followed suit. "Ahh!" I cried as a tall woman behind us pushed me into a pew to get by me, tripping Katherine. I bent over and scooped Katherine up before someone trampled her. Adrenaline flowed in my veins, and I wanted to leave that church immediately.

The sun was deceiving; its brightness diminished as we made our way outside, covered by intermittent clouds. Soft drops of rain fell on my head and face, but amid the confusion, I was determined to find John and the others.

"Stay together, girls!" I shouted above the chaos ensuing around me.

Women and children were frantically calling out to their fathers and brothers. Men looked for their wives and children, and others cried for fear of their lives.

The rain fell harder, and mud replaced the hard dirt streets. "John! John!" I cried.

Ellen screamed and pointed to a man lying face-down in the mud near us with arrows protruding from his back.

When I saw that the man had blond hair, not brown, and a yellow jerkin, I sighed in relief and immediately felt guilty for being so grateful.

Two more men, one wounded and one dead, sat by the eastern wall of the fort. I studied both of their faces as we made our way around.

"Mama, what if we go in circles to find each other? Shouldn't we stay in one place so Papa can find us? Maybe we should go back to the church?"

A part of me told me to keep looking, even if it was in circles. The weary looks on the girls' faces told me that Virginia was right; staying put was the better solution and less dangerous option. I looked down at Virginia. Her soft blonde hair and blue eyes sparkled with determination. At thirteen, it was as if I was looking at a version of myself. When had she grown up?

I gave her a small smile. "You're right, Virginia. We should go back."

We turned the corner of the old church, and I immediately recognized John's cap and the back of his head as he and several other men walked into the church to find their families.

"There is Mister Harris," Ellen said to Mama, pointing to a man with chestnut brown hair and kind eyes. "Remember, we met him on the ship."

She waved and he waved back at her with a look of relief. Behind Mister Williams, John appeared again.

"John!" I cried, waving. "Over here!"

John came running toward us and swung me in his arms.

Tears flowed freely from my eyes.

Papa, Anthony, and Jack were with us a minute later, hugging and kissing Bridget and Mama.

I looked around and did a mental headcount. "Is everyone here?"

Mama looked around too. "We are! It's a miracle. God be praised."

I put my hand over my mouth and let the sobs come. I finally felt like I could breathe again.

"What happened?" I asked.

John shook his head and looked down. "We were attacked. Jack, Mr. Percy, Chauco—they were right, the Powhattan were planning on attacking. I don't know what would have happened if Jack hadn't warned us when he did."

"But how did you get here? Our neighbors, did they make it?"

John swallowed hard. "Most did. I ran as fast as I could and knocked on each of their doors. Several listened, but the Thompsons refused to come. He said he'd rather stay fighting for his home. I don't know what became of them."

A chill ran through me, thinking of Nancy Thompson and her two boys. I prayed they'd made it through. I touched John's cheek, and my bottom lip frowned. "You did everything you could. The other neighbors are saved because of you."

"I tried to knock on as many as I could but the thought of you and the girls in the fort without me there to protect you almost drove me mad. I went back to the house and grabbed my musket, then helped the Williams next door carry their young children to the fort. Fortunately, we made it before the Powhattan, and the men at the gate let us in. A man informed me that the women and children were in the church, so I stayed and kept guard at the stockade with the others."

I sobbed into his chest, "I thought we'd never see you again." John wiped back a dark blonde strand of hair from my face, his shoulders slumped, and he gave me a tight-lipped smile. "I wasn't sure I would either, but I'm here, and by the grace of God, am not injured. So many weren't as fortunate."

I shook my head in disbelief and my heart soared. "We made it, we're all together," I choked out.

I looked around at my family again. John and my girls, Mama, Papa, Anthony, Ellen Jack, Bridget and little Sarah. I was afraid I'd wake up, as if all of it was a dream but it wasn't. We were all here, together in Jamestown.

John put his arms out for me and the girls. We held each other close and cried.

Chapter Forty-Four
RECOVERY

"Labor is light where love doth pay." – Michael Drayton

April 13, 1623

Jamestown Fort was one of a few areas left unscathed by the massacre of 1622. Reports gradually came in from the surrounding areas. The death toll amounted to nearly four hundred; four hundred souls—men, women, and children—taken to heaven within hours. It was heart-breaking. Some people were farmers, tradesmen, indentured servants, and families, many of whom I had known for years. Some mercifully survived, while others were taken to be traded off like cattle; such was the case of my dear friend Jane.

Hundreds more died that year from injury, sickness, or starvation. The Powhatan Confederacy burned down crops of farms they raided up and down the Chesapeake. Food was scarce, and only a few could get their spring crop planted.

We were shocked to hear of the damage and atrocities committed that day. Chief Opechancanough thought the

English would leave, but we refused. Men from the fort were sent on raiding parties, and more heartbreak ensued.

When King James heard of the massacre, he forced the London Company to place Jamestown under the direction of the English Crown. He also sent ships, guns, canons, and hundreds of people to colonize Virginia. The retaliation of the Powhatan people to the growing takeover of their land was ten-fold or more. But the English soldiers responded with equal force. Most were driven back or off their lands. My heart ached for the natives, but I also felt a great deal of relief as help and provisions arrived and I knew my family wouldn't go hungry.

This relief seemed to be felt by those remaining in the fort, as well. People started to trade each other for goods again, greet old friends and family at the docks, and rebuild English villages outside the fort.

Our family also began to settle in and find a place for themselves in our new home. One good thing came out of that fateful day. Ellen was paid a visit by Mister Harris and the two became inseparable thereafter. They married a month later and purchased ten acres of land a few miles south of Jamestown.

When the fighting died down as the presence of the soldiers brought more stability to our growing colony, I approached John with a new idea. "Maybe your son Thomas can join us now that King James is sending more people. They will need more tradesmen."

A sparkle lit John's eye, and he smiled. "Yes, I will write to him and ask him to join us now that my contract as a carpenter is complete. We have saved enough money to buy more land on top of the land promised us. There will be plenty for everyone."

The next morning, we walked towards the fort to meet Anthony. When we arrived, a clerk at the governor's office with a large, ruffled collar and pointed nose handed John and Anthony papers to sign.

"Your contracts, Gentlemen" he said, giving them each a firm handshake. "Pleasure doing business with you, gentlemen."

John turned around, swung me off my feet, and spun me around while Anthony grinned.

"It's here, Anne!" John said as he clutched the rolled-up contract in his hand. "It's finally here. The land deed we have been waiting for."

Anthony walked beside us. "I know I haven't been waiting as long as the two of you have, but can I celebrate too?" "Of course, now get over here." I said, as I pulled

Anthony into our arms for a big family hug.

I linked my arms between them as we walked back to tell Mama, Papa, and the children.

"I feel so free! I can't tell you how good it feels to not be under the Company's watchful eye," John exclaimed.

I squeezed John's arm, "And now Anthony has land next to ours."

Anthony chuckled. "To Elizabeth Town we go. Now, we must convince Jack and Bridget to move there with us," he winked.

The three of us talked and laughed as we walked arm in arm. I smiled as I looked back and forth between my husband and big brother. I could already envision the life of freedom that lay ahead of us. My family was finally together, the greatest threats to our safety had been subdued, we had land with room to grow, and we were building a future together as a family. I couldn't imagine anything better than that.

EPILOGUE

"Be not afraid of greatness. Some are born great;
some achieve greatness, and some have greatness
thrust upon them." – William Shakespeare

Spring 1640

The sun showed itself above the ridge of the fields. Various buds of pink, white, and purple reflected off the trees and showered the ground like flecks from heaven. John and I sat on the house's front porch like we did most mornings when the weather permitted. A warm breeze carried the sweet smell of flowers from the garden, and my thoughts turned to the last thirty years and all that John and I had been through.

I ran my hand around the side of my neck and face. The scars remained, but my heart had long healed. I still ached for the son I never had, but the hurt I felt inside somehow dulled over time. New memories were made of my children growing up and of my grandchildren, nine boys and seven girls. We had the privilege of not only seeing our children, but our nieces and nephews growing up near us as well. I ached for Mama and Papa after they passed but was grateful for the years we were able to spend with them in Jamestown and on our land.

I looked over the fields we had worked so hard to cultivate and I felt transported back to Norfolk, England, the land of my childhood, as I watched my young grandchildren play. It was as if I could feel the soft grass under my feet. I closed my eyes and imagined I was back in England as a little girl, running through the fields of Norfolk with my brothers and sisters in a place and time before loss, love, heartache, and peace converged into one. For the first time, I realized that Papa, Rebecca, Temperance, and John all were right: I was braver and stronger than I believed. I just needed to see it for myself.

THE END

A Letter to the Reader

Dear Reader,

I hope you enjoyed learning about the adventures of Anne Burras Layton. This book was based on the true story of her life. She, as well as Mistress Forrest, really were the first English women to come and survive in the New World! While homeschooling my three children during COVID, I found her story when researching my family history. At the time, we were studying American History, and what better way to appreciate and understand it than by looking into people's lives?

There are all sorts of articles and fun memories of Anne; there's even a statue in the Virginia State Building in Richmond, Virginia! However, no one has written a full novel about her life. I felt like her story needed to be told—so here it is.

Sometimes, as a writer, you only have part of the story and need to embellish or change bits and pieces a little. I felt like a detective and did my best to fill in the gaps in Anne's life. If you want to find out which parts are fact and which are fiction, please turn to the next few pages. Also included are a photograph of her statue, a copy of her ship record, class discussion/book club questions, vocabulary words, and the excellent resources I used to help create this book.

Happy reading! Tracy Smith

Acknowledgements

Thank you to my husband Grant and children Abigail, Asher, and Gwendolyn for countless hours of listening to me read my manuscript, brainstorming and supporting me. To my sister, Michelle, for always encouraging me to reach for more. To Laura Nielsen for being my friend, mentor, and guide. To my friends at SCBWI, the *Society of Children's Book Writers*, for our visits reviewing each other's work and for your insightful feedback. To Maddy Mortensen and Ashley de Tello at de Tello Publishing for giving me the feedback and direction I needed. To my editor, Melanie Kimball, who took the time to help me through the chaos. Finally, a big thank you to my supportive beta testers, Michelle Linder, Robert and Roberta Mercer, Jera Anderson, Lindsay Wilson, Laura Nielsen, Gretchen Knight, McKenzie Goodwin, Alicen Nielsen, Aubrey Olsen, and Lexi Yorgason.

I also would like to say thank you to the Jamestown Rediscovery and Jamestown Historical Society for bringing history to life and showing me and countless others what it was like to live in 17th-century Jamestown.

FACT VS. FICTION

Anne Burras:

Anne was a maid to Margaret Forrest, wife of Thomas Forrest, a wealthy investor in the London Company.

Anne had a younger brother, John Burras (who I renamed Jack), who arrived on the same boat to Jamestown and was labeled a Tradesman (meaning a craftsman). Anne and John boarded the *Mary and Margaret* for Jamestown along with Mistress and Thomas Forrest. They arrived on September 30, 1608.

Family records show that Anne was born and raised in Norfolk, England, hundreds of miles away from London. I wondered how she arrived in London, so I created a story of her grandfather's shipyard business failing and the family not having enough money to keep her and Jack. My idea for this came from the time period in which she lived. After Queen Elizabeth died and King James I started his reign, the economy was struggling, many people were out of work, and many middle-class families had to send children off to work. The Burras family would have kept Anthony because he was to inherit and Ellen because she was too little.

Anne's family records show that she had two younger siblings that died around the same time, Mary and Nicholas. The plague was in and out of England for years, so I attributed their deaths to that, but they could have died from a different illness or other causes. I don't know how Anne's mother, Elizabeth reacted to their deaths. I added her response to show the weight the family might have felt and how quickly children had to grow up then.

Anne's mother's maiden name was Eden, and family records show she came from a prominent family. The entire Burras family eventually came to Jamestown. When Anthony arrived, the ship's manifest marked him as a gentleman, so I assumed the family came from wealth but no longer had it.

It is unknown when and how Mistress Forrest died, but she most likely died after she arrived in Jamestown, or Anne would not have been able to marry. Sir Forrest returned to England alone and came back years later with his son Peter and Peter's wife.

Anne could have learned to read and write if she came from a prominent family, but it's not likely. Most girls, especially from unwealthy families, were not taught anything other than domestic matters. I added Anne's ability to read to add dimension to the story to see her point of view as well as that of her family members expressed in their letters throughout the story.

Anne's beating, imprisonment, and miscarriage due to the shirt-sewing ordeal were real events noted in historical records.

Jack Burras:

Anne did have a younger brother, named John. I nicknamed him Jack; I thought it would be less confusing later on when she married John Layton. Her brother very well could have gone by Jack, as it was a common nickname for John then.

Jack was on the ship's passenger list with Anne. He married Bridget Langley, one of the passengers shipwrecked on the *Sea Venture*. They are known to have had at least one daughter together. Jack was stabbed on January 1, 1628, by one of his indentured servants.

I imagine Jack and Anne must have been close, seeing how they worked for the Forrest family and went to Jamestown together.

John Layton:

There are many variations for the spelling of John's last name, including Leighton, Laydon, Leyden, and Layton. I chose to use Layton for this book.

We know that Anne married John Layton in November or December of 1608. Theirs was the first English wedding in the New World, and they named their first child Virginia.

Family records detail John Layton coming to the aid of the Forrest's and Anne's cabin by digging a trench around it to prevent flooding. Family records also describe him carving a chest with the initials A.B. for Anne Burras. I added the part of Anne admiring her mother's hope chest.

John Layton was with the first group to arrive in Jamestown. He arrived in Jamestown on the *Susan Constant* in May 1607 under Captain Christopher Newport.

Family records show that he had a wife and two children who passed away. They also show that his son Thomas survived and moved to Jamestown. It's unknown where he resided until he made his way to Jamestown with his wife.

The 1625 Jamestown muster shows John, age 44, a carpenter, living with his wife, Anne Burras, in Elizabeth City, Virginia, along with their four daughters, Virginia, Alice, Catherine, and Margaret. Catherine's name *was* spelled with a "C", but I spelled it with a "K" to add more to the background and show a connection to her paternal grandmother, too.

Pocahontas:

Pocahontas was known by various names. The people of her village called her Matoaka. When she was younger, she was known as Amunet to her family and close friends. She was one of many daughters of Chief Powhatan. Multiple accounts say that she had a brother that she would play with around the fort and that she initially learned English from Captain John Smith, whom her people kidnapped for a time.

She married Kocoum in her early teenage years. We know that he passed away before the English took her. There is also anecdotal evidence that she had a daughter she had to leave behind.

Pocahontas later married John Rolfe, a tobacco farmer whose former wife had given birth to a baby girl they named Bermuda while they were shipwrecked. Sadly, the baby did not live long, and Rolfe's wife died on the ship sometime between Bermuda and Jamestown. With other passengers, he made two small boats from the wreck and made their way to Jamestown only to find sixty or so people out of nearly six hundred. The Jamestown settlers got on their ships and headed toward Newfoundland (now Canada) to book passage back to England. While en route, they ran into the new governor, Thomas West, who told them to turn their ships ar ound.

Pocahontas and John Rolfe had a son named Thomas, and in 1617, they left for England to spread the word about Jamestown and to introduce Pocahontas to King James and his wife, Queen Anne. On the journey back, before they officially left England, Pocahontas and Thomas fell ill. They had to stop the ship in the small village of Gravesend, England. Pocahontas did not make it, but Thomas lived. John Rolfe had him live with his relatives. Years later, when Thomas was grown, he returned to Virginia.

John Rolfe remarried and had a little girl. Some say that his home was left untouched during the Massacre of 1622 because of his relationship with Pocahontas. Chief Powhatan died within a year of her death, and his brother Opitchapam took over as chief. However, Powhatan's youngest brother, Opechancanough, eventually assumed leadership. He was hostile toward the settlers, and many battles ensued.

Anthony Burras:

According to FamilySearch and ship records, Anne had an older brother named Anthony. Her father's name was also Anthony. There is no ship record of her parents coming over, but their death dates and the place, Jamestown, were written in their family chart. Anthony came to Jamestown on the ship the *George* in 1617 from the county of Norfolk, England (another link showed me that is where Anne is originally from). The ship records marked him as a gentleman.

I don't know for sure how and when Anthony died; some family group charts show he died on the same date Jack did—January 1, 1628—as did their mother, Elizabeth Eden Burras, but another article said he died years later and even testified in court on someone's behalf. There is no record of Anthony marrying, but a land record shows that he bought land with Anne and John.

Ellen Burras:

Ellen came over a few years later, on the ship *Marmaduke* in 1621. She married a man who was also on that ship, Sir William Harris. They had six children together.

Temperance Flowerdew:

Temperance was a passenger on the third supply ship that landed in 1609. Her husband passed away that winter during 'the starving time', the winter of 1609-1610. I added the part about her having a son and a sister who were there. She later remarried to George Yardley, a bodyguard of Sir Thomas Gates. Yardley later became governor. Temperance and Yardley had three children together. After Sir Yardley passed away, she married Sir Frances West, the next governor. It is unknown if she and Anne were friends or if she helped when Anne delivered Virginia, but they would have at least known of each other as she was part of the first group of women to arrive after Anne.

Jane Wright:

Not much is known regarding Jane and her family. Her name was mentioned in a short testimony of a woman who witnessed Jane and Anne being whipped for making shirts too short for the London Company. She may or may not be the same "Joan Wright" from Surry, Virginia, who was also accused of being a witch.

The Starving Period 1609-1610:

The winter of 1609-1610 was a brutal test of survival, one of the coldest on record. The Powhattan people, weary of the English, were unwilling to extend their help this time. Unlike other times of hunger, they were resolute in their decision to wait the Englishmen out. The native people themselves were barely surviving the harsh winter. The Englishmen were confined to the fort, their only source of sustenance being what remained inside.

Anne and her family survived the starving period that winter. Scholars suggest she and others volunteered to stay in Point Comfort for the winter, which very well saved her life. There, the people could eat seafood and trade goods for food with the locals.

The Sea Venture ship returned the lost boat from Bermuda to Jamestown early that spring. They were shocked that only sixty-one of the nearly five hundred people remained. I'm unsure if they stopped in Point Comfort first or if the people from Point Comfort met them at Jamestown. Regardless, the group joined them to try to return to England. It is true that upon leaving, they ran right into a British fleet, which ordered them to return to Jamestown. I could not imagine how terrifying it must have been to have to return. America might look a lot different now if they hadn't.

The First Enslaved People in Jamestown:

Heartbreakingly, slavery has been around for thousands of years. The term Slave, as used today, is derived from the word Slav, people from Eastern Europe who were enslaved in the Ninth century by Muslims in Spain. Slavery has existed in almost every nation at one time or another, and unfortunately, still exists today in some parts of the world. Enslaved people from Africa had been taken to South America by the Spanish and Portuguese as early as the 15th century.

In 1619, in particular, a group of a hundred-odd people were taken from the Kongo and Ndongo Kingdoms of Africa. They were forced to board a ship from Angola, Africa, towards Veracruz, a colony in New Spain, or present-day Mexico. Two English privateer ships under the direction of a Dutch patron took over the Portuguese ship, *San Juan Bautista*, that the enslaved people were on, hoping for riches to loot. When they found people in the cargo, the two ships, *The White Lion* and the *Treasurer*, divided the group in half and went their separate ways. *The White Lion* took the people towards Jamestown and stopped in Point Comfort first, where they traded the remaining Africans, around twenty of them, for food.

At the same time, the Africans onboard were forced to become indentured servants, something not uncommon to the people of Jamestown. Many individuals signed up to be Indentured Servants, and others forced them to do so in order to pay off a debt or to purchase passage to the new world by signing such a contract; however, the Africans were forced to do so. Some of the African people gradually earned their freedom from their contracts when the elapsed time was up, but some were forced to stay as servants for the rest of their lives. Gradually, more African people were taken from their homes and forced not only as indentured servants but as lifelong slaves.

I created the story of Anne seeing the first group at the dock in Jamestown to show what happened. Likely, she didn't see them as she would have been busy tending to her daily chores and children, besides the fact that they disembarked in Point Comfort, not Jamestown. She may or may not have seen them for years, as many were sent to work in fields or homes outside of Jamestown. Anne may have run into them at Jamestown early on, but she was bound to have heard of them eventually and met or seen a few of the enslaved people herself as more Africans were kidnapped and brought to Virginia.

The Bride Ship of 1620:

The London company saw the value of a long-term settlement in Jamestown. The low ratio of women to men made that impossible. The company devised a plan to set out advertisements for women in England to come to Jamestown and wed one of the men there. A man typically paid for his bride in tobacco, coin, or crops before her arrival before meeting her. The women needed letters of recommendation showing they came from a good family with specific skills such as sewing, cooking, and farming. The bride ship of 1620 consisted of ninety women. Many were eager to make the voyage while some were forced to cross the Atlantic due to a lack of prospects and money. All came to start a new life in Jamestown as a new bride.

It is unknown whether Jane Wright was on the 1620 bride ship, but I included it as part of my story to inform and familiarize the reader with what was happening during that time. The bride ship would have certainly affected Anne, changing the community dynamics. I imagine Anne was surprised and pleased to be around so many more women and families.

The Massacre of 1622

Chief Opechancanough, eventual predecessor and brother of Chief Powhattan, was angry at his brother for not getting rid of the English earlier. He coordinated an organized attack on the English Settlers on March 22, 1622. Wanting to get rid of the English "once and for all," he sent dozens of his people to the homes and settlements of the surrounding areas of Jamestown under the pretense of selling or offering goods such as venison and fruit. Precisely when the sun was at its highest, the Powhattan people attacked, resulting in the massacre of 347 colonists, men, women, and children, a quarter of the Virginia colonies' population at the time, not including dozens of women kidnapped and sold to other tribes or enslaved.

A young Native boy lived in the home of an Englishman named Richard Pace. He refused to kill Mr. Pace and instead warned him of the ensuing assault. Richard then warned the neighbors and sailed to Jamestown to warn the fort before it was too late. He arrived in time, and when the natives canoed up the river to Jamestown, the area was fortified and shut off, forcing the natives to leave.

John or Jack Burras lived near Richard Pace at the time, and records indicate that he and Anne's family survived the attack.

IMAGES

THE NEW COLONISTS
A.D. 1608.

Gent.

Thomas Graves.	Henry Collins.
Raleigh Chroshaw.	Hugh Wolleston.
Gabriel Beadle.	John Hoult.
John Beadle.	Thomas Norton.
John Russell.	George Yarington.
William Russell.	George Burton.
John Cuderington.	Thomas Abbay.
William Sambage.	William Dowman.
Henry Leigh.	Thomas Maxes.
Henry Philpot.	Michael Lowick.
Harmon Harrison.	Master Hunt.
Daniel Tucker.	Thomas Forrest.

John Dauxe.

Tradsmen.

Thomas Phelps.	Thomas Bradley.
John Prat.	John Burras.
John Clarke.	Thomas Lavander.
Jeffrey Shortridge.	Henry Bell.
Dionis Oconor.	Master Powell.
Hugh Winne.	David Ellis.
David ap Hugh.	Thomas Gibson.

[III. 73.]

Labourers.

Thomas Dawse.	Williams.
Thomas Mallard.	Floud.
William Tayler.	Morley.
Thomas Fox.	Rose.
Nicholas Hancock.	Scot.
Walker.	Hardwyn.

Boyes.

Milman.	Hilliard.

Mistresse Forrest, and Anne Burras her maide ; eight Dutch men and Poles, with some others, to the number of seaventie persons, &c.

151

"2nd Supply to the Virginia Colony Passenger List" is a public domain image. The original image can be found at https://en.wikipedia.org/wiki/Mistress_Forrest

273

"Anne Burras Laydon Statue" by Virginia Women's Monument is licensed under CC BY-SA 4.0. The original image can be at ht tps://commons.wikimedia.org/wiki/ File:Anne_Burras_Laydon _VWM_Statue.jpg

Book Discussion Questions

1. Why was family so important to Anne?

2. How is your life similar to Anne's? How is it different?

3. Would you have liked to go to Jamestown then? Why or why not?

4. How did being able to read and write help Anne?

5. If you had the choice to stay and be married in Jamestown or return to England as a maid, what would you choose to do and why?

6. Who was your favorite character in the story? Why?

7. How did Anne's relationships with Jack, John, and Pocahontas help her?

8. Why do you think the London Company was so strict? Do you think they were right to act that way?

9. Why is learning about Jamestown important? How does it affect us today?

10. How did going through hard times when Anne was young help her as she got older?

Vocabulary

- **Bodice**: The close-fitting upper part of a dress. A woman's dress top generally had whalebone sewn into it to keep its form.

- **Chamber pot**: Instead of using toilets, people would go to the bathroom in metal pots and then throw out the waste when they were done. At night, chamber pots were usually kept under beds; then the waste would be thrown outside the next day.

- **Coif**: A cap worn by women, usually made of linen that covered their whole head and came to a point on their forehead.

- **Hackney coach**: A horse-drawn carriage used at the time. Could usually seat up to six people, with a driver perched in his own seat in the front.

- **Kirtle**: A dress usually made of wool or linen that was placed over a woman's shift. The top was attached to the skirt and laced into place to close the gap. The front of the skirt was open, showing the petticoat and an apron was usually placed on top of the skirt portion.

- **Musket**: A gun with a long barrel. Gunpowder was

placed in the barrel, then ignited to fire the bullet. The gun was typical for light infantry and held near the shooter's shoulder to aim.

- **Petticoat**: A woman's skirt that was worn on top of her shift.

- **Plume-feathered hat**: A sizeable, brimmed hat men would wear with a feather or two sticking out of the side.

- **Shift**: A lightweight linen dress worn by women under their clothing. The long-sleeved arms and neckline would be seen under their bodice, and on their sleeves. Typically, another skirt would be worn over the shift under the petticoat if the petticoat design had an opening in front.

- **Well met**: A common greeting, such as "nice to see you."

Sources

1. Cotter, John, and J. Paul Hudson. "New Discoveries at Jamestown Site of the First Successful English Settlement in America." January 1, 2008.

2. "England Births and Christenings, 1538-1975." Database. FamilySearch. https://familysearch.org / ark:/61903/1:1:NB79-8WY. Accessed March 19, 2020. Ant Burrow, 1561.

3. "England Marriages 1538-1973 Transcription." First name(s) Ant.; Last name Burrowe; Name note -; Marriage year 1579; Marriage date July 11, 1579; Marriage place Thurlton; Spouse's first name(s) Eliz.; Spouse's last name Edon; County Norfolk; Country England; Record set England Marriages 1538-1973; Category Birth, Marriage & Death (Parish Registers); Subcategory Parish Marriages; Collections from England, United Kingdom; Repository: FamilySearch Intl.

4. Fishwick, Marshall. "Jamestown." April 23, 2019.

5. "For age of Mrs. John Layton." "Pedigree Resource File." Database. FamilySearch. https://familysearch.org/ark:/ 61903/2:2:3KDC-1BG. Accessed September 27, 2022. Entry for Mrs. John Layton cites sources; "Jennings

Flemming Family Tree" file (2:2:2:MM6J -YK3), submitted November 6, 2018, by Kristin Jennings Flemming [identity withheld for privacy].

6. Historic Jamestowne. https://historicjamestowne.org.

7. Smith, John. "A True Relation of Occurrences and Accidents in Virginia, 1608."

8. Johnston, Mary. "To Have and To Hold." 1899.

9. Hannah-Jones, Nikole. "The 1619 Project: A New Origin Story." August 18, 2019.

10. Potter, Jennifer. "The Jamestown Brides." 2008.

11. "Renaissance Costume Glossary: Men's Clothing Terms: Costumes by The Tudor Shoppe (17th century clothing ideas)."

12. "Pocahontas: Her Life and Legend." Historic Jamestowne. Part of Colonial National Historical Park (U.S. National Park Service). https:// www.nps.gov (Kidnapping of Pocahontas).

13. Smith, John. "The Generall Historie of Virginia, New-England, and the Summer Isles." 1624. Reprint in Jamestown Narratives, edited by Edward Wright Haile. Champlain, VA: Roundhouse, 1998.

14. Thane, Elswyth. "Williamsburg Series vol. 1-7." 1934-1957.

15. "The Starving Time at Jamestown – Humans For Survival." https://humansforsurvival.com.

16. Townsend, Camilla. "Pocahontas and the Powhatan Dilemma: The American Portrait Series." January 1, 2004.

17. Smith, John. "Pocahontas: My Own Story." January 1, 2006.

18. Williams, Tony. "The Jamestown Experiment: The Remarkable Story of the Enterprising Colony and the Unexpected Results That Shaped America." January 1, 2011.

19. Steward, Ted, and Chris Steward. "Seven Miracles that Saved America: Why They Matter and Why We Should have Hope." January 1, 2009.

20. "List of Passengers of the Second Supply." Research and compilation by Anne Stevens. packrat-pro.com.

21. "Death of son, Anthony Burras 1 Jan 1628." "Find A Grave Index." Database. FamilySearch. https://www. familysearch.org/ark:/61903/1:1:ZR6Z-WHT2. Accessed October 20, 2022. Anthony Burruss; Burial; citing record ID 208883403, Find a Grave, http://www.findagrave.com.

22. Order of Descendants of Ancient Planters: Anne Burras, by Noelle Ortiz (posted November 6, 2017, accessed November 6, 2020). (Updated via WaybackMachine, accessed August 4, 2022).

23. Global, "Find A Grave Index for Burials At Sea and Other Select Burial Locations, 1300-Current."https://search.ancestry.com/cgi-bin/sse. dll?indiv=1&dbid=60541&h=173421845&tid=167522

280&pid=4021965590077&usePUB=true&_phs-rc=Yt
G2460&_phstart=successSource.

24. "Marriage of Anthony Burras and Ann Eden,
Ann's parents." "England Marriages, 1538–1973."
Database. FamilySearch. https://familysearch.org/ark
:/61903/1:1:N2P5-7QY. Accessed March 12, 2020. Eliz.
Edon in entry for Ant. Burrowe, 1579.

25. "Death of Elizabeth Eden Burras." "Find A Grave Index."
Database. FamilySearch. https://www.family search.org
/ark:/61903/1:1:ZR6Z-GXZM. Accessed September 10,
2021. Elizabeth Eden Burruss; Burial; citing record ID
208887092, Find a Grave, http://www.findagrave.com.

MEET THE AUTHOR

Tracy Smith is a debut author and historian at heart. She loves learning about different cultures and places. She has a Master of Arts in Teaching Elementary Education from Western Governors University and a Bachelor of Arts in Political Science from Brigham Young University-Hawaii.

She has spent several years teaching inside the classroom and online. Tracy loves stories of ordinary people who face extra-ordinary circumstances and rise to the occasion.

She, her husband, and three children live in Northern Utah with their two dogs and thirteen chickens. Her favorite pastimes include spending time with her family and friends, traveling, kayaking, reading, board games, relaxing near the water at a lake or a beach, and playing the guitar.

Tracy's goal in writing historical fiction is to teach young readers to understand and appreciate history and the influence it has on us today.